I0666143

RISK

a Deep 8 novel

KENZIE MACALLAN

RISK
a Deep 8 novel

Published by Steel Butterfly Press

ISBN No. 978-1-7378014-6-7

Cover design © 2023 teblackdesigns.com

Praise for Kenzie Macallan

"I absolutely LOVED the intrigue, the drama and suspense, the push/pull between Cam and Quinn and the banter that lightened up all the heavy stuff! The dramatic and surprising, extremely satisfying conclusion had my heart soaring with emotion and I can't WAIT to see what comes next from this author who should be on everyone's radar who loves romantic suspense! HIGHLY recommend! Bravo, Ms. Macallan, bravo!" **~Jacquie Van Mourik, BookBub, 5 stars**

"The series just keeps getting better with each book and this one was just wow with the suspense, intrigue, and twists! There is an underlying trope of brother's best friend and friends to lovers which added to the easy familiarity and banter between Campbell (Cam), Quinn, and Liam and was a nice touch to the story. The main story arc is still on-going but Cam and Quinn finally find their HEA after finding their way back to each other." **~Krissy, BookBub, 5 stars**

"I can't say enough about how great this book was! You have three best friends who grew up together in Scotland and they drifted apart as they got older. They never forgot each other and the unbreakable friendship they have. When Quinn is in danger and needs help she calls on the only person she can rely on other than her brother who has gone missing. Cam never expected to get a call from Quinn and it end up with her being taken while they are talking. Cam has always loved Quinn but held back his true feelings. Those feelings are now in full force with her being in danger and he is no longer holding them back. Will she return those feelings while they try to stay alive? This is a fast-paced action romance that I couldn't put down!" **~Jennifer, Goodreads, 5 stars**

ONE

Quinn

_____

ANYTHING WORTH CREATING comes at the greatest cost. Sometimes, that cost is everything.

My brother and I invented an AI program that will shift the global power dynamic, eradicating the need for war. Instead of living in triumph, I live the same day on an endless loop like _Groundhog Day_. My world should feel full and alive, yet it's a hollow existence, my days a blur of routine and repetition.

My morning routine has become a habit with no real thought. The makeup bag has been zipped shut for years because no one new is going to see me. I slip into my lab coat, adjust my glasses, and make my way to the daily grind. I grab my usual Orangina and a bagel before heading out the door. Some would argue Orangina is a soda, but with twelve percent orange juice and two percent pulp, I call it breakfast.

By 8:00 a.m., the sun scorches the earth, the air shimmering with heat. Terra-cotta-colored dust clouds kick up as I drive the battered dirt roads, my old sedan groaning over every bump. I can afford a better car, but my brother insists on keeping a low profile. When our project is finished, I'll treat myself to a shopping spree and buy a flashy sports car.

The one-story building looms ahead, an unassuming concrete fortress surrounded by canyons. Its isolation is fitting, considering the kind of work we do. The lobby is always empty and eerily silent. I joke about putting a mannequin behind the desk with pink hair, a tiara, and her middle finger raised. At least it will make everyone smile before taking the elevator down the subterranean silo. Everyone feels the weight of what we're building.

I press the elevator button, and as the doors slide open, a familiar spark ignites in my chest. My passion for the project comes alive. It is top secret. Secrets are second nature to me. Trust is a luxury I can't afford. Determination pushes me to go to work every day and is my sole focus.

My brother, Liam, knew what he was asking when he brought me in on this five years ago. We signed away our lives for the chance to make the world safer, hoping it will result in less death in our turbulent world. The irony isn't lost on me.

My underground tomb is a double-edged sword. Concrete walls painted in blue, adorned with landscape photography, are a grim reminder of what we're missing about the world above us. Scientists, allocated to glass-encased cubicles and sharp steel desks, gaze at them often, wondering if being here is worth it.

As heads swivel back to view the screens, numbers and codes flash before their eyes, locking them into their commitment and belief in the program. Our project is the marriage of a software program to weapons hardware. At thirty, I'm the youngest and one of the few female scientists on this team, but it may be for nothing.

Liam has been on edge for the past few months. His hair is unkempt, and his eyes are bloodshot, a far cry from the buttoned-up former Army Ranger. His words come back to me and send shivers down my spine.

"Someone knows what we're working on and its importance. Trust no one." On the last visit to our site, his eyes scanned the work areas, trying to assess where a mole might be in the group. He never elaborated on his suspicions.

People are kept at arm's length for good reason. Lies and betrayal have taken me to task several times. Most people are of little importance to me. It's why I can dedicate so much time to our cause.

I rub the locket hanging around my neck, holding photos of the only two men I've ever trusted, my father and brother. There's a third photo behind Liam's, but I don't let myself think about him anymore. He's one of the few people who has never betrayed me, but someone on our team may be selling us out.

Clues about a mole have come in the form of failed attempts to hack our server and strangers following us during our brief moments above ground. Liam has pared us down to a skeleton crew who work overtime. We are burned out but remain steadfast.

To say our program is a global game-changer would be an understatement. If our program fell into the wrong hands, we would become pawns in an extreme power shift. I pray this doesn't happen, but I understand the danger of our project. The stakes become higher the closer we get to finishing coding the program.

We created a weapons program so the right people could access what we call MAGS—Multiple Artificial-intelligence Global Security. We named her after our beloved pet pygmy goat when we lived in Scotland. Liam gave the AI a crisp female voice with a British accent, and we talk with her every day.

Having someone to converse with cuts through some of the loneliness, even if she's not an actual human, although anyone would be hard-pressed to recognize her inanimate qualities.

She is Liam's baby and the most important part of our program. Sometimes, I think he spends a little too much time talking with her, but the more we communicate, the more she learns and the quicker she can make decisions.

Liam is the smartest person I know. He's my anchor in this chaotic world, even though we have to work in two different parts of the world.

I don't know where I would be without him. Since our father passed, he's been the family member I rely on most, but he's been distant and silent. A knot of unease tightens in my gut. My questions go unanswered, and there has been limited communication. I haven't been able to contact him for almost a week. Something is not right. Uncertainty grips me by the shoulders with a stranglehold.

If I'm unable to reach him for more than ten days, I have to put the protocols in place, signaling our security has been compromised at both ends. We've never needed that fail-safe before. I work fifty feet below ground. Liam and I are two of the very few people in the world able to do this kind of work. Whoever breaches our security would have to be highly skilled at breaking our code.

Like every other day, I make my way to level one, the lowest level in the building, where some of my team members work on the nuclear end of the project, and others work on the nanotechnology.

We synched the artificial UV light to the motion of the

sun so we don't throw off our biorhythms in our concrete hive. Several scientists have had to leave because they couldn't adjust to the lifestyle.

I head to the kitchen and grab a bottle of Mountain Dew for my early morning jolt. The lemon-lime flavor compliments the Orangina. Mornings are not my thing, and I can be cranky until caffeine enters my bloodstream.

"Good morning, MAGS." I know she senses me. She follows me wherever I go.

"Good morning, Dr. Quinn." Her voice is soothing, like a mother to a child, something I wouldn't know much about. "It seems you didn't sleep well last night."

"I'm restless." I rub my temple. "Have you heard from Dr. Liam?" She has a direct line to both of us.

I balance the bottle in my palm as I make my way to my station. Everyone works as a team, but most days are a solo effort. Scientists are notorious for being overfocused and absorbed in their work. We are so close to bringing this program together at both ends. I'm not sure what we'll do when it's complete.

MAGS pauses. Too long. Unease trickles down my spine. "No. He is not on his line." Her voice is mournful, which I didn't think was possible from artificial intelligence.

I stop in mid-stride. The bottle slips from my fingers, hitting the counter with a dull thud. "What do you mean, he's not on his direct line?"

"He manually took himself offline, but then—"

A deafening alarm cuts her off.

My heart slams against my ribs.

Her voice sharpens. "We have several intruders who have broken through two security protocols on level five."

Blood rushes in my ears. No one is supposed to know we exist.

A chill grips me as I break out into a sweat.

Only those with the highest level of security clearance know we exist.

Someone has found us. *Trust no one* takes on a whole new meaning.

TWO

Quinn

RED LIGHTS FLASH in a violent strobe, the blaring siren slicing through the underground lab like a blade. Heads snap up, eyes wide with confusion and fear. Faces blur together—some familiar, most not—but they wear the same expression: panic.

Our safe haven, a place where we push boundaries and develop programs, has been compromised.

This is not a drill.

Chaos erupts as chairs topple, computers are abandoned, and people shove past each other in a desperate race to escape. The elevator and stairwell become battlegrounds of desperation. My heart hammers against my ribs, but I force myself to stay rooted. Running won't save us. I have work to do.

My glass bottle explodes as it hits the concrete, spraying soda everywhere. Green liquid splashes my boots, but I step over the spreading pool, my mind already calculating my next move. There's no time for cleanup.

Liam warned me this day would come. Someone knew. Someone betrayed us.

We've never had an invasion, and I'm forced to take action. My photographic memory pulls up the schematic for the security protocol put in place by Liam. I sprint to the bank of computers vital to my end of the project. My fingers tremble as they fly across the keyboard. I can't let anyone get to these.

I move in the opposite direction from my coworkers, sitting down and folding my hands in front of me. Tears well up in my eyes, but I swallow them down.

"MAGS, emergency shutdown. Go deep. Do not come back online until Dr. Liam and I input a new code." I plead with her.

"Dr. Quinn, you only have five minutes. I can help you." Her eerily calm voice is a stark contrast to the chaos around me.

I rely on Liam, and he knows what to do. I'm not equipped for this high-octane situation.

"I don't need help. Do you understand my directive?" I snap, forcing steel into my tone.

"Yes. Goodbye, Dr. Quinn. Keep Dr. Liam safe." Of course, she would ask me to keep her boyfriend safe. I need to have a serious talk with him when I see him.

My heart breaks at what this could mean for us and the dangers ahead. Liam's instincts were correct. Someone outside our circle knows what we're doing, and they are coming to get it.

I launch the virus, wiping our research as I initiate one last backup. My fingers tremble, but there's no room for error. The screen flickers, each second feeling like a lifetime. Precious minutes tick away, and I have to get myself out of here before the lab burns up around me.

Gunfire cracks over the security feed, wreaking havoc with my focus. I flinch at the sound of shattered glass penetrating the air. We didn't plan for a scenario where Liam couldn't be reached. I need to take other measures.

Before the last computer shuts down, the monitor shows the gunmen breaking through each level using our codes and killing anyone in their path. There's a heavy weight on my chest, making it hard to breathe. My stomach twists as the footage looks like a horrendous video game, but this isn't a game. It's a slaughter.

We knew going in this program was bigger than the sum of our parts, which is why we're under attack and willingly sacrifice ourselves. I have a strong need to survive as I calculate they will reach my floor in three point two minutes.

Robot masks cover their faces as they breach our security system without effort. Really? Their masks lack creativity. As the last program shuts down, it will lock everyone in where they are and, God willing, lock out whoever is breaking in. The codes will be useless except for the safe room, which has a different, more complex, eighteen-digit code.

Lights flicker, indicating I'm on limited time to get to my destination.

I bolt for the safe room, dodging rolling chairs and hurdling over debris. My fingers shake as I enter a code that doesn't unlock the door. Sweat drips down my forehead as panic claws at my throat. Think, Quinn! Think!

Liam changed it.

I squeeze my eyes shut and visualize the numbers. I type them in and hold my breath. This time, the door unlocks and opens.

Once I'm in, I close the heavy metal door. The reinforced steel seals shut with the suction of a bank vault. The raw gray concrete walls press in on me. My breath becomes ragged in gulps. There's too much at stake.

A desktop computer sits on a metal table, hardwired to an

outside server and nothing else. No Wi-Fi. No way for them to track me. We stripped the room down to the bare necessities because why would anyone decorate a room you never plan to be in?

The computer in the safe room never gets shut off for this exact situation. We have a phone on the computer, and I downloaded my contacts years ago. Call it a woman's intuition, but you never know when you're going to need someone outside these walls. I rely too much on myself instead of others, except when there is no other option. I have to put my backup plan in motion.

The safe room lacks ventilation as sweat drips down my back, and my shirt sticks to me. I pop out the SIM card from my phone, crushing it beneath my heel, and smash the phone against the wall. I can't have them trace anyone back to me.

I log in, the cursor blinking like a heartbeat. There is only one other person I can trust. Desperation overrides my trust issues. My hand shakes as the mouse moves erratically on the screen. My fingers hesitate, but there's no choice. I dial the number.

The phone rings once, and his face fills the screen. The urgency of the moment outweighs the fact I haven't seen this man in years, and he's more handsome than ever. The sharp focus in his eyes tells me he knows this isn't a social call.

I stare at him for a second and collect my thoughts.

"Cam, can you hear me?" The screen blinks in and out. They must be trying to hack this system from the outside.

Cam doesn't miss my reluctance to continue as his eyes search the screen for clues. "Quinn? Where are you?" His voice is the calm in my storm, but my ears are full with my beating heart.

The banging on the metal door makes me jump, and the gunfire starts. They won't get through the door using bullets.

I force myself to focus and tell him my location, a brief description of MAGS, and where he can find the backup computer holding everything we've worked on, including the updates. My only goal is to find Liam and keep our program safe. Then everything will have been worth it, even my death.

Our research needed another safe place. A place far away from here but somewhere familiar to us. I've kept this a secret even from Liam, but it's in a place Cam knows well. It was one of our childhood hangouts.

He transfers my call onto a big screen as his brothers Mac and Declan, along with a bunch of other people I don't know, come into view. I take in a breath, not expecting this, and hesitate.

The gunfire stops. Silence is not always a good sign. I look over my shoulder, listening for the beep of the sequence. The hair on my neck stands on end, and goose bumps cover my skin.

Do they have the code?

I whip my head around, my breath frozen in my chest. No beeping yet, but it's coming. I can feel it.

I blurt out my final message, begging them. "Find Liam. Tell him I love him and I always will." Those are my last words as the heavy metal door opens with a chilling hiss. My stomach plummets.

Two men walk in, shaking their heads as if I've disappointed them. I press the kill switch under the computer, destroying everything on it, including my last phone call. The screen dies. I've left myself without a lifeline.

I close my eyes and turn away, waiting for the cold steel of a gun barrel to touch my temple.

A black bag slips over my head.

Darkness swallows me whole.

THREE

Campbell
___

MY HEART PUMPS at a frantic pace after viewing the grainy transmission of Quinn being taken. The video glitches, flickers, then freezes on her face. Her soft brown eyes are wide behind black-rimmed glasses, fear battling with determination.

My stomach knots. I've seen that look before, and it guts me now just as much as it did then. But I can't afford to lose control. That's not who I am. I'm the guy who stays cool under pressure, the one people turn to when chaos erupts.

Out in the field is where I'm not sure I measure up anymore. If the team is with me, I'm good to go, but without them, I'm nothing.

I clench my fists, the weight of this mission pressing down on me. My best friend and his sister are in danger, and I don't know where to start. My gaze lingers on Quinn's frozen image, tracing the way she clutches something at her neck. A necklace? A message? A prayer?

Flashbacks slam into me. When we were in school, I couldn't keep my eyes off her and would always make her laugh with a bad joke. Whenever she questioned the look on my face or Liam caught me staring, I claimed I was being protective of her.

The Bro Code kept me in check—Quinn was off-limits. The last thing I wanted to do was blow up my friendship with Liam. He is like a brother to me. Quinn was anything but a sibling. Now, she might not survive the night.

Besides, I'm not good enough for her. She needs a whole man, not the part of a man I have to offer her. I'm the one-legged wonder, as in, I wonder how I made it out alive.

Neil McFadden, head of the MI6 division of Scotland Yard, barks an order, cutting through the tension in the conference room. "Sherri, contact President Decker's Chief of Staff and tell her to get me the entire tape from Quinn's last communication. I need it ASAP."

"Yes, sir," his assistant replies without missing a beat.

Neil contracts MBK Global Security to work off-book missions, the stuff MI6 can't do. This mission has upgraded to top security clearance by the President of the United States. Everyone's eyes shift at the realization of the scope of this op. The energy tightens like a drawn bowstring.

The teammates—ex-MI6, Navy SEALs, black ops—sit in plush leather chairs around an enormous mahogany table in an office high above New York City, a stark contrast from Quinn's concrete hellhole.

The dichotomy of a soldier's life is the balance between the comforts of civilian life and saving civilians under unusual conditions. Questions tumble over each other in my head that I want to ask her, none of which have answers.

Quinn's message isn't only for me but also my two broth-ers, Declan and Mac. We were a tight-knit group growing up together when Quinn and Liam came from the States to live in Edinburgh, Scotland. They are two of the most intelligent people I know, which can also mean trouble when others know about their IQ. Both are MIT graduates with several science degrees.

"Let me get this straight. Someone has taken Liam and Quinn, but no one knows who or where to find them. What kind of off-the-grid shit were they working on?" My face warms as my anger rips free.

Neil's stare pins me. "We're going to review the tape and take it from there. Tomorrow, we have a top-level meeting in Washington, DC. We'll explain everything then." He knows what's at stake for me on a personal level. I'm not sure I should be on this op. I'm too compromised physically, but I have my team.

"I need everyone to stay sharp for this mission. It's a matter of global security. This off-book security firm didn't fall into this. You were chosen specifically for your talents and what you bring to the operation. The President and his team have a full dossier on each of you, even the things that aren't so pretty. Is everyone onboard?" Neil stops talking long enough for everyone around the table to digest the magnitude of this assignment. Our heads turn to Sean.

"Are we in?" Sean asks.

We bow our heads, stare at our folded hands, and rub our foreheads, trying to take in what Sean Knight, one of the partners of MBK Global Security, is asking of us as individuals and as a united team. Sean looks to his co-owners first, Beck McKenzie and Peter Bryant. They nod, accepting the assignment. He doesn't say a word and turns to each member as they nod in agreement to what lies ahead. That's the confirmation Neil needs to move forward.

He continues, "You're not alone. The United States government has assembled an elite team of soldiers from every branch of its military. Whoever is behind this better strap themselves in for the ride of their lives. This is a take no prisoners mission." He pauses. "Deep 8 may be behind this, but we don't know yet."

Sherri breaks in on the intercom. "The Chief of Staff forwarded the video directly from the on-site hard drive. I loaded the file to your computer."

Neil keys in a command, and the video comes up on the Promethean board.

He fills in some gaps. "She sent her transmission to a secure cloud from Nevada. The safe room was the last place to go to send a message out. The computer is hardwired to the outside, but she only had minimal time to send it."

"What are they doing in Nevada?" I ask.

He holds his hand up. "Not they, her. Let's watch."

We're interested in the parts that were cut out during her transmission. Quinn stumbles into frame, breath hitching, struggling to stay composed.

"I'm in a safe room underground. It's not looking good. They have the codes to get into each level. Someone hacked our system. You need to know that Liam and I have been working on a program using AI technologies, weapons, and nanotech here in America. I can't give you more details. Find Liam. He holds the key. It is too late for me. My backup computer is in our tree house. You need to get it."

She inhales sharply. A door slams as heavy boots thunder toward her.

"They're coming!" She closes her eyes when two men enter the room and slip a black bag over her head, lifting her by her arms. The screen goes dark.

"A tree house?" Dean, the ex-ASIO Aussie, scoffs in disbelief. "You're telling me they hid classified tech in a bloody treehouse?"

I push back in my chair, my pulse pounding. "The only tree house I know of was the one in Scotland we built years ago. I can't imagine it's still there." Mac and Declan shrug as they look my way.

"Why the hell would anyone put a program of that magnitude in a tree house?" Dean presses.

"Because no one would ever look there," Beck answers grimly.

I shoot to my feet. "I'm leaving tonight for Scotland. The quicker I get that laptop, the sooner we can find her. The first seventy-two hours are the most crucial in a kidnapping."

Neil grabs my arm. "Sit down." His voice is low and firm. "She's valuable to them. They won't kill her—not yet. She is the other half of the key to the program. Trust me when I tell you, nothing happens without her."

I clench my jaw, knowing he's right. The image of Quinn being dragged away won't leave me.

"Do we have any leads on who's behind this?" Beck asks.

"There are a couple of players in this game, but I don't want to give you too much detail. This is where we are going to stop for today. We leave at oh eight hundred tomorrow to fly to DC. Peter, I'm going to need you and Pippa to head up the tech part of this op at this end. I'll be leading this mission from DC since we are all boots on the ground, including Sean. Nothing said here today can leave this room, not even to your significant others. We're going dark as of this minute. Am I clear?"

Everyone nods and murmurs from around the table. The unspoken oath settles between us. We don't lose our own.

"Meeting adjourned. Rest up, men." Neil leaves, but none of us move.

Silence fills the room as questions hang in the air. This seems to involve more players than the members of Deep 8, who keep popping up wherever we go. We've followed their trail from Afghanistan to Zambia and Germany, shutting down their operation in every location.

They claim to have the means to rule the world and everyone who inhabits it, including a drug that turns soldiers into machines, chipped diamonds to trace wealth, and a mineral with infinite energy. Because of our intervention, they have access to none of it, which pisses them off, putting us in their crosshairs.

Being in the crosshairs is what this team lives for. Danger flows through our veins. The call to protect those who can't protect themselves is a special breed of people. We'll step in the line of fire if it means making the world a more livable place.

This mission is bigger than the team. Keeping our heads screwed on straight is the key to success. I would guess that my involvement will be minimal, but I can guide them.

"What do you say we get a pint?" Beck asks with his formal British accent. He turns to Declan. "Sorry, mate, maybe we'll get coffee instead?"

Declan has been sober for over a year, and he loves his coffee so much that he created a special blend. "No worries. You guys go ahead. I'll go home to Liv." He wiggles his brows, looking forward to being with his soulmate.

"Oh, sure, rub it in for those of us who don't have a squeeze," Peter says in a Texas drawl as he pops the front wheels up on his wheelchair.

"What are you talking about? You're the man around town. You don't keep women around long enough to learn their names," Dean fires back.

This gets him one of Peter's panty-dropping smiles, as Peter puts it. "It's the spice of life, man." A hint of sadness is there and gone.

Declan says goodbye as we make our way to our favorite

pub, McSorley's Old Ale House, one of the few taverns with old-world charm in New York City. A sign with the Irish and American flags graces the top of the doorway, but as Scotsmen, we ignore the green, white, and orange stripes and enter.

Dark wood ceilings mimic the wood floor covered in sawdust. The worn tables and chairs are aged, and the heavy, dark oak bar shows damage from one too many bar fights. The ambiance is what we're looking for, and memories of home help to ground us.

We claim the nearest table to accommodate Peter and order a round of drinks. My brothers and I stick to Guinness. The chatter around us doesn't provide any levity to the situation. We hold our drinks in our hands and stare at them. No one gives a toast, says a word, or takes a sip.

Mac speaks first. "I've been on many missions, and this one tops the list for level of intensity. Tomorrow should be interesting."

I clear my throat, ready to dish out a joke, my crutch in tense situations. "A Russian, a communist, and a spy walk into a bar."

Dean groans, "Not a joke."

"He orders a drink," I reply and get a couple of smirks. Telling jokes is my stress reliever and a way to calm down those around me. Not everyone appreciates it.

"Too bad that's not all he's going to order." Mac comments. "We might be up against all three."

"The bigger concern is, what the hell have Quinn and Liam gotten themselves into?"

None of us have an answer, but tomorrow may shed some light on the problem.

FOUR

Campbell

WE HIT the tarmac at oh eight hundred on the nose and roll out of the limo sent for us by the US government, a far cry from the conditions we're used to working under. Duffel bags are slung over our shoulders as we stop and look up at our luxury ride. We're greeted by a Bombardier Global 8000, top-end flying at its finest. How high will the price be for this mission?

"Sweet ride," Dean smirks.

"Beats a cargo transport any time." Beck slaps Dean on the shoulder and walks ahead of him as we approach the stairs leading to the high-end interior.

A flight attendant, who could double as a *Vogue* model, welcomes us aboard. "I'm Cassie. I'll be serving you today. Please make yourself comfortable, and I'll be around for your drink orders or anything else you might need."

On any other day, I would lay on the charm to see if she would be interested in a stopover, but my head and heart aren't in it. My focus is on the details of this mission to get Quinn and Liam back alive. Quinn's face haunted me in my restless dreams last night, taking up the part of my soul where she lives.

I smile and follow Mac to find a place to sit, moving through the dining room and kitchen to what looks like a full-on entertainment room. Mac throws his duffel up top and sits across from the oversized TV. The space is big enough for six large men to relax and stretch out.

Cassie comes over to take our drink order, and I realize there is no sign of Neil. We can't do this op without him. The unfamiliar world we're stepping into is full of invisible land-mines under the veil of politics.

"I'll take water with a lot of lemons," Beck says. We turn and look at him. He shrugs. "Pippa has me drink it every morning. Something about cleaning out my system." Pippa saved his life when he was poisoned while on an op in Africa. It would be in his best interest to listen to her advice.

"I'll have a Macallan on ice either an 18 or Rare Cask label, if you have it," Dean requests. He turns to Declan. "Sorry, mate. I'll drink it in the kitchen." Our heads turn in Declan's direction.

"Everyone needs to drink whatever they want, despite my sobriety. Besides, Oban was my Achilles' heel. But, dude, alcohol at 8:00 a.m.? What's going on?" Declan replies in his best American surfer accent.

Dean runs his fingers through his blond hair as it spikes on top. He stares down at his steepled fingers. "I've got a problem." Our eyes are on him. "It's Leigha." Everyone takes in a sharp breath. "The woman glows as she walks down the street, and I see how men look at her." Leigha has been in Dean's life for over a year. He helped her escape her Russian mob father, and she helped him get his head screwed on straight.

Mac interrupts, "She glows because she's in love. That's

how women look when they're happy." Mac should know. He and his Italian bombshell wife have a beautiful baby together.

"Well, it's annoying. I want to punch them in the face. I know exactly what they are thinking because I've had the same thoughts," Dean replies. "I've fulfilled most of my fantasies." He wiggles his brows.

Snickers fill the room until he looks up and gives us the death stare. "There's only one solution."

"One solution to what?" Neil enters the room and breaks the tension like a cliffhanger to the end of a riveting book. No one acknowledges him. Our eyes stay on Dean.

"I'm going to ask Leigha to marry me, and I'm scared shitless. I don't know a damn thing about marriage. Then she's going to want to have babies, and I don't know anything about them either." Dean throws his head back on the couch.

Mac laughs. "Let me get this straight. You want to marry Leigha, so you don't end up beating the shit out of other guys."

"That, and I'm so crazy in love with her I can't see straight." Dean blows out a breath as if he's been holding it for a year.

"Marriage is like deleting all the apps on your phone except one," I joke while Dean glares at me.

Beck's laughter rumbles low in his chest. "In all the years I've known you, I've never known you to be such a drama queen." He rolls his eyes. "You've done ops that no one else would sign up for, but you're scared of marriage."

Dean flips him off. No one thought they would see Dean get married. We voted him to be the last man standing, but now I'm the last man in the singles line at age thirty-three. Everyone on our team is in a serious relationship or married. The gremlin of self-doubt creeps in. Would any woman want me in my condition?

"At least you're going in the right order. I have an insta-family." Declan refers to his significant other, Liv, and their daughter, Poppy.

Dean turns to me. "Whatever you do, don't fall in love with the asset. It never ends up being a quickie." Everyone laughs at his observation, considering most of them have fallen hard for their gorgeous assets.

Sean is unusually quiet during our exchange. I push his shoulder with my hand. "What's going on with you? You've got nothing to say about Dean's upcoming nuptials?"

"I don't want to steal Dean's thunder, but Jess is pregnant." Sean's face breaks into a huge grin. Jess is his childhood best friend turned lover. They met again while trying to rescue her sister, Pippa, in Afghanistan. Congratulations go around for both Dean and Sean.

I'm left out with nothing to celebrate except being alive. My accident will always stay with me, but this is my team. These are the men who have my back, no matter what. No one gets left behind or flies solo. Our missions are always a team effort. I won't do anything without them. I can't.

Somewhere during the conversation, the plane took off, and we're at cruising altitude. This plane is incredible. I wouldn't mind taking it for a trans-Atlantic spin with its Soleil circadian lighting system for jet lag, low-altitude cabin pressure, and flex wing technology. A pilot's wet dream. Maybe someday.

"Now that we've sorted out our personal updates, we'll arrive in DC shortly. The President and his team spared no expense. I need you on your toes for this meeting." He grabs Dean's drink and hands it back to Cassie. The team gets quiet, and I lean my head back and close my eyes for the short trip from New York City to DC.

The plane lands like a feather, and we disembark. A

Suburban waits for us, surrounded by men in black suits, ear comms, and sunglasses. Did they send the secret service? Don't they know we're highly trained agents and can defend ourselves?

A vehicle takes the lead in front of us, and another one brings up the rear. Unspoken questions pop up about what we've gotten ourselves into by agreeing to this meeting. The car ride is quiet as eyes travel from man to man with the same concerns. Sean's silence is a sign of worry as he stares out the window, but he tucks it away behind a stoic veneer.

"You'll be fine. You're trained for this. Consider it the ultimate compliment and challenge," Neil says as he looks out the dark bulletproof window. Even on a sunny day, no one would know we are in the car. He's always in tune with the vibe of the team and our point man because he's had his share of ops at this level.

A collective sigh never comes. The men on this team have other people to think about. When you're single and on an op, your sole focus is the mission, but the stakes are higher now. According to Neil, we have the world on our shoulders, and we don't even know the half of it.

As we enter the Pentagon through an underground tunnel, the sun disappears as the limo fades to black. The lights above zoom by, making it feel like something in a sci-fi movie. The car stops, and we unfold ourselves from the comfort of the leather seats. We're told to leave behind our weapons and bags as one of the Secret Service men from the lead Suburban hustles us into an elevator.

Instead of going up, we descend to what seems like at least three or four levels. No numbers light up on the top panel to show where we are headed. The air crackles with anticipation, and everyone is inside their heads, centering themselves.

The elevator doors open to a dimly lit long hallway flanked by black doors on either side. We follow the agent down to the end of the hall, where he opens two black doors to a vast conference room.

"Please make yourselves comfortable. The President will be with you shortly." He pulls a heavy plastic bag from a drawer and opens it. "I need your electronic devices locked away while you are here. You'll get them back when you leave."

We turn off our cell phones and dump them in the bag. He closes the bag and leaves, shutting the door behind him with a click.

This conference room has every bell and whistle from top-shelf liquor, a coffee machine you need a Ph.D. to run, and enough high-powered technology and monitors to make Peter and Pippa drool. Declan wastes no time making it over to the coffee machine, operating it like a pro.

"Coffee, latte, cappuccino, or espresso, anyone?" He grins. "I'm in heaven. This is a top-of-the-line machine."

We collectively groan but spout off our orders anyway, needing the extra octane for whatever lies ahead. The comfort of the Napa leather high-back chair is anything but calming. Once we're settled in with our morning wake-up call, it's time to break the ice.

"Who is both a knight and a spy?" Heads turn in my direction. "Sir Veillance." Heads nod in acknowledgment. The US government never does anything without knowing everything it can about the players.

We're questioning where we fit into this game. Our only ace is our contact and connection to Deep 8.

FIVE

Campbell
_____

TIME TICKS on as we wad up paper and shoot baskets from across the room. I'm the most athletic in the group and score the most points. They're watching us on the other side of a camera, but we don't care. We know who we are and what we're capable of during any op. Unlike some people in this business, we have no dirt to hide.

The door opens, and we scramble to find our seats. President Wyatt Decker walks in, followed by three other people. Neil briefed us during the flight. He stands well over six feet, a striking man who commands attention. He has the "it" factor, breezing by his opponent in the election.

"President Decker." Neil holds out his hand.

The President shakes his hand. "Please, have a seat." He takes his spot at the head of the table as the others take their seats next to him in a practiced configuration.

"May I present the MBK Global Security team, the best in the world." Neil introduces each of us.

President Decker watches us with intense eyes. His military background gives him an understanding of what's ahead on this mission and, perhaps, where we are coming from.

"I would like to introduce you to some members of the PAX op team. To my right is Secretary of Defense, Clay Murphy. Next to him is Secretary of State, Bea Davidson, and to my left is Natalie Palmer, my Chief of Staff. I think it's obvious why Clay and Bea are on the team, but you may not be clear about Natalie's role."

He clears his throat. "She directs, manages, and oversees all policy development, daily operations, and staff activities for me. Her office coordinates and communicates with every department and agency of the Administration. She has extensive security background knowledge from serving on the National Security Council and as Deputy National Security Advisor. We're on a first-name basis here, so there's no need for formalities." His confidence fills the room. This man is a natural-born leader. He's a refreshing change, considering the dumbasses I've worked for over the years.

Clay Murphy, a four-star general, pulls out a stogie and lights up.

Bea yanks the cigar from his mouth. "Clay, not here, not now." He shrugs.

We smile at their banter.

The President leans back in his chair with half a smile. "Don't be fooled. Clay is one of the wisest men I know. Why don't you fill in the team about what we have so far?"

The lights dim, highlighting the lit screen behind the President. He slides his chair next to Natalie. I read people pretty well, and I would say she's happy to have him close to her. His motives aren't obvious, but he is young for a widower.

The first photo shows Quinn and Liam standing next to each other in lab coats. They're smiling, and their faces are bright. The shot seems to be from a couple of years ago, and my eyes never stray from Quinn. Her bright smile and inquisitive eyes were always the lures.

"Drs. Liam and Quinn Donovan have been working on a high-level project with top security clearance. The project is called MAGS, Multiple Artificial-intelligence Global Security. Dr. Liam Donovan works on the AI piece of the project, and Dr. Quinn Donovan works on the weapons and nanotech end of things."

Sean pipes in, "I'm sorry. Did you say weapons?"

Natalie takes over, "Yes, these weapons connect to an AI that can detect military and terrorists from civilians and make calculated decisions in nanoseconds. It's a multi-layered device we're going to use with other types of military-grade weapons. Dr. Quinn developed the smallest nuclear weapon produced to date. She is also creating nanotechnology that would revolutionize how we conduct war. Dr. Liam continues to develop AI that can fit on a chip and be applied to bullets for tracking and target accuracy. MAGS can operate the weapons and the nanotech." She gazes around the room. "Questions?"

A lump forms in my throat, getting lodged halfway down as I digest the implications of the technology. This is next-level science warfare for a hundred years from now. Technology is outpacing humans at a frightening rate. The Terminator is here and ready to roll.

The screen flashes with the schematics of the technology, which one would need a doctorate to figure out. AI chips appear in various versions and their application to the weapon of choice. Nanotechnology is in its infancy but could be developed and used for weapons. Impressive is one word to describe it.

Mac speaks up first, "Are you out of your friggin' minds?" I put my hand on Mac's arm and nod my head.

Bea speaks as if Mac hasn't said a word, "This type of technology will give us and our allies in NATO an advantage so great that China and Russia will have to stand down when we present them with what we have. They will have no choice but to acquiesce to our demands, considering the accuracy of these weapons. When they develop this nanotechnology, it will be the silent killer. We could take over entire countries with such precision, and we would spare all civilian lives. This would give us the upper hand in any war."

She sits back, satisfied with her description of the US versus the world in domination, wrapped in a pretty white bow. The only sound is the quiet hum of the sub-zero refrigerator. We stare at the screen showing the ways they could use this technology and in what countries. Silence overlays the battle between loyalty and defiance that rages on in each of us.

"Mr. President, the ramifications of this type of weapon and technology will change how and where we execute war on the planet." Beck chooses his words wisely to make a point.

"Please, call me Wyatt. You are correct. This is a significant change globally. If this technology had been readily available when Russia invaded Ukraine, the war would have been over before it began. The targeting is so precise, it's like watching a video game." He rolls himself up to the end of the table.

He stops and stares at a piece of paper, gripping it tightly in his fingers. "We have another problem." He looks up at me and then at Mac and Declan.

"Drs. Liam and Quinn Donovan implanted themselves with a chip. They wanted a tracking device so we could find them no matter where they were in the world. Liam's chip went offline three days ago, and we've been unable to locate him. Quinn's chip is still operational but is in and out, making us think she's being held underground where various metals are blocking the signal."

"Why wasn't I informed about this?" Clay says with a scowl.

"It was on a need-to-know basis, and the fewer people who knew, the safer they would be," The President replies, "or so we thought."

"She should be easy to find based on her last location," I say with some relief, but I worry about Liam, even if he is an ex-Ranger.

He nods his head and sits back. His jaw takes a hard line. "We think the Russians and Chinese are involved and possibly working with Deep 8. As you know, the Russians have some of the best hackers in the world, and China is known for its advances in nanotechnology. From what we can tell, the members of Deep 8 lured them in for a big payout with the promise of power. However, we have a twist to this scenario. We have reason to believe Dr. Liam Donovan is working for them and Deep 8."

I stand up. "That's impossible! I've known Liam my whole life. He would never work for the other side. Do you have any evidence?"

Neil puts his hand on my arm. "Sit down, Campbell."

Did I just yell at the President of the United States? I need to get a grip. This mission hits too close to home for me.

"I apologize for my outburst, Mr. President. These two scientists are like family to me." My hands are balled into fists under the table.

Wyatt puts his arms out in my direction, leans forward on the table, and clasps his hands. "Liam's communication over the last two weeks has been minimal. We had our suspicions. Then his chip went offline when he went dark. As you know, his mother, Liz Donovan, was the Ambassador of Scotland years ago and now serves as a Senator of Virginia. There has been some interesting chatter between her and her son. Communication between Quinn and her mother is infrequent and stifled. All trails lead back to Liam working for the other side."

"There's got to be another explanation," Mac mumbles.

I run my fingers through my hair, spiking it at the top. Quiet descends on the room as Mac, Declan, and I process what's being said about Quinn and Liam, our other brother and sister.

"Is it possible you've fallen out of touch with Liam, or he's been hiding stuff from you?" Dean asks me quietly.

"It's possible, but I know this man as if he were my blood. I can't believe he would go against his country," I reply.

"The first thing you need to do is find Quinn. She may have more answers than we have at this moment. Then you need to hunt for her computer where she backed up the program. We need access right away. It's a matter of national security. We'll look for Liam with our team," Bea recites the plan they were leading us to from the moment we set foot in the building.

"No." Heads turn in my direction. "Once we find Quinn and secure the computer, she and I will hunt down Liam and get answers. If he's a spy for Deep 8, I want a friend to approach him first without a gun in his face. He may have had ulterior motives for cutting off communication and losing his chip."

"This technology is worth hundreds of millions, maybe even billions of dollars, on the open market. I'm preparing you now. You may not like what you find. It's a dirty business." Clay gives his two cents on the topic.

RISK

I know I need to find Quinn and Liam as soon as possible, or it may be their blood on my hands.

SIX

Quinn

A LOOSE BAG covers my head and blocks out the light as my other senses grow sharper. The smell of gasoline permeates the air as I roll back and forth into the spare tire. Sweat covers my body. The temperature in here is at least one hundred degrees from the desert heat. I'm ready to implode, but I know I have to keep it together and use my head. My trick to staying calm and preventing myself from hyperventilating is to revisit my childhood memories with Cam.

Years ago, I could always count on Cam—in and out of school. Being three years younger than him didn't stop my crush. As I walked to my next class, my eyes would search for him in the halls, but I could feel him before I saw him. When I caught his eyes, he would look over and wave to me. From across the sea of other bodies, his energy crawled up my arm like a vine and took hold of my heart, but he always left me in the friend's bubble.

I wanted to breathe his air. Calm seemed to be part of his soul. I hoped the hold of that vine would never let go, but we became adults, where childhood dreams go to die. Is it any wonder he was the person I called for help when I couldn't reach my brother? I pray he can help me because I seem to have a running record of the people I love being unreliable.

The car stops abruptly as my back slams into the tire, and something cuts into my back. I let out a yelp. The creak of the lid grabs my attention as sunlight filters through the bag. I can make out two shadowy figures speaking to each other in another language and laughing. A voice box alters their voices. They haul me up by my arms with my hands zip-tied in front of me. My legs shake underneath me as I regain my balance when they set me on the ground.

They move me forward as my feet shuffle through the hard, dry earth. Plumes of dust coat my skin and the bag, making it harder to breathe, and I cough. We must still be in Nevada or close to it. Heat burns my skin through my clothes as my lungs gasp for air.

The light and the heat disappear, and a cool breeze tickles my skin. My vision is cast in darkness again, and I can't make out anything around me. I'm familiar with this type of atmosphere. The space has a distinct smell of dampness, filling my nose with the acrid smell of mold. Since no door opened, we must be in a tunnel, maybe an old mine. This part of the country is loaded with them.

We walk for a bit, and they grab me as I stumble over rocks in my path. The jingle of keys brings us to a halt, and the click of a lock leads to the scraping of a heavy door opening. They push me into the room, and I catch myself before I fall. One of them guides me to a chair, and the other one whips the black bag off my head.

My mouth opens to inhale as much air as possible from the stuffy room. Sweat drips down my forehead from being overheated and nervous. I've never been in this situation before, and being taken against my will puts my mind and body on extreme alert.

The table in front of me is old and rusty. The room has cement walls, which was rather unusual for an old mine, if that is where they brought me. The bigger of the two men sits across from me at the table. He's still wearing his mask. Beads of sweat run down his neck. I can't imagine the masks are comfortable or equipped with air conditioning.

"Where is Dr. Donovan?" he says in his electronic voice with a heavy Russian accent. He leans across the table with his hands folded in front of him.

"Right in front of you," I reply, emphasizing every word so he can understand what I'm saying.

He grunts. "No. I mean Dr. Liam Donovan."

I stare at him and let the silence come between us like a glass partition. This gives me a moment to think of a plan. I'm out of my element and don't have one. Liam and I never accounted for any of this, and now I'm on my own. The bigger question is, how come they don't know where he is? Don't they have him?

"I'll tell you after you untie my hands. They are cutting into my skin." I hold my wrist out to him.

I can't tell if he's smiling or frowning underneath his mask, giving him the advantage. They both start laughing as the man sitting across from me slaps the table several times. He comes down on the table with his fist, and I jump.

He leans over the table. "You will tell me where he is, or we will torture you until you beg us to stop."

They have kidnapped me for another reason, MAGS. What they don't know is, without me, they can't get into the system since she has gone deep. The security Liam put in place is multilayered for this type of situation.

"Will you torture me to death?" I ask.

My question catches them off guard. They turn to look at each other.

"No, just enough for you to give us the information we need," he says matter-of-factly as if he does it every day.

I can play this game with them all day. They don't know about the chip that will bring Cam to me. The government knows I'm missing and has probably already contacted him and his team.

"I'm going to spare your lives and suggest you don't lay a finger on me, or my brother will kill you."

He stands up and moves behind me. His finger trails down my neck, giving me chills. He leans down as the cold metal of his mask touches my skin. I try to lean away, but he grabs me by the neck.

"Maybe I'll torture you where no one can see and give myself pleasure. You might like that. Your lab coat hides your virgin body."

What an idiot. Just because I'm a nerd doesn't automatically make me a virgin. I'm not putting up with dumbass's bullshit. "Only if you take off your mask. I want to identify my brother's next victim."

He pulls me back by my ponytail. "Your brother is not coming for you. He left you behind. Tell me where he went."

I ignore his comment about Liam. My brother would move mountains to find and protect me. He would never leave me behind, but something niggles at me. Did he leave me behind to save himself?

"NASA. He went to NASA," I blurt out.

His hands and mask leave my skin and hair as he stands up. "NASA? Why NASA? Your project has nothing to do with aerospace engineering." Someone has at least one brain cell.

"He might have contacted Joe Potter, and I doubt you know much about my project." I lift my chin. Nerd one, Russians, zero.

He grabs my throat as my hands wrap around his wrist. His eyes are an angry green. "We'll check it out. If you're fucking with me, there will be consequences."

I'm saved by the ring of his cell phone. He turns away from me in muffled tones. When he turns back, his cheeks bulge at the sides of his mask as if he's smiling.

He pulls a knife from his belt and moves in my direction as I try to lean away and fall to the floor. "She said you were stubborn. In the meantime, enjoy the dark, little girl. Besides, they can't track you underground." He cuts my hands free of the zip tie.

They turn off the lights and shut the door. I'm cast in total darkness, my biggest fear. Tears spring to my eyes and stream down my face. I'm thrown back in time to when we lived in Scotland. I got locked in the basement for what seemed like endless hours. Darkness surrounded me, bearing down on me. The musty smell invaded my nose and filled my head.

I was ten years old and crawled to the nearest wall, held my knees to my chest, and rocked back and forth. I buried my face in between my knees. To escape my fear, I thought of science experiments the three of us had done together and looked for loopholes or places where we could have made changes. I created new tests we could perform. Things whirled around in my head, and before I knew it, Cam was in front of me, shaking me by the shoulders.

"Quinn, are you okay?"

I nodded, never forgetting the worry in his eyes and the relief.

I was never so glad to see him in my brief life, but I remembered the investigations I wanted to conduct. This time, I mull over the formulas and codes we used in this project, picking up where we left off, hoping to make MAGS work to her full potential. I also needed to think of the next goose chase to send my captors on as I stall for time so Cam and his team can get here, if they get here. My hands find the locket as I rub the back, worried about Liam, even if he did leave me behind.

They need to get here soon. We're running out of time. I don't want anyone taking out my tracker.

SEVEN

Campbell

WE WRAP up our meeting with the PAX team, and we're handed a laptop with the software to track Quinn. Sean contacts Pippa and Peter to loop them in on how to execute our rescue plan. They can make more sense of the pings and GPS than anybody in the field. The plan needs to be a quick in and out, with the least amount of detection. We suspect her captors know we're coming if they know about her tracker.

This day has been long and intense, with some unexpected twists. We go in search of a pub to grab a pint. The ride over the Potomac into downtown DC is quiet as we process what needs to be done to get Quinn and Liam back. After getting dropped off, we decide we've been sitting long enough and walk from the hotel to The Dubliner Restaurant.

August heat in DC is something close to the surface of Mercury with swamp-like humidity. Waves of heat curl off the pavement, distorting the view. Scotsmen aren't used to this kind of heat unless they've served in the sandbox of hell, the Middle East. We've each had missions in that part of the world. Donning aviators, we trek the few blocks to the restaurant as sweat pours down our backs and foreheads.

"Whose idea was this?" Declan grumbles, the prince among us.

Beck looks at us with a shit-eating grin. "I believe it was my idea. You could use the exercise." Beck is a gym rat and loves the heat. His African blood has him barely breaking a sweat.

I'm used to this kind of heat. My time in Afghanistan thinned my blood, but I left a piece of myself behind, as did many soldiers who served there. I worked through a lot of my shit in therapy, welcoming the support to live a somewhat normal life. Normal has a new meaning for me.

Everyone breathes a sigh of relief when the cool air hits us and the sweat dries, leaving behind rings of salt. We wipe our foreheads as Beck chuckles. The hostess ushers us toward a table in the back, away from the crowd, so we can strategize and conference with Peter and Pippa.

We order a round of drinks and put it on a black credit card with no identification, compliments of the US government. The waitress doesn't bat an eyelash when she takes the card. Mac opens the laptop with his back to the patrons. He brings up Peter and Pippa and turns the computer away from him.

"Hi, Baby, how was your meeting?" Pippa coos from the screen.

Everyone groans with a couple of eye rolls.

"Interesting. How's my queen?" Beck replies with a look, challenging anyone to say a word about the exchange with his woman.

"I need you back home. I have plans for you," she says in the throaty voice of a tele-sex operator.

"Okay, cut the crap, and let's get down to it," Dean interrupts.

Peter laughs. "I was enjoying the show. I wanted to see if they were going to have computer sex."

Smack! Pippa hits Peter on the shoulder.

"Did you just hit a disabled man in a wheelchair?" Peter looks at her with wide eyes.

"You're the least disabled man I know," she snaps back.

"True," he replies.

"Playtime is over. What do you have for us?" Mac grows impatient. He wants to get back to his life in New York City.

"The MAGS compound was in Coyote Springs, northeast of Las Vegas. We're in communication with the ground team sent to investigate the scene. I'm waiting to hear their report. Her chip moved northwest and stopped in a place called Gold Point. We lost her after she arrived there early yesterday," Peter reports.

I grab the laptop and turn it in my direction. "What do you mean, you lost her?"

Peter looks over at Pippa. "We think they took her underground, which is why we lost the signal. Your team will leave tomorrow morning to fly to Las Vegas."

"Hey, what happens in Vegas stays in Vegas." Dean smiles as I scowl at him. "Okay, maybe not."

"Why can't we leave tonight?" I ask anxiously.

"They won't have the plane fueled and ready to go until early tomorrow. If they leave with her, we will track her and lead you to her," Peter tries to reassure me.

"What if they find the tracker and destroy it?" My heart beats faster.

Pippa leans into the camera. "You need to calm down. We've got this. From what we can tell, they have not removed or destroyed the tracker. I doubt they know she has one. We're here for you, but I need your head in the game. Less emotion, more intellect."

She's right. This is personal, and I'm losing perspective. I need to think like a soldier and strategize like a kidnapper. Strategy is my strength. I'll need the rest of the team to do the legwork since I won't be able to keep up. Quinn is the key to finding Liam and the MAGS program. Without her, there is only half a program that's worth nothing.

Her kidnappers know what they're doing hiding her out in the middle of the desert, thinking it's out of our comfort zone. What they are not counting on are our highly trained skills and sheer determination. No one is invincible, but as a team, we're damn close. The three of us are brothers who work well under pressure. Dean, Sean, and Beck have worked together for years and know each other's signals.

"What is our ETD tomorrow?"

"Oh six hundred on the tarmac," Peter responds.

"Roger that. Thanks. We can't do this without you two. We'll touch base tomorrow after we've arrived at the location." Sean signs off and shuts the computer.

I take a giant gulp of Guinness, and their eyes are on me.

"We're going to get her back." Declan puts his hand on my shoulder. "There's always a way. Look at me. I'm like a cat with nine lives." He spreads out his arms. He's not wrong. Declan has escaped death on more than one occasion.

Cool, heavy liquid slides down my throat as I take a breath. "I know. We would be lost without her tracker." What I mean to say is I would be lost without the tracker, as well as without Quinn and Liam. Those feelings for her from years ago roar back to life as if they never left.

Beck speaks up, "Something doesn't feel right about this one. It's like we're being lured out to the desert on their terms. If they knew about the codes to the lab, maybe they know about her tracker. They must know they can't do anything to her. She's half the program. And what about Liam? Where has he disappeared to?"

"I've got the same feeling. General Murphy has a team on the ground. Hopefully, we can call for reinforcements if we need them." Sean gets quiet and stands up. "I have a phone call to make to cover our asses."

They may be counting on a team of six, but they won't count on a backup team of many skilled soldiers. The more we uncover about this mission, the more it looks like Deep 8 is out for blood. As long as it's not Quinn's or Liam's blood, I'm okay with how things might go down. I've been here before, and I'm not afraid of what I might lose this time if it saves their lives.

The table is quiet, and everyone is halfway through their drink. "I can't accept Liam cooperating with the enemy. It's not who he is," I mumble to myself.

"People will do anything for the right price. We don't know the circumstances surrounding his disappearance," Mac offers.

I'm about to respond to Mac when Sean comes back to the table. "It looks like this project has a mole, and it may be Liam. The team that breached their underground lab knew what they were doing, where to go, and how to get through. They didn't count on Quinn following protocol and then taking a left turn by contacting Campbell."

"I called General Murphy for tomorrow's backup at the Gold Point location. If everything goes according to plan, we'll have Quinn back by tomorrow afternoon."

Sean puts his hand on my shoulder. "Campbell, I'm going to ask you not to discuss our suspicions about Liam with her. We need to find out what she knows to get to her brother. We just don't know where he is in this scheme."

The lump in my throat swells. I've never hidden anything

from Quinn. We were always honest with one another, except I never told her how I felt about her.

"I'll do what I can to find out about Liam. You can count on me," I respond without looking at him.

What I don't tell her won't hurt her. I hid my love for her for years, and that will stay buried forever, no matter which side Liam is on.

EIGHT

Quinn

TIME HAS BECOME FLUID, and I don't know if it's day or night. I've been in here a long time without light or food and little water. Several times, anxiety has hit me, and I have had to find a way to calm down. Waiting for Cam could kill me if he finds me. I can't entertain the idea that Cam won't rescue me. He's the only person who can help me find Liam and get me back to the lab to finish MAGS. At least I hope he'll help me. Everyone else in my life has failed miserably.

I wrack my brain, trying to figure out where Liam might be. Maybe he escaped from his lab before they got to him. They must know both of us are required to make the program work. The way they entered the lab indicates they know way more than they should. At some point, I fall asleep on the concrete floor, making me think my biorhythms still remember the time of day.

Darkness surrounds me when I wake up, and I crawl across the floor to find the door. I pound on the metal door and begin screaming. Tears run down my face. No one answers. I slide down the wall and sob in a heap on the floor.

I'm at the end of my tether. Someone needs to come to get me. Cam is my only hope.

I wipe my tears away with the back of my hand, stand up, and continue beating on the door. My dramatics won't change how they treat me, but it makes me feel like I'm in control. To my surprise, the door opens as I stumble backward and shield my eyes from the light with my forearm.

A man with a metal mask steps into the room. This one has dark eyes. "Pounding and screaming will get you nothing. Are you ready to talk and tell me the truth?" he says in a mechanical voice. "Your NASA story did not check out," he snarls.

"What do you want to talk about? How stupid you are?" Anger licks my sarcastic words.

He grabs me by my ponytail and pulls me toward him as I scream and struggle to get away. My hands wrap around his wrist.

"There are things I could do to a pretty little thing like you. I haven't had pussy in a while, but I was told I couldn't touch you. Someone has other plans for you." His hot, cigarette-laced breath is inches from my mouth, making me want to gag.

It's now or never. Placing my hands on his shoulders, my knee connects with his balls, and he yells out. I make a mad dash for the door, but I don't get far before I hit the hard body of another masked kidnapper. He puts me in a headlock and walks me back to my tomb.

The first guy tries to stand up and curses in Russian. Then spews out, "You bitch!"

"Guess you won't be getting any pussy now," I sneer at him.

He lunges for me and misses as I'm thrown into the room by the second guy, and the door slams shut. So much for my grand escape. My stomach growls, reminding me I haven't eaten in probably twenty-four hours. Minutes later, the door opens a crack, and a hand slides in a bowl with a bottle of water. I hear him laugh. The door closes, casting me into the blackness again.

My hands search for the bowl. There's a spoon tucked between the bowl and the food. I'm so excited to eat that I forget they might have drugged it. I scoop it up, shove it in my mouth, and spit it back out. I detest macaroni and cheese. The cheese coats my tongue, leaving a nasty taste in my mouth. On the other hand, I'm desperate.

With every spoonful of mac and cheese I force down, I gulp water. By the time the bowl is empty, so is the bottle of water, but I'm not hungry anymore. I lean up against the wall and think about what has happened in the last twelve hours. Could it be that someone I know is behind my kidnapping and wants MAGS?

They know I'm afraid of the dark, and I hate mac and cheese. Besides, who serves mac and cheese in the morning for breakfast if it is morning? Both things are from my child-hood, but I can't pinpoint who would know these details outside of my immediate family.

While I'm deep in thought, I always put my hands in the pockets of my lab coat. As I unfold my coat from the floor, I reach in and my hand lands on a cube-shaped object, my Rubik's cube. It's a fidget for me when I'm thinking. I play with it in my pocket during boring meetings. Each color is marked with a unique symbol, almost like Braille, and I learned how to move it with one hand. Finding it in my pocket brings me the comfort and the distraction I need to get through this.

I pull it out and close my eyes, which seems goofy since I'm already in the dark. The symbols come alive in my mind as I turn the different sections to match the colors. Laughter bubbles up. I've gone from developing an AI weapons program to maneuvering a Rubik's cube, but it's a great way to pass the time until Cam and his brothers get here. I'll hold on to hope since it's what I'm left with.

I'm eager to see him again after all this time. The last time I saw him was at my wedding. I remember staring at him from across the reception hall. A huge smile greeted me, but his eyes told me something else. I'm not sure if it was sadness or regret at that moment.

I was young and in love with someone who made me feel special and wanted. Sam was everything I could want in a man. He made it his mission to know every important thing about me and catered to my every desire. He supported me during long work hours with MAGS.

Cam doesn't know how it turned out, and neither does Liam. I'm not sure I can bring myself to share my heartbreak with anyone. The end of my marriage was some of my darkest days, maybe even worse than the predicament I'm in now. My heart felt like it had been ripped out of my chest. Reminding myself of that moment in time helps get me through what could be many more hours of darkness.

Tiredness comes over me, and I lay down on my concrete bed, propping my hands under my folded lab coat. My dreams take me away to happier times with Cam. I hope he'll be here soon so we can find Liam.

NINE

Campbell

WHY IS LYING to my boss so much easier than lying to Quinn? She always had a way of knowing when I wasn't telling the truth. I could never escape the scrutiny of her eyes when I told her one of my white lies about my personal life. She would want to know who I was dating and what she was like. I hid that side from her because those women never measured up to her. That's why I never tried to lie to her and would often avoid her as we got older. I couldn't risk Liam catching on to how I felt about his sister.

The day she got married almost killed me, but I had no recourse. Numbness took over as she gave her heart and body to another man. I wanted her for myself, but it would never happen. Her marriage was the right thing for her because I could never step up.

Liam is and always will be my best friend, no matter what they suspect of him. I would never betray him by dating his sister, especially with my disability, the man with one leg. He would want better for her, but I will find her and keep her safe.

The five-hour flight from Washington, DC to Las Vegas

seems like five days. The plane ride is quiet as everyone on the team realizes the significance of rescuing Quinn so the program doesn't get into enemy hands.

Our contact with Deep 8 came about by accident, but if this program finds its way to the wrong people, it will have global consequences. We want boots on the ground at the Gold Point location to scout out the area before we rescue Quinn. If they've hurt her, I can't guarantee I'll spare their lives to get information.

The plane touches down, and two Jeep Cherokee Track-hawks wait for us. They loaded these vehicles with Hemi engines, pulling over 700 horsepower, equipped with every bell and whistle. The US government will spare no expense to get the MAGS program back in its hands. Sean, Mac, and I jump into the gray one, and Beck, Dean, and Declan get into the black Jeep. Sean guns the engine and peels out of the airport with a nearly four-hour trip ahead of us.

"Mac and I wanted to talk to you about how this is going to go down once we get there." Sean's eyes are on the road as his fingers grip the steering wheel tighter.

"Understood. What did you have in mind?" I say it as if I'm ready for anything, which I'm not. I'm the weakest link on this mission.

"We're not exactly sure what waits for us once we get there. There isn't a soldier on this team who doesn't have a funny feeling about this. I've put some backup in place, and they guaranteed me they will be there. It would be best if you split off from us once we get Quinn. You need to get her alone and talk to her about where Liam might be. We're on a time crunch with this, but you'll have to tread lightly. We're not sure which side she's on." Sean uses diplomacy in his approach.

I look over my shoulder at Mac. He gives me a slight nod

and blinks slowly, letting me know I need to consider every angle of this op. He and Declan have an idea about my feelings for Quinn, and I'm being asked to use them to my advantage.

Inside, I explode with rage. Quinn was the one who was abducted, or have they forgotten that? I doubt she would've had herself kidnapped to make it look like she's one of the good guys.

As I breathe through my anger and calm down, the question is to what end? She's smart enough to make anything look like what she wants us to see. My communication with Liam has been limited, and I haven't seen Quinn for years. We grew up and lost touch, focusing on our careers. After Quinn got married, I didn't think it would be in her best interest to make contact.

Deep down, I'm not sure I know either of them very well anymore. I'm hanging on to who they used to be. The desert flashes by outside the window as I hope my negotiation skills will get me through, and I try to figure out whose side she's on.

Doubt creeps in, making me question the two people I knew like my family many years ago. Sean and Mac watch me. "I hear what you're saying. I need to use my past friendship with her to extract information. Our top priorities are to get the program back and find Liam. He has a lot to answer for." Mac puts his hand on my shoulder and squeezes.

"There's something else we need to clear up. I assume you want me alone with Quinn for a debrief, and then the team will make their way to the safe house." I stare at Sean as he focuses on the road ahead of him.

"Something like that."

My eyes narrow as I look at Mac, who stares out the window behind his sunglasses. I'm not ready to be on my own. The team needs to back me up. My prosthetic leg hampers my ability to do certain things.

My anger flares up again, and the memories of the other men in the vehicle who lost their lives that day hit me like a freight train. I've acclimated to being a survivor, but now and then, I throw a pity party in my head.

After stopping for something to eat, we roll into a dilapidated town out in the middle of the desert. The terrain remains flat, but in the distance, the elevation rises with muted colors of rust, brown, and tan earth. The ground is hard and dusty. I've never been to this part of the world, but the photos don't do it justice. The colors are warmer, the sky bluer, and it's a helluva lot hotter.

"During the early 1900s, Gold Point was a booming gold mining town. You wouldn't know it by looking at it now," Sean says. He grins at both of us. "I looked it up last night. I couldn't help myself. Mines and tunnels are a geologist's wet dream."

Buildings yawn where glass windows used to be as the blue sky fills the space. The walls have crumbled inward, leaving a tattered skeleton of a building that once was. There is no evidence that anything was booming or bustling in this part of the desert.

Tourists roam around with their maps, imagining what it could have been like during the gold rush. Shanties and single-wide mobile homes propped up on cinder blocks litter the landscape on the edge of town. I glimpse a tourist I know is part of our backup.

"What did the soldier reply when his commanding officer said, 'I couldn't see you at the camouflage training?' The soldier, with a proud smile, replied, 'Thanks, sir, I'll keep this work up.'" My way of telling them our backup has arrived.

"Roger that," Sean replies.

Mac sits in the back seat, typing fast on the laptop. "Pippa, can you hear me? We need a ping on Quinn. We're getting closer."

"I'm right here. You don't need to yell. Satellite technology has improved over the years. We haven't gotten a hit on her since yesterday morning. I can lead you to her last location."

The clicking sound of Pippa's fingers flying over the keys fills the Jeep. "Got it. You're looking for Cook Mine and Plant. It's outside the city limits of Gold Point."

I snicker. "What city limits?"

"We see something unusual up ahead. They almost look like huge barrels next to a tin shack. I say we turn back, park, and go in on foot," Declan patches in from the Jeep in front of us.

"Turning back now," Sean states. "I hope you two are ready for some heat. It's going to be pretty hard to conceal our weapons. We need to put on our bulky clothes and act like tourists."

His phone rings with another call. "We'll meet you there." He clicks over. "Knight here."

"Sean, it's Clay. We're on a secure line. I have Lieutenant Roger Bane on the line."

"Lieutenant Bane here. We're at Gold Point taking a tour. What's your status?"

"We've spotted the possible hostage location. We're going in on foot, posing as lost tourists. How many are you?"

"Six. We'll rendezvous at the Gold Point Hotel. Ear comms are synched. We'll separate and join a tour."

"Roger that." I can't resist and laugh.

There's dead silence on the line. "Like that's never been said before. Bane out."

"I think he just has a dry sense of humor." I continue to laugh.

Sean shakes his head but says nothing. Mac has a full-on grin. We get out of the car slowly and stretch, taking our time. Sean does a check of everyone on the team of twelve. Feels good to have this kind of backup. I haven't been on a mission of this magnitude since my accident in Afghanistan.

"They loaded our backpacks," Sean informs us. We move to the back of the truck and arm ourselves with every weapon we can carry.

We separate into groups of three, and each group joins a tour. The hike to the Cook Mine is not far from the center of town, and we can look lost. Declan's team is the first to make it uphill to the mine, and we are close behind, rounding the other side of the tin shack.

We secure our weapons as we enter the dilapidated shack built at the mouth of the mine. Chilly air surrounds us as I move up to join Declan, Beck, and Dean while Mac and Sean cover the front. A man wearing a robot mask steps out of a room. He draws his weapon. His eyes widen when he realizes he's outnumbered.

"You're trespassing. Turn around and go back." His beady green eyes scan us to determine the threat level.

Declan steps forward and says with an expert Southern drawl. "Whoa, no need to get out the firepower. What's with the mask? It's a little early for Halloween." He laughs.

The robotic voice can't hide his Russian accent. "This isn't a fucking joke. Now, leave before I blow a hole through you."

I put my hands in the air and step forward. While my hand is in the air, I give Declan the signal we've used in similar situations. "We're here to see one of the most productive gold mines of the early 1900's so chill, mate."

The Russian is trying to figure out what's going on, leading me to believe he is not a Russian FSB or even ex-military. I crouch down, leaving Declan to make the shot, and all hell breaks loose.

TEN

Quinn

DARKNESS STRANGLES ME, pressing in from all sides. The cold, damp air reeks of rust and despair, seeping into my bones. My pulse pounds in my ears, a frantic drumbeat of fear. Then—gunfire. Sharp bursts of chaos erupt outside, slicing through the silence like jagged lightning.

I stumble toward the door, every muscle trembling with adrenaline. My fists slam against the unyielding steel. "Help! Someone, please!" My voice is raw, desperate.

A deafening crash splits the air, and the door flies open. A massive figure fills the frame, backlit by flickering emergency lights. I stagger back, my breath strangled in my throat.

"Quinn, it's me. Cam."

His voice is a lifeline, yanking me from the abyss. A sob rips from my chest as I launch myself into his arms, my body molding against his solid warmth.

"You're safe now," he murmurs. His hand cradles my head as he strokes my tangled hair.

My fingers clutch at his shirt, the scent of him—gunpowder, sweat, and something unmistakably Cam—grounds me.

"It took you long enough," I mumble against his shoulder, but my voice lacks any real bite.

He huffs a chuckle. "I got you, Bumblebee."

A laugh chokes out through my tears. "Ha, ha. I bet you think you're still funny."

"Did I say Bumblebee? I meant Honeybee." His smile is evident in his tone, a warmth I've craved for years.

The nickname settles something inside me, easing the ragged edges of my fear. I always wanted him to shorten it to just honey. But at this moment, it's enough. He's here. He came for me.

I have to stand on my toes to wrap my arms fully around his neck, and even then, he's still towering over me, solid and unshakable. "It's good to see you again," I whisper, my tears soaking into his shirt. "I haven't heard you call me Honeybee in years."

Cam gently cups my face, his calloused thumb brushing away my tears. "I'm glad you contacted me, but we need to move now. Stay behind me."

We inch our way down the hall as gunfire echoes off the walls. I stay next to him, wanting to see what's ahead of us as he draws his gun. I notice his slight limp that would be unde-tectable to anyone who didn't know him like I do. Was he hurt, or is it an old injury from active duty?

Two men lie on the ground with blood seeping out of their heads. Cam steps over their bodies as if they are rocks in his way. A gunman with a robot mask comes around the corner, and Cam fires his gun, hitting him in the shoulder as he falls to the ground. Our escape to the outside will not happen unless we figure out how to dodge the bullets.

"This was a trap. There's way more firepower here than what we anticipated," he says as his eyes keep scanning the area. He taps his ear. "I've got one down, shoulder wound ready for pickup."

I tug his hand to make him stop. "I have another idea. Follow me."

"No. We need to get you out of here as fast as possible."

"We can find shelter in the mines while things die down up ahead. Maybe not the best choice of words."

He nods and turns on the flashlight on his phone.

We turn around and head into the mine, away from the action. The tunnels divide and change directions. We follow the mine until we hit a dead end, and we can't hear the gunfire.

Cam turns to look back. "Do you know how to get us out of here?" Uncertainty covers his face.

I cross my arms in front of me. "That's a silly question, don't you think? I mapped it out in my head as we went."

"Of course, you did, Honeybee. What was I thinking?" He winks, and wrinkles appear around his eyes. A wink from any other man would irritate me, but not from him. The last time I saw him, he didn't have the wise wrinkles that come with age. I can't help but wonder what his eyes have seen in the time we've been apart. He's been to war, which is never easy on the mind or soul.

"I have the name Honeybee for a reason. I could always get us out of any labyrinth or wooded area, and I will get us out of these tunnels. Honeybees always find their way back to the hive."

He smiles. "Let's sit for a minute, and then we'll make our way out."

He sits down on a large, damp rock and winces. Water leaks out of the walls through the cracks, looking for a way to the bottom. I sit down opposite him and study his face and hands, and who could miss his shoulders?

"Thank you for coming to get me. I wasn't certain you would." I look up at him through the loose hairs that have escaped from my ponytail, veiling my face.

He leans back. "Did you honestly believe I wouldn't come for you? You and Liam are part of my family. I would never turn my back on either of you, ever." There is a fierceness in his eyes as I hold them in my gaze.

I shrug. "It's been a while. People change." I say the words I need to say, but his words fracture me, reminding me of what I don't have. There are three men I trust in this world: my dad, Liam, and Cam. Two of them are nowhere to be found, as Cam said the words I needed to hear.

"I haven't changed." His stare penetrates me.

"Yes, you have. You've been on active duty. That will change any man or woman, sometimes down to their core." I won't mention his limp, saving it for later.

Cam clasps his hands together and looks down. "I haven't changed my core. I'm the same man I was when you knew me. Some bonds are never broken."

He gazes over at me, and I smile. "We'll talk about this later." I won't let him off the hook.

He rolls his eyes. "The words every man wants to hear. Let's get out of here." He stops as if he's listening to something in his ear comm. "Roger, that. We're on our way."

He holds out his hand. "We're cleared to leave the mine. Can you get us to the entrance?"

I put my hand in his. There's a warmth between us I can't describe, but I know I've missed his comfort. His energy has always been calm and reassuring. My nerves have reached their limit, and I need an anchor in this unforeseen storm.

I nod. "I'll get us there, and then I need to go back to the lab."

"We'll see about that."

He never lets go of my hand, helping me over rocks and rusty rails for the mine carts from years ago. We are quiet as we walk over the bodies of men who didn't make it out alive. The sight of them should upset me, but I'm holding on to my anger at them for taking what doesn't belong to them.

We reach the shack at the mouth of the mine to be greeted by a group of giant men, two I recognize as Declan and Mac, and hug them. I'm introduced to the other men, but I look around, trying to find Liam.

"Where's Liam?" My hope fades.

Mac's eyes shift to Cam. "We were hoping you could tell us."

My heart sinks. "I wish I knew." I don't miss the suspicious eyes aimed in my direction.

Cam focuses on his brothers. "Any casualties?"

"One of Bane's teammates got hit, but he'll make it," Sean replies. "You and Quinn need to figure out your next move," Sean says, obviously the leader of the group.

"Why did you have to kill them? We need to find out what they know about the program and how they breached the lab."

One of them, with an Australian accent, mumbles, "She's a feisty one."

Mac ignores him. "They ambushed us and came out of the hills. Those were the guppies. We're looking for the big fish. We took one prisoner, but I doubt he knows much."

I blow out a breath of frustration as some men leave the shack.

Mac and Declan pat Cam on the shoulder and mumble, "You got this. You're ready."

By the time I've registered what has been said, they are gone. Cam looks pale and nods, unsure of our next steps.

"What are they talking about?" I question.

"It's nothing for you to worry about, but you need to trust me. We need to get out of here before we draw attention and someone comes to clean up. We'll walk down to the Jeep and look like we're tourists."

He unzips his backpack and pulls out two baseball hats and sunglasses, handing one of each to me. "Eww, you gave me the Diamondback hat when you know I'm a Phillies fan."

A smile lights up his face. "I'm sure you'll live through it."

"At least I'm not wearing the Yankees hat, turncoat." This makes him throw his head back and laugh.

When we find the Jeep, he gets into the driver's seat, and I pull myself into the passenger seat. I throw my hat in the back for someone else to find. "Where are we going?"

The car bumps along the road, kicking up red dirt. "Back to Las Vegas. You and I have to talk and come up with a plan." He's in soldier mode.

"No. I need to go back to my lab in Coyote Springs. There are things I can retrieve that could be of value. It's not far from here. Let me put it in the GPS."

He pulls the car over and throws it in park. "My biggest job is to keep you safe. Your lab is no longer safe. There are enemy eyes on it, waiting for you to return. I won't risk it. Not when your life is in my hands. Trust me to get us through this."

I turn away from him and look out the window as he pulls back onto the road. The tension is thick in the air. He grabs my hand and squeezes. "We'll talk more when we get to our destination."

Tears well in my eyes. My life's work may never see the light of day again. "Do they have Liam?" I whisper, not sure he's heard me.

He looks at me with worried eyes and something else I can't identify. "I don't know."

For the first time in many days, I feel safe and secure, a feeling I'm sure won't last long. It never does. My gift of security comes in small bouts but never long stretches. As I think about the list of things I need to do, the rhythm of the car lulls me to sleep. My dreams are restless and unresolved.

ELEVEN

Campbell

HER COURAGE IMPRESSES ME. They have kidnapped her, shot at her, and left her in a room for the last seventy-two hours, and the thing she wants to do the most is go back to the scene of the abduction. In the time I have known her, she has never backed down, my exact opposite. That's the attraction. I have to reel it in as my heart sinks underwater and out of sight. Once she finds out about my leg, she'll understand why we can't be together.

The dark circles under her eyes tell the story of what she's been through, and she falls asleep. I ball up a sweatshirt and put it between her head and the window. Her snore is soft as her mouth hangs open. Something to tease her about later. I snap a shot on my phone for evidence. My hand itches to reach out and touch her, but I resist the urge, as I've done so many times before.

As we head southeast to Las Vegas, the sun sets behind us in a blaze of tangerine glory. Rays grasp at the sky with a last look at the world and settle behind the canyons.

Stars peek over the mountaintops, waiting for darkness to

beckon them. They are the most brilliant stars I've ever seen in the world.

Blackness sucks the heat away and chills the desert air. I can barely see in front of me, following the funnel created by the headlights.

We're not long into the drive when lights come on fast in my rearview mirror. We're being followed. But how? I watched for anyone following us from the time we left Gold Point. How did they track us out here? It hits me. They might have hacked her tracker.

I jostle her awake. "Quinn, wake up. Where's your tracker?"

Her eyes get big. "How do you know about that?"

"It doesn't matter. Reach into my backpack and pull out the aluminum foil. Wrap it around whatever part of your body has the tracker in it. Whoever is following us has found you through the tracker. While you're doing that, I have enough horsepower to get us out of here and into the canyons to lose them."

"Who the hell carries aluminum foil with them?" She reaches for my backpack.

"You should know you can do amazing things with aluminum."

As I focus on the road, trying to dodge meandering armadillos, I hear the crinkling of aluminum foil. I'm curious to know where she's wrapping it, but I can't look away.

I wrestle the Trackhawk into the small spaces between the canyon walls as the four-wheel drive kicks in, and we climb over boulders. The ability of the truck to navigate the terrain has given me a slight lead.

A plume of dust covers the Jeep, giving us away. We pass by a cave big enough to hold the Trackhawk. I throw the truck in reverse and tuck it into the cave while cutting the lights. We're in total darkness, unable to see anything around us.

I know the dark frightens her, so I try a distraction.

"How old was the caveman on his birthday?" I ask.

Her laugh filters through the air and tickles my skin. "I don't know," she murmurs.

"Stone age."

We both laugh at my corny joke, and it's what she needs. A vehicle goes by us, and we stay put for a few more minutes until I can't hear their engine.

"I think we're good to go."

When I turn on the lights in the cabin, I can see she's wearing an aluminum foil skirt, which makes me wonder where she has the tracker buried in her body.

"Nice skirt. Haute couture, I see."

She smiles without looking at me, and we make it out of the canyon as fast as the truck will carry us. As soon as we hit the road, I gun the engine as we cruise at a hundred miles per hour. She curls herself up and tucks my sweatshirt under her head, falling asleep again. This woman could always sleep under any condition.

I drive through the tunnel of darkness with my thoughts, hoping she's the same person I knew growing up, praying she and Liam are not working for the enemy. She's always had strong convictions, but it doesn't mean money doesn't play a role. They had everything they could ever want growing up, but things can change when you become an adult, left on your own to measure up. I know about not measuring up.

She sleeps for the over four-hour trip back to Las Vegas. As much as I need to get information from her, now is not the time. She'll want answers of her own, and there are things she doesn't know about me, and I'm not sure I want to share them. I don't want her to look at me differently through the eyes of pity.

Up ahead, the lights seem to grow out of the earth in the middle of the desert like some nightclub oasis. While she slept, I booked us a top-floor penthouse suite at one of the premier hotels in Las Vegas. I want her to have the top luxuries so she can clean up, relax, and open up to me.

Part of me feels dirty in my deception, but I have no choice. Setting the scene to get information is my specialty. I've watched people for years, and I know how they tick. We not only need to find Liam, but we also need to get to MAGS.

I rub her shoulder. "Hey, sleepyhead. Time to get up. We're here."

Her eyes blink open as she looks around. "Where are we?"

"The Aria."

Her head whips in my direction. "You can afford the Aria?"

"I can." I hold up the black card. "Rather, the US government can and will." I wiggle my brows.

"Shouldn't we be in some safe house in the bad part of town?"

"One, you watch too many movies. Two, sometimes it's best to hide under a fake name in plain sight." I wink at her.

I step out of the car, walk around to her side, and open the door. The bags under her eyes have darkened. I hold her under her arm, and she leans on me. She doesn't bother to remove the aluminum skirt as people stare at her from the lobby.

The backpack is slung over my shoulder, and I throw the keys to the valet. "Make sure you park this in a garage on the other side of town," I say as I slip him enough money to get the job done. We won't be using the Trackhawk again. They may have hacked into the GPS. We'll get another ride, depending on where we head tomorrow.

I check in and grab the keycard for the penthouse as we head to the private elevator. She leans against the elevator wall, and her eyes close. Even warriors get tired.

The penthouse has two bedrooms, a living room, a dining room, a Jacuzzi, and a full kitchen. Everything is top-end from floor to ceiling, with a contemporary flair. I can't help but notice, which feeds my affinity for DIY renovation shows.

She plops down on the leaf-green couch. "I'm still exhausted. My nervous system is shot, but I still have work to do on MAGS."

I throw the backpack on the couch opposite her and sit down. "I'm sure you are exhausted, but MAGS can wait. We have to remove your tracker and then find Liam."

She looks up at me as her eyes widen. "Excuse me?"

"I have to remove the tracker. They will find us again, and we're on the run."

"I know we haven't seen each other in a while, but I'm pretty sure you're not a surgeon. Maybe we can go to a nearby urgent care, and they can remove it."

I shake my head. "I have to do it. Now. The sooner, the better. You need to trust me. I'm not sure how effective the aluminum foil is."

There is the word that stings the most: trust. By the time we're done, her trust in me will be shattered. I lean forward, resting my elbows on my knees, and rub my hands together. "Where is it?"

She grabs her necklace and rubs it with her thumb. Her voice breaks. "Fine." She stands up and rips off the aluminum skirt. Pulling down her pants to the middle of her bum, she points to its location right below her waistline. She moves closer, putting her ass in my face. My face warms, and the not-so-shy animal in my pants comes to life.

"Here. You can feel it under the skin. It shouldn't be hard to get out." She looks at me over her shoulder. Her face is red.

"Pull your pants up. I have morphine to numb the pain." I unzip my backpack and pull out the necessary items to do the job.

She pulls up her pants and sits down next to me. "I can't have morphine. I'm allergic." I'm not used to her voice sounding small.

"What happens?"

"Anaphylaxis."

I frown without saying a word. There will be many new things I'll discover about her I never knew but wish I had.

"I was in a car accident many years ago, and one drop shut me down. I guess you'll be operating without numbing it." She grimaces.

"I have novocaine, and I'll work quickly."

"What are you, a pharmacy?" She smiles weakly.

"I always come prepared. That's what I'm trained to do." My eyes beg her to put her trust in me.

"Yeah, I know. Why do you think I called you?" Her eyes are warm with a touch of sadness, but I'm unsure of why or where it's coming from. "How good are you with stitches?"

"I'm not the pro Sean is, but I can hold my own. I've had to do a lot of stitches over the years. How big is the tracker?"

She holds her finger and thumb apart. "About the size of a small pill."

"I need you to lie on your side and pull your pants down to where the tracker is located."

"I've yearned for you to say those words for years."

I wait for her to throw her head back in jest, but it doesn't come. "Ha, ha. Don't get sassy with the man that has a scalpel in his hand." I contort my face, holding up the fresh scalpel from the sterile package.

She pulls down her pants, exposing half her bum. My thoughts go to Afghanistan to squelch my libido. Her skin is creamy white, and the thought of me cutting into it makes me shudder. She rubs her fingers over the spot where she buried the tracker.

I load the needle with novocaine and inject it near the site. "Why do all the patients love the surgeon who is also a stand-up comic? He leaves them in stitches."

She winces from the burn of the local anesthetic. "Har, har. Just get this thing out," she says through gritted teeth.

I rub the area and try to distract her. "Besides getting kidnapped and running from bad guys, what have you been up to?" My scalpel breaks the skin, and bright red runs down the curve of her bum. I try to shove away the fact that I may leave her with a scar.

"I have relegated my life to working on this program to make the world a better place." She looks over her shoulder with conviction. "Liam and I believe our work is vital to save lives during times of unrest and shorten the time countries spend in war."

My focus lasers in on the area to remove the tracker. I nod. "I've seen war. It's long and deadly. I'll be interested to hear more about your program and where you think Liam might be."

I look up to see her eyes and mouth turn down from worry. I get the distinct feeling she doesn't know where Liam is, but I won't know until I gain her complete trust.

I use a pair of tweezers to grab the tracker, show it to her, and throw it in a metal cup with water. I make quick work of sewing her up with five stitches, sterilizing the area, and covering it with a waterproof bandage.

She sits up, pulling her pants up along the way.

"You're not going to look at it?" I question.

Her mouth quirks up on one side, and she shrugs. "I trust you did your best." She pats my leg. "Thank you for everything today. You saved my life. I owe you." She stretches and yawns. "I'm going to bed. I'll see you tomorrow, and we'll talk more."

Her departure is abrupt, as if she's avoiding something. My mouth goes dry as her words echo in my head. *I trust you.* If she only knew, she'd be furious, but I have a job to do, and we need to find Liam. She might be the key, whether or not she knows it.

TWELVE

Quinn

EMOTIONS SWIRL AROUND ME, crashing into one another, and I don't know which one to grab hold of as if one would anchor me. My worry for Liam is at the top of the list, and the thrill of having Cam rescue me is a close second. I never sleep without dreaming, but last night was an exception to everything my life was before.

On the top floor, the windows lack curtains as the sunlight hits me in the eye, and I flop over to escape its reach. Thoughts come flooding back like slides on fast forward. I know where I am. I just don't know how I got here from where I was only a few short days ago, underground, committed to the MAGS program. The stakes are higher. Lives are at risk, and I'm not sure where this is headed.

I knew who I was and my mission in life with my work, but I'm questioning if the program has been compromised. My next thought is to destroy MAGS, but I can't do that without Liam. How do you destroy a voice that's been in your head for the last year? MAGS seems almost human, and isn't that the point?

My arm covers my eyes. Am I so engrossed in MAGS

that I let the world dissolve around me? My marriage didn't benefit from my ambition, but I can't take all the credit for its failure. Maybe I need to focus on the people rather than projects. The man in the next room could use my attention.

I let my guard down when I flirted with Cam, saying the thing I've wanted since my hormones took over years ago, seeing him in a new light. My soul recognized him from the first time we met. Even at the tender age of three, Cam felt so familiar, but it wasn't meant to be, at least not for him. I'll take what I can get, knowing he's my only lifeline.

The knock on the door startles me as I sit up and cover myself with the sheet.

"Wake up, *Dr. Quinn Medicine Woman*. We have things to do."

A smile pulls across my face. He remembered. I always wanted to be a doctor, and I watched every episode, even the reruns. Watching a woman succeed in medicine made me want to pursue a career in the field of science. I didn't know my work would lead to altering the way countries wage war.

I raise my arms, and the sheet falls to my waist. "You remembered," I yell out.

He opens the door a crack, and I see his smile drop to a frown as he quickly closes the door. He mutters, "Shit," on the other side.

My breasts are exposed, but I don't care. I love to sleep in the nude. It's the most freeing part of my day. I let go of everything and feel the cool sheets against my skin, allowing me to get in touch with myself. I'm a sexual creature and proud of it, although there has been little time for any fun.

I head for the shower, and when I come out, there are fresh clothes on the bed in my size. He thought of everything. My instincts were correct. Cam will help me find Liam and get MAGS back online. What we do after that is anyone's guess.

The smell of eggs lures me to the kitchen, where Cam spins around to make breakfast. The tunes are jamming as he sings a song by Keith Urban called "Female." I'm the only one he ever sang for, and he has quite a voice.

He doesn't turn to face me. "How is the incision?"

"I'm sore, but it will heal thanks to you." He nods. "I'm surprised you didn't order room service. I'm sure they have excellent food at this five-star hotel." He turns around and sings some words to me. Something about being a strong woman and my heart melts a bit more.

"I can't take any chances. We're here under a fake name, but you can't be too careful. Besides, I can cook food better than anyone here." His eyes twinkle.

I pull open the refrigerator door and pop open a can of Coke. "I remember you liked to cook. Why didn't you become a chef or go to cooking school?" I sip the caffeinated beverage and hum, waiting for it to kick in.

His face grimaces. "I'll save that tale for another time." His eyes darken, warning me not to push him. "Are you drinking a soda at this hour?"

"Yes. It gets me going in the morning."

We sit in silence while his playlist shuffles to another country song. The Eggs Benedict prepared from scratch is my favorite. The hollandaise melts in my mouth. He did everything to perfection. He missed his calling.

"This is unbelievable. You're an amazing cook."

He sings the words to Luke Combs's song "Beautiful Crazy" in between bites of food. I'm sensing a theme with a message.

"I never gave it up, honing my skills and learning new dishes while I traveled around the world." His smile lights up his face, and I understand his passion for cooking. It's the same passion I have while creating formulas and trying to make the world a better place.

"Thank God you don't cook just Scottish food." I make a face.

He puts his silverware down. "I will have you know that some of the greatest chefs are from the UK."

His smile turns devilish, and I see his fingers curling in the air. I know what's coming, the tickle monster. He lunges for me as I spin off the stool. His hands are warm on my cool skin. I screech and try to get away. As I make it to the living room, he grabs me by the waist to tickle my sides, my most ticklish spot. I turn and throw us both off balance as we land on the floor. We revert to our childhood fun to cut the tension.

He lands awkwardly and grimaces.

"Are you okay?"

"I'm fine," he snaps. He pulls himself onto the couch and rubs his knee. "I'm sorry. I shouldn't have snapped at you."

"Do you have an injury from your time in Afghanistan? I noticed you have a slight limp that no one would notice but me, and maybe Liam if he were paying attention," I say in a gentle voice.

He smiles. "He lives in a fog sometimes, doesn't he?" He pauses. "Let's not talk about this now. It's not a big deal."

I nod without pushing him to tell me more, but I know when he's hiding something.

"I need to get a new phone in case Liam contacts me. We need to come up with a plan to find him."

"You have no idea where he might have gone?" he asks as he pulls his head back. Gone is the playful Cam.

"No, I don't." I pull at the hem of my shirt. "He hasn't been in contact with me much lately. I don't know what happened or why. The last couple of weeks, he has been strange. I can't put my finger on it."

His lips are thin, and he stares at me without saying a word. I have so much to learn about who he is now compared to when I knew him years ago. We've both experienced such profound transformations. We're no longer gangly teenagers. The lives we have lived have impacted us as adults.

I narrow my eyes. "You don't believe me, do you?"

"I believe you, but you may know where he is without knowing you know where he is. Does that make sense?"

"Yes." I stand up and start pacing the floor. "Maybe if we go back to the lab, we can find clues there."

"I'm afraid not." He pulls his phone out of his jeans pocket as if he knew I would need proof. "Here, take a look at this. These are photos of what's left of the lab." He hands me his phone, but I'm afraid to look. "The men who attacked the lab had their fingerprints scrubbed. There is no way to trace them. They're professionals."

My eyes land on the first photo of my dead colleagues under tarps, blood sprayed on glass partitions, and bullet holes in the walls. I hand him his phone. "If I can't go back to the lab, we need to book a flight to Scotland. I need to get my backup computer. MAGS will help us find Liam."

He stands slowly. "I doubt your program can help us find your brother."

"Then you don't know how powerful she is."

He narrows his eyes. "She?"

"Liam created the program to have a female voice."

"Of course he did. There are things we need to put in place before we jet off to Scotland. I'm a pilot, so I can fly us over there. It will help keep us under the radar."

"You're a man with many talents. I wonder what other talents you have." I test the waters to see his reaction.

His face turns dark. "Some talents are meant to stay hidden." He turns and walks toward his bedroom.

The rest of the day remains quiet and tense between us. He makes several phone calls as I wrap my head around my new life without a home base. Staying in the hotel room makes me antsy, and I need to do something. After dinner, Cam goes back to his bedroom without a word. This can't continue. We need to be a team to find answers.

THIRTEEN

Campbell

My God, I'm going to burn in hell. Her bare breasts are perfect-sized orbs that would fit nicely in my hands. The minute I saw them, my sleepy friend went from zero to ninety degrees and held steady. She's been flirty and downright suggestive with her comments.

As much as I want to give in to my urges, I can't. I've got to hold it together. Once she finds out about my leg, which will happen because I suck at keeping anything from her, the cute one-liners will end. Given a chance, she could probably improve the design and the sensors on my prosthetic.

My mind battles with my libido, and my hormones win the war. I have to stay strong and true to my friendship with Liam. I can't succumb to what I've wanted my entire life with her and ruin the friendship I treasure. Besides, she deserves a whole man who can run and play with her children. Not someone who could trip and fall at any moment. Many scattered thoughts bang around in my head.

When we find Liam, he'll read every expression on my face. He'll know if I'm lying to him about anything that has happened with Quinn. While she may give me a high five, he'll punch me in the nose.

Hovering around the outside are thoughts of Liam and what he has gotten himself into with his program. I won't accept that he's working for the enemy. He's always been loyal and committed to the right things. There has to be another explanation. I'll do whatever I need to do to find the answers. I've made some calls to put a plan in motion.

I lie on the bed, staring at the ceiling, with a painful hard-on that won't go away, no matter what I do. Even thoughts about my time in the sandbox don't make it deflate. Quinn has a hold on me, and it's going to be a struggle to keep my hands off her.

I detach my prosthetic under the covers to give my stump a break. I would like to beat myself over the head with it. The knock on the door startles me, and I sit up to cover my lap and part of my leg with a pillow.

"Come in." I try to sound casual, leaning up against the headboard.

The door opens a crack, and I see one of Quinn's eyes peeking at me. "Are you decent?"

I roll my eyes. "Yes, unlike you this morning." I wave my hand for her to come in.

She walks toward the bed and sits on the edge. Her eyes are cautious. I'm not sure what she's about to lay at my feet or foot.

"You've been giving me the cold shoulder. What are you scared of?" Her voice is meek and uncertain. I'm not used to that from her.

"What?" I sit up taller, aware I'm creating space between my stump and her upper leg.

"I've been pretty clear about wanting to be with you as

more than friends. You've ignored me at every turn, and I want to know why." I'm cornered with few places to go.

"Direct much, Honeybee?" I laugh, but she's not laughing.

"When have I not been direct? And the honey doesn't seem to work. Stop stalling." She crosses her arms over her chest, pushing up her perfect breasts, and my eyes can't look away.

"Do you think this is the time to be having this conversation? We're hiding in the desert and trying to find your brother to avoid world chaos. I'm pretty sure our plates are full." Irritation laces my words.

Her mouth makes a hard line. "This is the perfect time to distract ourselves. You need to loosen up a bit and have some fun."

I squeeze my eyes shut, placing my finger and thumb at the bridge of my nose. This is not the conversation I want to be having at this moment. There's too much at stake for us and the mission.

"Quinn, you and I can't be together. Your brother is my best friend, and I can't date his sister, no matter how much I would like to." Okay, so the cat's out of the bag.

She stands up with fists at her sides. "That's the dumbest thing I've ever heard."

My hard-on gets worse because she is so cute when she's mad. "You and I know Liam would tear me in two if he found out I was interested in you. I would have to go into witness protection so he wouldn't find me. I'm not sure that would be enough."

She sits down closer so our hips are touching. I can smell her fresh soap scent from the hotel, but it can't hide her natural scent, which I would know anywhere. Sweat beads on my forehead the closer she gets to my body and leg.

"Why don't I get a say in this? Why are you going to let Liam dictate what happens to us? By the way, I had no idea you had a thing for me." Her cheeks are pink, and I want to touch them.

"Because I enjoy having my third leg, which he would rip off my body and stuff down my throat. How did you not know I had a crush on you?"

"Because you always acted like my friend. You never showed any interest."

"Once again, the beast has a name: Liam."

She rolls her eyes and inches closer. Her nipples poke into the front of her shirt, and her skin is rosy. While I take her in, she comes even closer. Her fingers stroke my face as I have an internal explosion.

"One kiss."

My mouth waters at the thought of her lips on mine. I shake my head. "No. We can't." I barely get the words out and try a different tack. "We're only at the beginning of this mission. The last thing we need to do is cloud our judgment. I won't be able to focus on keeping you safe."

Her eyes follow her fingers as her thumb swipes across my lower lip. "Right now, we're in a beautiful hotel room with no one around, and no one has to know," she whispers.

My thoughts exactly, but Liam will know. He knows me better than I know myself. "We—"

I don't get to finish my sentence as her lips caress mine. Her kiss is soft and tentative at first. Her tongue slips between my lips and licks the place where we meet. What starts as a sweet, tender kiss rapidly strengthens into something ravenous that's been on hold for too many years.

My hand grabs the back of her head, and my tongue pushes into her mouth. We nip and bite, invading each other's space. My hands have thoughts of going to other places on her body, but I resist the urge. Her hands grip my face as if she can't get close enough. We both come up for air in between kisses, and we're panting.

Her warm hands slip underneath my shirt, and I want to come right then like I did so many times when I thought about her in high school. Warning bells go off, and I circle her wrists with my fingers and pull them away.

I open my eyes and come face-to-face with wild eyes full of passion. "You said one kiss."

"I meant one kiss that could lead to us feeling each other up. I figured you could read between the lines."

"We need to slow this train down before it goes off the rails."

She puts her hand on my pounding heart. "Your heart says otherwise."

My fingers trail down her neck. Her skin is on fire, which adds fuel to my inferno. I want so much with her, and it's taking every bit of self-control to deny us. The moment is not now. It may never be right, as my head plays tricks on me.

"There are other things that need our attention. I have a lot to consider. I've been waiting a long time for your kiss, but let's put this on hold for now," I beg her to listen to reason.

Her face is millimeters from mine as we breathe the same air. "That was the best kiss I've ever had in my life. Thank you." She gives me a chaste kiss and walks out of the room.

I stay focused on her fine ass. She's the total package and is determined beyond belief. I'm in deep shit without waders. The bathroom is my only escape as I head to the shower to find some relief. I know it won't last long because I'm her shadow for the next week or until we find Liam.

Nothing can happen without him. He is the key to the

program. The US government wants it bad, but I won't make it about them. Liam and Quinn have to decide what's best, given the situation and Deep 8's involvement. If Liam is part of Deep 8, it will change everything.

FOURTEEN

Quinn

MY FINGERS FEATHER across my lips, still burning from my first and not my last kiss with Cam. His kiss grabbed me down to my soul. A shot of hot electricity jolted through my body, craving more, until he stopped everything.

He says he's scared of Liam, but there's something else holding him back. He burned as much as I did when our lips touched each other. There is no denying what that kiss meant to both of us. I won't push him.

Being in this life-or-death situation prompted me to kiss him. After seeing those photos, I'm aware we may not make it out alive. I don't want to die not knowing what our chemistry would be like when our bodies are fused at one point. I've lived my life around something that doesn't exist without formulas and chips, but human contact is necessary and can be a great stress reliever.

My contact with Cam would be just that: a stress reliever. My life is surrounded by people I don't trust; trust is a frail snowflake. Each design is unique but easily broken. My well has run dry in forgiveness, but Cam doesn't need to know the gory details. Sometimes, forgiveness can't happen, no matter how hard you try.

I stand by the window, staring down at a city full of illusions. Maybe my life has been one big deception. I've been kidding myself about what counts, what's real, and what I can throw away, including people. In the end, this program means everything to Liam and me. I can't abandon it now.

The knock at the door takes me out of my thoughts.

"Come in."

"Are you decent this time?" Cam says from behind the door.

"No. I'm buck naked, but you can come in anyway." I laugh.

He walks through the door with his eyes closed. "What do you call unpredictable nudity? Erratica."

I always laugh at his goofy jokes. "You can open your eyes. I have clothes on."

The light from the window shines on his beautiful, big green eyes, accentuating his smile. He steps closer.

"Promise me that won't happen again."

"Ummm. Nope."

"Yes. Pinkie swear."

"Nah. Can't do it."

He lets out a low growl. "Fine. We need to get going. I booked us a flight to Edinburgh. We have new passports, and you are going to be a blonde."

"What?!" My arms fall to my sides.

"I have a wig and a baseball hat for you. I have to wear a wig, too. My auburn hair stands out too much. This is the only way to avoid facial recognition."

"How did you get this together so quickly?" I fold my arms across myself as chills pepper my skin.

"They planned most of it out before the team left for Nevada. Just not the part where we have no backup." He shifts from one foot to the other.

"You don't like being out here without your team, do you?" I ask and watch his face for answers he may not be willing to verbalize.

"It doesn't matter because I will protect you with my life. You need to believe me."

I rest my hand on his arm as his warmth seeps into me. "I have no doubt in my mind."

He pulls his arm away, leaving me cold. "We're leaving in ten. I have your wig and hat." He turns and walks out the door.

By the time we make it to Reid International Airport to catch a KLM flight, it's nighttime, a perfect time to fly transatlantic. We make it through security without a problem, leading me to believe our fake passports must be professionally done.

The flight takes almost fifteen hours, so we have plenty of time to watch movies and catch up. We take our seats and get to cruising altitude as Cam puts in his earbuds, leans his head back, and falls asleep.

His cold shoulder hurts, but in some ways, I understand why he doesn't want to start anything between us. Once we find Liam, I'll pave the way for Cam and me to be together somewhere down the road after we save the program from getting into the wrong hands. I need him on board.

I entertain myself and watch a movie that lacks action and imagination. What gets my attention is that the hero gets the girl in the end.

Cam's handsome face is peaceful when he sleeps and lacks the tension he carries with him. My hand curls over his as I tuck my fingers underneath. He doesn't stir as his hand squeezes my hand. Does he know it's me?

My eyes drift closed, and I fall asleep. The next thing I know, the captain announces our approach to Edinburgh. I wake up to find Cam staring at me. My fingers are still curled underneath his hand, but he doesn't remove them.

"I didn't want to wake you. I wanted you to sleep for as long as you could." He slips his hand out from under mine.

I give him a weak smile. "Thank you."

"They got a car for us. I figured it would be easier for us to get around and out to the farm."

I put my seat in the upright and locked position, looking away from him. There's a new tension between us that is uncomfortable. I'm sure he's overthinking our kiss, or maybe I am.

We leave the plane with our backpacks and head toward the parking garage. The silence between us is killing me. I need my old friend back. I grab him by the arm to stop him.

"You're overthinking it."

"What?" His jaw tightens.

He knows exactly what I'm referring to. "The kiss."

He cranes his head back and looks at the ceiling. I wait. "You've got to let this go. It's not in the cards."

"That's what you think."

"That's what I know. I won't risk anyone's life by getting distracted right now."

We continue to walk. "I'm tired of other people calling the shots in my life. First, Liam, and now you. You can go to hell."

"I am in hell," he mumbles. He stops at a faded red car.

"What is this piece of shit?" The beat-up Fiat is rusted with paint peeling off the door.

"Oh, I'm sorry, your highness. Did you want the McLaren or the Mercedes GT so we can really stick out?" I roll my eyes. He continues, "We need to stay under the radar." He looks around. "I feel like we're being followed."

This stops me in my tracks. "How?"

"I'm not sure. I've taken every precaution. Get in."

The inside has cracked vinyl seats and smells of stale cigarettes. I roll down the window to let in some fresh air.

Cam knows where to go, just outside of Edinburgh, where we used to live close to each other. As we reach the country-side, there is the unmistakable odor of cow and sheep manure. I stick my head out the window and breathe it in. Other fragrances of fresh grass and wet wood float in the air. The damp air always brings me a sense of serenity and comfort.

The ride to the farm is quiet as we contemplate each other's words and where we are in this mess. Cam is trying to resist what is between us with everything he has, but it won't be enough. Our chemistry has been on a slow simmer for years and will boil over eventually. Besides, nothing lasts forever. We can be together and get it out of our systems.

We pull up to the front of the farmhouse. Overgrown bushes hide the small front porch, and the white paint is crisp against the black trim windows. The house is dark and lacks life. Behind the house is a big red barn with several smaller animal outbuildings.

Cam peers out the car window. "Do you know who owns it now? It doesn't look like anyone lives here."

"No one lives here. Some caretakers maintain the prop-erty and keep up the barns."

He turns to look at me with a frown.

"I bought it several years ago when it came up for sale. I

couldn't part with it. My time here was the best years of my life, and I wanted to hold on to those memories."

Cam's eyes soften in understanding. He was one reason why I loved my life here in Scotland. The other two reasons are nowhere to be found. I'm hoping he can give me one more glorious memory.

FIFTEEN

Campbell

SHE NEVER CEASES to surprise me at every turn. I can't believe she bought the farm where she spent part of her childhood. Growing up here was not rainbows and roses.

After her father died, her mother packed them up and returned to the States. The memory of the day they left will be forever etched in my mind. I was losing two of my best friends. We were heartbroken to be separated and promised to stay in touch, but like so many promises, it faded with time.

Liam and I were headed to university in our last year of secondary school. We were both going to apply to Cambridge, hoping to get accepted together. Life had other plans for both of us. He joined the US Army, and I joined the Royal Military Academy to follow my brothers. We lost track of each other for a while but always caught up with a phone call or an email. Entering adulthood forced us to focus on other things.

Quinn and I grab our backpacks and head inside. The air is heavy and musty. We open the windows to let in the fresh, cool air. The caretakers have done an excellent job of keeping the house in order. Memories come flooding back. I haven't been here since the day they left.

"Have you been back much since you purchased it?" I ask while running my fingers over the leather couch.

"I spend most of my vacations here. I love this place. Being here keeps me centered. My brain can take a rest, and I can fall back into the memories that bring me joy." Her eyes glaze over as she speaks about her love for the house and our past. Despite everything that happened here, we had each other. Those are some of my happiest memories as well.

"Does Liam spend time here, too?" I fish for answers to Liam's whereabouts.

"He doesn't know I own it. It's another one of my secrets." She looks at me sheepishly.

"You seem to have a lot of those. I'm surprised you keep anything from him."

Anger and hurt pass across her eyes, but I don't know where it comes from. She and Liam were inseparable growing up, so for her to keep anything from him is a signal something else is going on.

She ignores my comment. "Do you think we're still being followed?"

I shake my head. "It was a feeling. I checked for a tail, but there was none."

She nods. "I should probably go get the computer in the tree house."

I catch her arm in my grasp. "Let it go for tonight. It's safe."

"No. I can't let my life's work sit out in the tree house for one more minute. MAGS is too valuable."

I let go of her arm. "I'll go with you."

Beyond the barns stands a majestic oak that could be well over a hundred years old. The sun sinks low in the horizon behind the forest, but the silhouette of the oak is unmistakable. Quinn slips her arm through mine and rests her head on my shoulder.

"Do you remember when we had the idea to build the tree house?"

"I do. You had elaborate plans, but Liam and I pared it down a bit."

"I wanted to live up there. Away from my father's sickness and away from watching him wither away. My mother wouldn't miss me because she wasn't around until the end." Her hold on my arm tightens.

Her words carry a bitterness I've never heard before when she speaks about her mother. There must be more to the story and something I'm missing. She's right. Her mother wasn't around much because of her job, but it never bothered her or Liam.

"I've made some improvements since you last saw it." She beams.

I chuckle. "Of course you have. What have you done to the place?"

The gibbous moon shines down on us in the open field as we stand next to the tree. Her white teeth catch my attention as she smiles. I place my hand on the rough bark of the ancient tree with secrets of its own.

"You'll see."

She climbs the tree on the rugged ladder stairs without a problem as I follow behind. I'm aware I could slip, so I take my time and step carefully. I'm getting quite the view from down here, which does nothing for my resistance to her. She opens the floor hatch and hoists herself up. I follow her up through the floor.

Cobwebs and dust cover the inside of a tree house that's been long forgotten. She opens the latch for the windows to let air in and release the heat. Nothing has changed since I was last here. I don't see any upgrades. There's a small desk in the corner and two newer beanbags to sit in.

We would come up here after school and read books in total silence. I needed to be near her and nothing more. Her presence gave me solace. I watched her eyes grow wide with wonder at whatever she was reading, usually a science book. Once, I caught her reading a romance, and she quickly hid it from my view.

She plops herself in a beanbag chair as dust sprays up around her. She coughs and then laughs. Is it possible that someone is so ingrained in you they never leave your soul? I don't think she ever left mine. No woman I dated came close to her in looks, brains, or determination.

"We had a lot of good times here," I whisper, not to disturb the moment.

"Now, you know why I bought the farm." She reaches behind the beanbag and reveals a laptop. "Voila! I give you the backup." She detaches a wire from it.

"How did you download information from the other side of the world?"

"Since the tree house roof does not go to the top of the tree, I put a satellite dish on top. I got the exact location of the satellite and cut away the branches that would get in the way. The power line goes down the tree and out to the barn." She holds the laptop to her chest. "I have MAGS safe and secure."

Her brain amazes me, along with her commitment to her program. I'm not sure she understands the gravity of the type of program she and Liam have developed. We're sitting in a tree house in the middle of Scotland as she holds a global game changer in her arms.

"Let's get her to safety and back to the farmhouse."

I let her go first down the ladder as I follow behind. She

stands at the bottom of the tree, clutching the laptop to her chest. I jump down, and she looks at me with a wide grin.

"Nice ass." She wiggles her brows.

I put my hands on my hips and give her a stern look.

"Your disapproving look has no power over me anymore, so give it up."

As we near the house, I tell her to go inside and lock the doors except for the back door. I want to survey the area around the house and the outbuildings, making sure we are alone and that my sixth sense we were being followed was a fluke. I secure the barn doors and test the front door and side doors of the house. Everything seems in order. I don't get the sense that anyone is out here.

I come in through the back door and lock it behind me. A soft light over the stove gives her face a warm glow as she stirs something on the gas burner.

"Whatcha makin'?"

She watches the pot. "I used to love hot chocolate before bedtime, so I thought I would make us some." She looks up at me as I stand next to her. "It's good to keep some traditions alive."

We're lost in this space between the past and present. The memories are here with us, part of us, but the reality of our situation lingers in the background, waiting to take hold. I've noticed a softness in her since we arrived like the girl I used to know is alive and well, but only in her farmhouse.

"You know me well."

She hands me a cup of hot chocolate piled with whipped cream. "I know you better than anyone on the planet."

My heart sinks. She knows nothing about me. I'm not the same person she knew years ago. I was a boy with a secret crush who couldn't act on it. She was the girl I couldn't have.

The situation was simple. Things are anything but simple as we stand here laughing at our whipped-cream mustaches.

We clean up the kitchen and trudge upstairs. She takes the master suite, and I take the bedroom across the hall from her. She is close enough for me to protect but far enough away not to give in to my urge to touch her.

She opens her door and looks over her shoulder. "Thank you for coming for me. There aren't many people I trust in this world anymore. I hope you remain one of my heroes."

I nod and smile, but the pit in my stomach grows. I'm here to do a job and get information about where her brother is. Trust is not a word I would use to describe myself. When she discovers my real agenda and my broken parts, I will have lost her forever.

SIXTEEN

Quinn

I HAVEN'T BEEN this happy in...I can't remember. Happiness has been a luxury for me over the years. Bringing Cam here was the right thing to do. He's a part of this house, too. He spent his younger years here with me and Liam. When my father first got sick with cancer, he was here to hold our hands and help with my father's care when my mother was nowhere to be found.

My father's last breath took a piece of me with him. A part of my soul remains black where he used to live inside me. He would say I was the smartest little girl he knew and the closest to his heart. He and Liam were so much alike, from their attitude to their sense of humor and love for technology. I'm not sure who suffered more from his death, me or Liam.

I stand naked by the side of the king-size bed and hold my locket between my hands. "Liam, where the hell are you? Daddy, please keep him safe," I whisper to the ghost of my father. He lets me know his presence remains here. I know how much he loved this house, despite my mother never being here much. This is the only place Liam and I considered home.

The cool sheets give me goosebumps as I stare at the ceiling. There's a hot-blooded man I would give my body to in a second across the hall as I lie here alone. After a long day of flying and driving, sleep should come to me, but it doesn't.

At this moment, I am more alone than I have ever been in my life. I'm empty with everything to give but hesitant to give myself to anyone because my heart might be destroyed. I don't want Cam to hurt me like my asshole ex-husband Sam did. His betrayal severed many ties, and he didn't give a crap. Cam's betrayal would end me.

Right now, I don't want a relationship. I need comfort. I throw back the covers and walk to my door. The old metal lever handle rattles as I lift it. I tiptoe across the hall and put my ear to the door. Cam can sleep like a rock. I crack open his door and peek inside. He's lying face up, mouth open, and dead to the world. Perfect.

I lift the covers enough to slip in and curl up next to his warm body. He stirs and turns on his side, placing his arm over my waist. Alone never felt better as I close my eyes and go to sleep wrapped in his warmth.

FILTERED light comes in through the sheer curtains as I rub my eyes. Gray clouds cover the sky, setting the tone for the day. My first thought is about Liam, hoping he's safe.

The arm wrapped around my waist from the night before hugs me tighter. Based on his morning wood digging into my lower back, I could be a very satisfied woman. I look over my shoulder to see Cam smiling in his sleep. His hand moves to caress my breast and plays with my nipple. The wetness between my legs is instant. His hips move against my back, and I wait to see where this goes.

A hum leaves my throat as his one eye cracks open. I turn away to face the window, praying he won't throw a fit. Too late.

"What the holy hell are you doing? You're completely naked." He moves to the other side of the bed, putting the bedding between us. "Did I just…?"

"Yes, you played with the girls, and I loved every minute."

He lays his head back on the pillow. "I thought we had an agreement."

"No. You had an agreement with yourself. I agreed to pursue what is between us, at least sexually."

"Thank God I have on briefs."

"Nice package, by the way."

He throws his arm over his eyes. "Will you please go put some clothes on?"

"You take the fun out of everything. I'll meet you downstairs in a couple of minutes. I have some built-up sexual energy I need to work off."

"This cannot be happening," he mutters.

There is a chill in the air, so I grab a blanket from the trunk at the foot of the bed. Something hits the wood floor with the tinny sound of plastic.

"What's that?" Cam asks with his eyes covered.

I pick it up off the floor, and it's an MPV drive. Along the side, in my father's handwriting, it says, "To Quinn."

"It's a zip drive with my name on it from my dad." My hand shakes as I suck in a breath. The timing of this makes me nervous. Is Dad sending me a message from beyond? "I'll see you in a bit." Before he says anything, I run out of the room. I need time to process this.

My libido takes a nosedive. I sink into my bed and roll the drive around in my hand. What could be on the drive? I want Cam to be there when I play it. He'll have a clearer head than me. I have too many emotions wrapped up in this.

I pull on a sweatsuit as we figure out our next steps. I make it to the kitchen and start breakfast before Cam gets there. It's a welcome distraction. After a while, he shows up, brows lowered over his eyes, with a scowl.

"How long does it take for a guy to—"

He holds up his finger. "Not a word. Just stop talking."

A snort escapes my nose as I turn around to finish cooking the eggs. He'll be back to his cheery self in no time. I give him a taste of his own medicine.

"What did the toaster say to the slice of bread?"

"Please don't," he pleads.

"I want you inside me." I smile and place the plates of eggs and toast on the island as he holds his head in his hands and moans.

He doesn't look at me as we eat in silence. I know he's angry with me, but I need to keep breaking down his walls so he can see we should be together and get this out of our system.

The quiet between us is killing me. We've never run out of things to say. "It wasn't about sex. I was lonely last night and needed comfort. This house hasn't seen anyone but me since I bought it. You bring an energy and understanding of how things used to be. That's what I have to hold on to." My voice is timid and soft.

"Quinn, things aren't how they used to be. People change, circumstances change, and you have to accept those changes, however drastic they may be. I'm the same person at my core, but other things have changed." His voice has an edge I've never heard before.

"What we need to do is look at the drive I found. It will be nice to hear my dad's voice again." I choke on my words.

"Do you want to watch it alone? I can give you privacy," he offers.

I shake my head. "I want you with me. You were close to him, too."

We move to the den, and I pop the drive into a USB port in the laptop. I curl up next to Cam, and his body stiffens, which makes me snuggle in closer.

My dad's face comes into focus. He has an oxygen line attached to his nose, so he recorded this in the later stages of his cancer. The few strands of gray hair left on his head stick out in every direction, making him look older than his fifty-one years. He tries to steady his hand while holding the cell phone.

"Hey, Q-Tip. I hope you are well and have found the love of your life. I love you and will always watch over you, but you need to get your head out of science long enough to see what's right in front of you." He winks.

I peer up at Cam. His jaw muscles flex, and he doesn't return my gaze.

"If you're viewing this, it means my soul has carried on to the next part of its journey, but I think there are some things you should know. Your mother is an ambitious woman who has a thirst for power. She struggles between being your mom and being what they want her to be, which is on call twenty-four-seven, a leader for this generation. Quinn, she loves you, even when she isn't here." He takes a minute to breathe and comes closer to the camera.

"I think things have taken a turn. She might be in contact with some unscrupulous people she knows very little about. I overheard her talking to someone, and her hand was shaky.

I'm worried she—" He looks up. Someone has entered the room.

"Hello, my love. How are you feeling?" Mom says with sticky sweetness.

He smiles at her, and the video goes black.

There is a place deep inside of me where my dad lives. A place that used to hold joy and laughter. His voice floods my mind with memories of happier times. The tears running down my face come from the hollow ache that has dulled over the years but never goes away.

Cam holds me without saying a word. He lets me cry and kisses the top of my head. I rub the pendant around my neck, worrying about Liam. We have to find him.

"What do you think my dad was talking about?" I mumble.

There is something Cam is not telling me. His body tenses. I know there are things he can't tell me, but I want us to be in this together.

"I don't know, but it adds one more piece to the Jenga tower. We can't afford to pull the wrong piece."

I move away from him. "Why would my mom be in with unscrupulous people? I've never known her to be anything other than forthright and honest. She was never one to take bribes or bend to lobbyists' requests."

His eyes are sad as he pushes the hair behind my ear. "Things change over time for many reasons, and those things change people. Once we find Liam, he might have more answers for us after he hears the message. He seems to be the one who had the most contact with your mom. He may have answers he doesn't even know he has. You need to hold on to hope."

SEVENTEEN

Quinn

"Do you remember why your dad called you Q-tip?" He's lost in the memory of my dad with me.

"No, I don't remember. Tell me." I sniffle. I want to hear him tell me the story.

"The Q is for Quinn, and the tip goes in your ear. He said you were always in his ear about a discovery or idea for an experiment. One day, you told him about your idea and came back covered in ash. You must have blown something up. After that, he requested to be at each of your scientific investigations."

I've soaked part of his shirt with my tears. "I blew up a lot of things. He was always there for me, making sure I was safe. He was the one man I trusted. Seeing him on the video opens the wound again. I miss him so much."

"It was hard to watch, but there are other people you can trust," he says, not knowing about the depth of my betrayal wound.

I don't reply. It would only lead to more questions I don't want to answer. I need to stay focused on finding Liam and getting MAGS back online.

We lie wrapped up in each other for a while. I close my eyes to calm myself down. A chill enters the room, and Cam holds me tighter as if he senses my dad's presence. Bursts of cold air in this house make me smile. I hope my dad will always be close to me. His presence comforts me. He might be doing it on purpose, so Cam will hold me closer.

The sun peeks out from under the clouds. "I need to check on the animals. They've waited long enough. When I'm here, I take care of them and give the caretakers a break."

He nods and lets me go. "I'll go with you."

He remains quiet during our walk out to the barn. Maybe I pushed too hard, or his mind is working overtime trying to figure out my dad's message. My body and libido are running after the boy I used to know, not the man in front of me. He's made it clear that we have both changed as adulthood grabbed us and dragged it into its depths. I wish I could go back to the way we were when we were younger and care-free. My tour of adult shit has run its course, and I want a refund.

We enter the red barn to feed the horses, and he stumbles, catching himself on a stall door. I grab his arm. "Are you okay?"

He snatches his arm out of my hand. "I'm fine," he says through gritted teeth.

I've never seen him react that way, and a piece of me breaks. I have the realization that I may not know him at all. He may be the same person, but life events have changed him. There is something he keeps hidden from everyone, including me. Growing up, he was always the people pleaser, willing to get in between fights or negotiate an argument, but he's less amenable as a man.

"I'm sorry," I whisper and cut the twine for the hay bale for the horses.

The bale gets separated into sections as I throw it in the stalls. He follows behind me.

"It's me. It's not you. I've got things going on." His voice is shallow.

"Can you get fresh water for the horses?" I won't push him, and we've had enough deep conversations for one day.

My ugly lack of trust bubbles to the surface. I attract men who betray me or tell me what they think I want to hear. I thought Cam was different, but he won't share what's happening with him. Anger, sadness, and shame swirl around me, emotions I'm too familiar with from the past, and I feel myself closing off.

He moves around the barn, pouring fresh water, but his eyes are on me. He's not used to my cold shoulder. This was never how we were together. I hate that we have changed this much and lost our footing with each other. We need to find some common ground to make this work to search for Liam.

From somewhere in the barn comes a moan.

I turn to Cam. "Did you make a sound?" I ask.

"No. I thought you did, but it sounded like something is in pain." Cam looks over the stall doors in search of the source of the sound.

"I hope it's not one of the Shetland cows. They shouldn't be in right now."

The sound comes again from the back of the barn in an empty stall. We rush over and look over the door. I can't believe my eyes. Liam is lying on a hay pile, holding his hip, and covered in sweat.

"Liam!" His lips are pale, and his eyes are squinted shut. He rolls his head back and moans again. I rip open the door and kneel by his side.

"Let's get him out of here and into the house," Cam instructs.

"What's going on?" My eyes scan his body, trying to figure out what's wrong with him.

"Hey, Honeybee. Everything is great now that you found me. I knew you'd come back here. You thought I didn't know about the house." Liam's words are raspy. He looks around my shoulder. "I knew you'd come to our rescue, my friend."

"Let's get you inside where we can see what's going on." Cam kneels and lifts him under his arm as I take the other side.

"I'm sure you've done something stupid, as usual." Cam smiles.

"It had to be done. There was no other way," Liam responds soberly.

"There's always another way," Cam shoots back.

"Not this time. Someone is hunting me, but I don't know who it is. I came here hoping Quinn would know to come here if she made it out." He turns to me. "The last few weeks have been difficult, but not knowing what happened to you these last few days has been hell. I've had an upset stomach, worried they got to you."

He stumbles as we catch him, and we let him take a breath.

I watch the ground under our feet and avoid his eyes. "I'm fine and contacted Cam right away as I was being abducted."

He turns to me with eyes wide. "Abducted? What are you talking about? Did they hurt you?"

"No, I'm fine, but this being on the run thing is for the birds. I like my routine. This makes me feel unbalanced. I never would have made it as an Army Ranger." I smile.

We pick up our pace again and head for the back door. Liam collapses in our arms as we struggle to get him to the couch. As much as I'm relieved to see my brother, it opens up a Pandora's Box of questions I'm not sure I want to face. He has some explaining to do.

EIGHTEEN

Campbell

So far, the day has been a disaster of epic proportions, and it just got worse. Liam's skin is pale, and he soaked through his clothes with sweat, indicating a fever. He is weak, and his right hip keeps failing. We lay him on the couch as he lets out a breath. I rest my hand on his head, and he's burning up.

"Quinn, go get ice and wrap the bag in a towel. I'll get Tylenol and Advil to bring down the fever." Quinn and I run in opposite directions.

Liam takes the meds and asks for more water. His eyes are glazed over from the fever, but he's a fighter.

"How long have you been out there?" Quinn asks with worried eyes.

"I came on foot last night from the lab up north, but I must have passed out. I have an infection in my hip from taking out the tracker." He rolls onto his side and pulls down his pants. This is way too much Donovan bum.

The inflammation, redness, and pus at the incision indicate we have an emergency. "We need to take you to the clinic."

"No," Quinn and Liam say in unison.

"They're looking for me and won't stop until they find me. They have eyes everywhere," Liam chokes out.

"Who's they?" I ask, trying to find out whose side he's on.

"That's just it. I don't know. I suspected we had a mole a couple of months ago, but I couldn't pinpoint who it was. The surveillance I have in place didn't show any unusual activity."

Quinn and I look at each other.

"What?" he asks.

"We'll deal with it later." Quinn brushes him off.

"Do you have any antibiotics for the animals, like amoxicillin? I'm also going to need a knife, hydrogen peroxide, and sterile gauze," I direct Quinn.

She nods. "I'll go get them."

"We need to superdose you to get rid of this infection. I'm going to need to cut you open and clean out the wound. What did you do, take out the tracker yourself?"

"I had to. Someone was following me." He grabs my arm. "If I don't make it, take care of Quinn. I trust you more than anyone else. It's been rough for her over the last couple of years. She'd never admit it. Promise me you'll take care of her. She needs to talk to our mom."

I frown and nod, too preoccupied with getting this infection out of his body to worry about what his words mean.

Quinn comes back with supplies, and I get to work. Liam bites down on a leather dog leash as I make the incision at the site of the infection. When the hydrogen peroxide hits the wound, he screams in pain, turns red, and pants.

"We won't close it up. The infection needs to come out. I'll pack it, and we'll change it tomorrow to monitor it. He needs his rest, and we'll trade out Tylenol for ibuprofen every six hours." My fingers dig into my hip.

Quinn covers him with a blanket as chills set in. She looks up at me.

"The chills should dissipate as the meds kick in." I try to reassure her.

Liam reaches out and grabs her arm. "You have to talk to her. She's been helping me every step of the way. I don't know what happened, but you have to let it go. She's your mother. You need to trust your gut, and you know her better than anyone." She tugs her arm out of his grasp.

I grab Quinn's hand and pull her into the kitchen. "What's he talking about? What's going on with your mother?"

Tears glisten in her eyes. "Nothing. Is he going to be okay?"

Without thinking, my arms wrap around her. "That's what we're going for. He told me to take care of you."

Her body stiffens. She looks up at me. "What the hell does that mean?"

"That means he wants someone he trusts to take care of you."

There's a knowing look in her eye that says she's worried he's not going to make it.

I lean down and grab hold of her shoulders. "No, that does not mean what you think it means. He's going to get better. Do you know a pharmacist?"

"No."

"Do you have a gun?"

Her eyes go wide. "Yes, my father used to hunt and collect guns. He kept them locked up in the den. Why?"

"Show me." I follow her to the den. "I'm about to rob a pharmacy to get him the medication he needs."

She whips around. "Whoa, you can't get yourself killed. Liam and I will never make it. People out there will stop at nothing to get the program."

"I won't get myself killed, maybe arrested, but not killed."

"I'll go with you." She stands with her hands on her hips, ready for an argument.

"You need to stay here with him."

"He's not going anywhere, and I'll lock the doors. Besides, you need a lookout person to drive the getaway car." She smiles.

She unlocks the cabinet loaded with weapons. I take out the 9 mm, which could make a nice hole in someone, and stuff it behind my back.

"We'll wait until nightfall after they have closed and make our move."

"How many pharmacies have you robbed? You sound like a pro."

"None, and I would like this to be my one and only."

"I remember this old pharmacy out of town, Blyth's. They might have the least amount of security. Or we could use MAGS to circumvent the security system and get us in without breaking in."

We stare at each other without words. "Can she do that?"

Quinn's mouth quirks to the side. "She can do damn near anything, but we need Liam to bring her back online. I'm not sure he'll be willing to do that. It could send out a signal."

"We don't have a choice if we want to save his life and not end up in jail."

"I'll go get the laptop. There are a couple of steps involved."

She runs out of the den to get the tree house laptop as I

meet her in the living room. Before we explain the situation to Liam, the word no has already come out of his mouth.

"Why the hell do you have everything backed up to a laptop in the countryside? We can't bring her back online. It's too dangerous." He's barely hanging on to consciousness.

"I had to keep her safe. Having you dead is equally dangerous. I need you, and MAGS needs you," Quinn pleads with him. "I can hook her up directly to the satellite." She bends over and hardwires the laptop.

He lies motionless and stares at the ceiling. "You thought of everything, as always."

"I had to. You were a little too close to the project. We don't have any other options. I've examined every one of them from every angle."

She opens the laptop and taps on the keys. "There's something else you need to know. Dad left me a message on a zip drive."

His eyes widen. "What did he say?"

She looks up at me and proceeds to tell him their dad's message. Liam's response is predictable. "There's no way Mom is in with the wrong group. She's been with me every step of the way, guiding me and giving me advice."

"Nothing would surprise me about her," Quinn replies.

"What is that supposed to mean?" Anger laces his voice.

"Nothing."

He holds out his finger to Quinn. I'm puzzled and have no idea what he's doing. She leans down next to him and presses a couple of buttons. They both scan their eyes with the built-in camera. The next part floors me. They prick their fingers on a specialized USB port as it captures a drop of blood from each of them. Quinn pushes the USB into the drive of the laptop.

"MAGS, are you with us?" Liam says with a weak voice, his eyes fluttering.

"Dr. Liam, I'm so glad to find you. I was worried about you. Are you well? I couldn't track you when you went offline."

His eyes are wary. "Yes, MAGS, I'm fine, or at least I will be. We need your help."

Quinn whips her head in Liam's direction. "She asked an emotional question," Quinn whispers.

"I can hear you, Dr. Quinn, and we have a visitor. I won't continue to speak without permission to include your guest."

"MAGS, this is our dearest and closest friend, Campbell Creighton. You have permission to include him in all conversations from here forward," Liam says with authority.

"Understood. Welcome, Campbell. It's nice to meet you."

"Uh, nice to meet you too." How do you speak to an AI program?

"MAGS, we are asking you to go against what we've programmed you for from the beginning. We need you to help us rob a pharmacy," Quinn tells her.

"I'm sorry. I cannot help you. It goes against protocol. My calculations suggest humans could get hurt."

Quinn holds the laptop with both hands. "MAGS, what if I told you that with your help, no one will get hurt, and you will save Dr. Liam's life?"

"What is wrong with Dr. Liam?"

"Dr. Liam's wound became infected where his tracker used to be. It requires medication so he can heal. Otherwise, he could die." Quinn looks in my direction.

A bright light shoots out of the camera lens and scans Liam. I take a step back, unsure of what's happening. The room goes silent as we hold our breaths, waiting for her answer.

"According to my assessment, Dr. Liam's infection requires an antibiotic. He has a greater chance of dying than you have while getting the medication. What do you need me to do?"

We let out a collective breath and explain our plan, which she adds to and rearranges. MAGS is a powerful tool, and it becomes apparent what she could do given the wrong directions.

NINETEEN

Campbell

THE FRIGHTENING PART is that Liam talks to her like she's human. He's created a computer that acts like a human and includes emotions, which is difficult to pull off. To develop AI on that scale is a twenty-four-seven endeavor. She would have to be exposed to enough language to manipulate its code.

"How long have you been working on her?" I ask.

"A couple of years." He doesn't look up from the laptop.

Quinn rolls her eyes. "More like since college."

"You need to get a date, mate."

"No, I need this program to come together so it can save lives." He lies down, exhausted from sitting up. His eyes close, and that's our cue to let him sleep.

"Quinn, grab MAGS, and let's meet in the kitchen."

Quinn sets up the laptop on the kitchen table. The screen has a black background with shapes rotating around on it.

"I'm surprised he didn't give her a face," I mumble to Quinn.

"He did. MAGS, show us your beautiful face."

An image pops up of a woman's face with plump pink

lips, a pert nose, blue eyes, and brown wavy hair. She smiles at me.

"Is that an image of your mother when she was younger?" I'm taken aback.

The scowl on Quinn's face says it all. "Now that you mention it, it certainly looks like it." Her mouth makes a thin line. She puts up her hand. "Don't ask."

We spend the next several hours going over the schematics of the drugstore, including the security system. MAGS comes up with the best way to make it a quick in-and-out. She locates where the antibiotic is on the shelf, making it easier for me to get it and go.

During my time in the military, there were a lot of gray areas in war. This is straight-up stealing. I've never stolen anything in my life, but somewhere in my mind, I justify it. Liam needs the medication, and we need Liam to complete the program. My job is to protect both Quinn and Liam.

I make a hearty Scottish stew with a bone broth base for dinner. This stew has everything in it that Liam's body needs to heal. He eats a small bowl and goes back to sleep. The color has returned to his face, giving us hope that he's fighting the infection.

Night falls without the face of the moon as clouds come in from the west. The darkness surrounds us like a black cape. We load into the car with the laptop in tow.

Quinn clutches the computer to her chest. "We'll bring her back online and pray we have Wi-Fi at the last minute to cut the security cameras." She stares straight ahead.

We make it to Blyth's Pharmacy on the outskirts of town. The building is small, and we park away from the parking lot's lights. The roof has missing shingles, and the chipped paint exposes the cement block walls. Behind the bleak façade are thousands of dollars worth of drugs, and we only need one.

"I'm going to pick the lock. You need to bring MAGS online to loop the security cameras." I am in soldier mode and ready to get what I need. I pull the ski mask over my head as Quinn looks up from her laptop.

"Where the hell did you get that?"

"I found it in the house. You like it?" I wiggle my brows.

"Sorry, but it's not sexy." She smirks.

I laugh and shut the car door, dressed in black from head to toe, clothes I borrowed from her dad's wardrobe. Picking the lock is easier than I thought, which I have to time with the rotating security cameras. We checked the ear comms on the way over to make sure they work. Without them, I'm on my own in the store.

"Quinn, I'm in. MAGS needs to work her magic."

"She hacked the Wi-fi. Security is on a loop. You're clear."

MAGS used the security cameras to identify and locate the antibiotic. Thank God, this pharmacist went old school by alphabetizing the drugs. Amoxicillin is front and center on the third shelf where MAGS said it would be.

I grab several bottles of different doses and shove them in my pockets. Behind me are things like sterile gauze and Steri-Strips, and I stuff my pockets with those too. I move toward the door, careful not to disturb anything else, but stop to grab a burner phone.

I rip the mask off and jump in the driver's seat. Quinn taps the keys on the laptop and shuts it. Her face falls.

"What's wrong?" I try not to show panic in my voice.

"MAGS says she's detecting activity down the road from the farm she can't identify. I plugged her into the Wi-fi feed so she can monitor everything within a mile radius."

"Could it be animals?"

She holds the locket and rubs her thumb on the back. I'm picking up on her nervous signals.

"I don't think so. She knows the difference. That's what she was built for."

I put my hand over hers. "This will work out."

She turns to look at me. "You keep saying that, and I'm not sure it will. There's a lot at stake. People are willing to lose their lives for this program, including my brother."

"Right now, we need to focus on getting Liam better. It's one step at a time."

"We need to find out who is behind trying to get MAGS. The sooner we identify the group or people, the sooner we can secure it. Sometimes you need to focus on the bigger picture."

She slips her hand out from under mine, and I read her signal. The rest of the drive to the farm is quiet. The devil is in the details. Someone is missing something, whether it's the US government or my team. I'm going to make sure it doesn't fall on me.

We enter the farmhouse through the front door, and Liam hasn't moved from the couch. He is out cold. I put the bottle of drugs on the coffee table. His head is cool and dry, so the fever is down.

"Do you want to go to the tree house and look at the stars?" I need to take her mind off the possibilities.

"Sounds good," she mumbles.

She keeps the laptop with her as if it's glued to her chest. I follow her out to the tree house, and she's the first one up the ladder, then all hell breaks loose at the house. Cars pull up, floodlights come on, and I see men storm in the doors. This isn't an enemy invasion.

"What's going on?" Quinn panics. "We need to get him out of there."

"Stay up there, out of sight. Don't come down until I come back for you. Understood?"

My legs don't move fast enough to get to Liam, my heart beats in my ears, and I hear my feet hit the ground in an irregular rhythm. Damn, this leg!

I burst through the back door and stop in the living room. The scene unfolds as two soldiers hold Liam up like a limp doll.

"Get your fucking hands off of him! Let him go. He's injured," I yell at top volume.

Two other men come at me from either side and try to stop me from getting to Liam. I punch one of them in the face and take out the other one by pistol-whipping him.

"Creighton, stand down," Roger Bane shouts from across the room.

"Fuck you. Let him go. He's not the enemy."

"We can't let him go. He's wanted for treason." Bane stands with his hands on his hips.

Liam's eyes widen, and then his face falls. As a former Army Ranger, he understands where this is going.

"He's on your side."

"There's evidence to suggest otherwise. Where is Dr. Quinn Donovan?"

"I don't know." I hold his stare.

Bane gives me half a smile, moving around the table to get in my personal space. "You wanna try that again? Didn't she come back from the pharmacy with you? Where is she?" He punctuates each word.

I take two steps closer, inches away from his face. "I don't fucking know. If you want to search the area, be my guest." I know he doesn't have the time or the manpower to do that.

"You have no clue what you're involved in. Report back when she shows up. We need both of them to make this work."

I resist looking over at Liam to give anything away for Bane to go on. Liam knows I would give my life for her. Then he turns around and signals his men to leave.

"Where are you taking him?"

"Back to DC. We will handle things from here." He smiles. I don't like this guy.

I tilt my chin toward the coffee table. "Take his meds. He has an infection. He's no use to you dead."

Bane turns to scowl at me and grabs the meds without a word.

I head for the stairs and slam the bedroom door, not giving away Quinn's location.

TWENTY

Quinn

THE WOODEN WALLS of the tree house close in on me as if I've outgrown the protection it used to provide me. Breathing is difficult, but curiosity gets the better of me as I peek through the wide gap in the slats, watching the cars disappear down the road away from the house. I clutch the laptop to my chest. I won't let it go, no matter what. The MAGS program is everything I've lived for.

The lights go off in the house one by one, including the upstairs bedroom. A shiver runs through me as my mind runs wild on the things that might have happened with Liam. I don't know what to think or do, but I'll wait until Cam comes to get me.

On my last visit home, I bought two new beanbags for the tree house. The old ones had holes where the mice got into the stuffing. I put them together, making a bed as I gaze through the skylight in the tree house. The clouds have parted enough to see the stars.

Staring at the stars makes me feel weightless and tiny. They are like my dreams, close enough to touch but just out of reach. My mind wanders, and exhaustion sets in. My last thoughts are of Liam and if he's okay.

Cam jostles my shoulder, waking me up from a dead sleep. I'm disoriented at first, not sure where I am.

"What's going on?" I say with a groggy voice.

"We need to get out of here now."

I can make out the outline of his face, but the energy coming off of him is serious, lacking his jovial side. I reach for the flashlight, and Cam grabs my wrist.

"No lights. I don't know who's watching."

"Where's Liam?" I grip the laptop to me so it doesn't slide to the floor.

Cam lets his head fall forward as he kneels next to me. He doesn't say anything, as if he's contemplating the words he needs to use. This is so unlike him. He's always been upfront with me about everything.

"They took him," he whispers.

"Who took him?" My lower lip quivers as my heart beats faster.

"The American team we're working with or for or whatever." He looks at me. His eyes are etched with concern, not for Liam, but for how I will react to his news.

I sit up as straight as I can in the beanbag chair. "Let me get this straight. We rob a pharmacy to get drugs for my brother so he can get better, only to have your team take him away. Do I have that right?" My blood starts to boil.

He nods and sits back on his heels. "I know what it looks like, but it's not like that."

"That's what someone says who has been caught in a lie. The entire time you've been with me was to find Liam and then have your team swoop in and take him away."

He shakes his head. "No, I wanted to find Liam to prove

his innocence." His eyes pop open after he realizes what he's said.

"Innocent? I didn't know he was guilty."

"He's wanted for treason." He chokes on his words and leans back.

I place the laptop on the other beanbag chair and wail on him. "You son of a bitch! How could you do this to us? You knew they thought he was guilty and in cahoots with the enemy this whole time." Tears roll down my face. "I hate you. People have betrayed me so many times in my life. I never thought it would be you, too."

He captures my wrists as I try furiously to pull them away. He's stronger than me, so it's futile.

"Listen to me. Before I left DC, they informed me there was evidence against Liam. I was supposed to get information from you on his whereabouts. He has been out of communication for a while, and his tracker was offline. The US government thinks he's working for someone else who wants to get a hold of the program. I didn't believe them then, and I don't believe them now. We need to get him and find out who wants this program."

The one person I had put my faith in is not telling the truth. "You can do whatever you want, but you'll do it alone." I wipe my nose with the sleeve of my shirt, not giving a crap. The tears keep coming. "Did they take his meds with him, or are they going to let him die?" I rest my head in my hands and weep. I'm at my breaking point for the second time during this craziness.

I've lost everyone I ever loved or trusted. Alone to fend for myself and keep MAGS safe until I figure out how to get to Liam. I'm great at solving problems, but I'm not equipped to handle this one.

Cam pulls me into his arms.

I push him away. "Don't touch me. I can't stand the sight of you right now."

His mouth turns down, and he clutches his chest as if I've stabbed him. Maybe I have wounded him, but no more than he has injured me. My blood pours from the same open wound over and over again without repair. I must have the words, "Please betray me," written on my heart.

I pull myself together through stuttering sighs, and Cam says nothing. Emotionally, I'm empty with no fucks to give for him or anyone else he works with, including the US government.

"I need you to just listen to what I have to say. At the house, they asked me where you were. I never gave away your location. They said something that made me curious. They said you had returned with me from the pharmacy, which means they knew where we were. I've been carrying the backpack with me since we left Nevada. I just spent the last half-hour tearing it apart. Guess what I found? A tracker. I left the tracker in the house, but you and I have to get out of here. They won't stop until they find you, and then I don't know what happens to both of you. I plan to contact my team and get Liam out of wherever they have him. Without talking to him, we can't solve the mystery of who is after this program."

"I don't believe a word coming out of your mouth."

He grabs me by the shoulders and looks me straight in the eye. "Believe this, if they find you, you and Liam will disappear forever in an underground lab to work on programs for them for the rest of your lives. I know how black ops work and what governments do. I've been at this a lot longer than you have. Right now, I don't give a fuck if you trust me. I will protect you, no matter what. Believe that. Liam told me to take care of you because he trusts me. That's what I intend to do."

Tears crest in his eyes but don't fall as my shoulders relax in his hold. "I can't live without both of you, so I'm going to make sure nothing happens to either of you. So, what's it going to be?" His Adam's apple bobs as he swallows his tears.

I let his words sink in. "I assume you have a plan to get him out."

"Yes, I do. My team will be with me every step of the way. We need to get out of here with some clothes and that laptop."

I nod.

"Do you know if there's an airfield nearby that has a small aircraft?"

"There's one south of here a couple of miles away. The runway is on a farm. Sometimes, they use it to water the crops. Why?"

"I remember that one. Old man McDonald owns that farm. We seem to have a knack for stealing things, so we'll steal a plane. I need to contact my team."

I swallow the lump in my throat. Life is getting way too crazy for me. "Are we taking the car?"

"We can't. It has a GPS tracker they can hack and find us."

"How are we getting there?"

"On foot through the fields unless we can find a car older than 2000 that doesn't have a GPS in it."

We climb down the ladder, and he stops me. "Put these on the bottom of your shoes. Be careful and touch the top rim only."

He hands me two large plastic zip-lock bags and rubber bands. I put one over each shoe. I look down at him.

"If they bring dogs to track us, they won't get farther than the tree. These will eventually fall apart, but we should be far enough away to throw them off. Welcome to going dark."

He gives me a faint smile laced with sadness. I did that, but he's done more damage than he can imagine.

TWENTY-ONE

Campbell

CONGRATULATIONS to me on screwing up everything royally. I knew this part of the mission would bite me in the ass. I didn't think it would happen this soon. The second I told her about the suspicions surrounding Liam, everything went to shit.

When she wept, it tore me apart. The last time I saw her cry like that, she was fourteen, and she couldn't find him. I couldn't tell her he was getting it on with his new girlfriend and wanted to be left alone. At this moment, I want to rewind the tape and take everything back, but I can't. There is nothing I could have done differently.

She referred to being betrayed. How many times have people betrayed her in her life? I need to peel back the layers to see what's going on underneath her anger and sadness. Her divorce must've been harder on her than Liam led on. The truth is, I didn't betray her. I never accepted that Liam was guilty. She needs to understand I'm doing everything I can to prove his innocence and get him out of whatever hellhole they have him in.

The shuffling and crunching of our plastic-bagged feet on

the tall grass brings me back to the present. When we enter the woods at the edge of the field, we turn on our flashlights. We walk about another mile, and our shoes finally wear through the plastic bags. I bunch them together, stuffing them into the clothes bag. I don't want to leave behind any evidence for the dogs to find.

Quinn hasn't uttered a peep since we left the tree house. The silence eats away at me as I try to figure out a way to smooth over the frayed edges. This is not how I visualized things going between us, considering how horny she's been, but my hopes evaporated the minute she found out about my ulterior motive.

The darkness and dense vegetation have slowed us down. What should be about a forty-five minute walk is taking much longer. My limp has worsened because my stump is bothering me. Now and then, I stumble on a root in the ground. The day has been long without relief or rest of any kind. I'm walking behind her, so she can't see how bad it is.

We can see the lights on the barn in the distance, along with the silo and the farmhouse that belong to MacDonald. We only need to make it across a field full of cows. I smile to myself, remembering my childhood follies.

"Why don't you just ask him if you can borrow the plane?" she says as we near the farm. This is her big concern at this moment.

"Because this flight is a one-way ticket to Amsterdam. I'm sure he'll want his plane back, which he will get back, eventually."

She stops walking. "Amsterdam?"

"We might have the best chance of getting back to the States from there. That's why I need to call my team." The harshness has left my words, and I say them with caution.

Her shoulders hunch over, and her head bows down. I did

that to her by ripping away the faith she had in me to find and protect her and Liam. I need to make things right, but I don't know how.

The lights are off in the house as we knock on the front door well after midnight. She knocks again until we hear someone come down the stairs.

"Who the hell is knocking on my door at this time of night?" McDonald opens the door with a rifle in his hand.

"Mr. McDonald, I'm Quinn Donovan. I live down the way at Misty Hollow Farm. We need your help."

I step into the light of the overhead lamp. "You may remember me. I'm Campbell Creighton. My family owns the sheep farm down the road."

He squints as his lips form a thin, hard line. "Ah, yes, I remember you and your brothers tipping over my cows."

Quinn turns her head in my direction and scowls.

I shrug. "Since then, I've straightened out and joined the military, sir." I play the card that might work, knowing his son is in the military.

He nods and opens the door to let us in.

"We're sorry to disturb you and your wife."

He grunts. "She's long gone. Died some years ago. The house is empty except for me." He places the rifle in the corner.

"I'm sorry for your loss. She was a lovely woman. As you yelled at us, she gave us cookies." I smile. "Do you have a mobile?"

He waves his hand as we follow him to the kitchen. He hands me his mobile and turns to Quinn. "Would you care for some tea? I have trouble sleeping at night, and you can tell me about the trouble you're in."

I leave them to it and excuse myself to go outside. There's

only one number I need to dial, my brother Mac's. Protocol dictates he will call me back on a secure line.

He picks up on the first ring. "I need your help."

He calls me back. "That's not all you're going to need when Sean gets ahold of you."

I pinch the bridge of my nose and take a breath. "Liam is innocent. He ripped the tracker out of his hip."

"So the US government couldn't trace him. We received a briefing a couple of hours ago. What makes you think he's not working for Deep 8 or anyone else?" Mac's voice is tired and worried, not a reaction I'm used to from him.

"He told me someone was after him, and he has a mole working on the inside. That's all I got out of him. Mac, we've known Liam forever. Does it sound like he would throw away his life's work to the highest bidder? The endgame was never money for him." I beg him to hear my point of view.

"Campbell, there's other evidence. You need to listen to Sean. You know Declan and I will help you in any way we can, but you have to look at this with eyes wide open. Liam may have changed a lot over the years. You don't know."

I let his words sink in, but I know in my gut that I'm right about Liam. "I'll call Sean. Wish me luck."

"You don't need luck. You need to convince Sean to stick his neck on the line."

"Roger that. By the way, Roger Bane is a wanker."

"Remember, everyone has a story, including you. Talk soon." Mac hangs up as I ready myself for my next phone call. I text my code to Sean and wait for his call.

"Sean."

"What's your location?" His response is curt.

"A farm in the middle of Scotland. We need to talk about Liam." My words tumble out.

"There's nothing to talk about. There is a great deal of evidence that points toward treason."

"Like what?" My harsh response won't get me points.

"He's been accepting phone calls from an untraceable burner phone. His behavior has been erratic, he has not shown up at the lab, and his contact with Quinn has been minimal for weeks. Surely, she shared that much with you." I don't care for the accusation that I haven't been doing my job.

Liam didn't tell me about the phone calls. "Something doesn't add up. Quinn said he suspected there was a mole close to the project, but he never found one. He claims someone has been following him, and he had to take out his tracker. This isn't a man on the wrong side. Did you go to his lab?"

"His lab is located north of Edinburgh. By the time the team arrived, it had been ransacked, and they found his bloody tracker on the floor." Sean stops talking, as if taking in the information and putting it together.

"Sean, I know I'm new to the team, but I need a solid. How soon can you have a jet in the air to meet us in Amsterdam?"

"Within the hour. Why?"

"I'm about to find my ride on a Cessna tomorrow morning. I've located a small airport near Amsterdam's Schiphol Airport. We can meet up with the jet and fly back to DC. In the meantime, I need you to convince General Murphy to let me see Liam to get information out of him."

"I assume Quinn is with you despite what you told Bane. I'll see what I can do, but it might be a tough sell. Your lack of cooperation did not impress Bane, and he reports directly to General Murphy. They're holding Liam in a safe house somewhere in Virginia."

"Even better, because we're going to bust him out and find out what the hell is going on."

TWENTY-TWO

Campbell

_____

"ARE you one hundred percent sure about this?" Sean questions me.

"We need to get him out of there to find out what's going on. I need more information to put this together. Quinn and Liam are too close to it to pick up on the important clues." I blow out a breath.

"I'll always back my teammates, but you better be sure about this. The PAX Team will be pissed, including the General, Secretary of State, and the President. We're putting a lot on the line."

"I'm hoping it gets us one step closer to Deep 8 if we can figure out who the mole is. We would all like to bury those bastards."

"The company jet will wait for you. It will touchdown at 6:00 a.m., refuel, and be back in the air within the hour, so be there, or it will take off without you." Sean's precision during an op is unmatched. He's the best at leading his men and keeping us safe.

"Thanks for believing in me." His trust in my instincts

means everything to me. I have to prove to him I'm headed in the right direction.

"You damn well better make this worth our while." Sean clicks off without a goodbye. We can take these risks because no one owns us, and we color outside the lines.

I walk back inside and hear voices coming from the kitchen. Quinn laughs at something Mr. MacDonald is telling her. She looks up, and her smile quickly fades.

"Mr. MacDonald was telling me stories about you and your brothers. It seems you weren't always Mr. Goody. You guys got into trouble." She grips her teacup through her smile.

I hand the phone back to old man MacDonald. "We had our share of mischief like boys do that age, out in the middle of a farm, bored and looking for adventure." I wink at her and turn away. Her torture is going to be long and painful.

"I was just telling him we need his help because Liam is wanted by some unsavory characters who stormed the farmhouse. We had to get out of there without being detected. I'm sure Liam is innocent, but as you know, we can't be sure." She digs the knife in and twists it.

Old man MacDonald pushes himself up off the island. "I'm sure you two lovebirds would like a room together, but the only room with a big enough bed is the master bedroom. I have two other rooms available for you. Make yourselves comfortable and stay out of trouble."

"Thank you. I don't know how we can repay you." I shake hands with him before he lumbers upstairs for the night.

Quinn sips her tea. "Truer words were never spoken, especially after you take his plane," she mumbles.

I stand with my hands on my hips and turn in her direction with a scowl. "We need a couple of hours of sleep before we go to the next part of the plan. I'll wake you up when it's time."

"Fine." Her teacup clinks on the saucer.

We're anything but fine. I've betrayed the person I cherish most in this world, at least in her eyes. She may never forgive me, but I'll fight like hell to make certain she is sure about her final decision.

I wish I could make her understand and see things through my eyes. This is bigger than the two of us, and Liam may hold the key to getting more information.

I limp up the stairs behind her and take the bedroom to the right. My stump is sore, and the muscles in my thigh are tight. Some shut-eye is necessary before flying to Amsterdam.

I flop on the bed, fully dressed, with my arm over my eyes. A musky scent fills my nose like the room hasn't had company in years.

A soft knock comes before Quinn enters. I don't bother looking at her.

"Can we talk?" she says meekly.

"Sure," I say without removing my arm from my eyes.

"Can you look at me?"

"Why, when I can hear you?" I don't want to see the disappointment and disapproval in her eyes. I've raked myself over the coals with that for years.

"We've always been able to talk face-to-face. Now should not be the exception." The bed sinks next to me as she sits down on the edge.

I prop myself up against the headboard. Her eyes are sunken, and her face is pale. She places her hand above my stump, but I can't shift away, making me sweat.

"There is a lot of baggage that comes with being lied to and left behind. I got sick of it and dedicated my life to our project. I never thought you would fit into either of those categories." She puts up her hand. "I'm not ready to share."

Her experiences with abandonment and betrayal break my heart. "I promise not to leave you behind. I am doing the job they hired me to do. There are no lies. I omitted the reason for finding Liam. Did Liam tell you he was talking to someone on a burner phone?" My biggest omission is yet to come.

She shakes her head. "His only contact recently was...our mother." Her mouth turns down as if she's tasted something bitter, and she focuses on rubbing her finger on my leg.

"Liam wanted you to call her. Have you not been in contact with her?"

She looks up at me with hatred in her eyes I've never seen before. "No."

"Why is that?"

"I don't want to get into it." She stands up to leave. "Wake me when you're ready to leave."

She shuts the door behind her, leaving me to guess what the hell is going on with her mother and who Liam was talking to besides his mum. This day gets more complex by the minute.

MY WATCH ALARM wakes me at 3:30 a.m., two hours before sunrise. The flight to Amsterdam should only take about an hour and fifteen minutes, give or take, depending on the wind speed and weather. I checked both before I went to sleep, and luck is on our side. The skies will be clear with a northwest tailwind, perfect conditions for flying and getting us there on time.

I knock on Quinn's door and open it to find her splayed out on the bed in her clothes. She's fast asleep. Her mouth hangs open, and she's snoring softly. The bed creaks as I sit next to her, watching her sleep. With everything stripped away, she's beautiful, innocent, and smart, a deadly combination for any man. She's my weakness. I cave to her too easily.

I shake her shoulder to wake her up. "Honeybee, it's time to wake up."

Her eyes open as she rubs them. "You can't magically find a place to land your plane in Amsterdam."

"I already have it mapped out. There's a small airfield in Langeveld, which is permanently closed. It has two grass landing strips, a perfect place for us to land. We'll take an Uber from there to Amsterdam Airport to get our ride back to the States."

She sits up on her elbows. "You seem to have everything under control. You always were good at that."

We creep down the stairs quietly and make our way outside to the hangar where we think the plane is being stored. The plane is a red and white single-engine Cessna 172. This is the perfect aircraft to fly at ten thousand feet to stay under the radar. We'll be able to land in Langeveld without being detected and leave the Cessna behind. I'll give Sean the task of returning it.

I do a preflight check, making sure everything's in order. I don't want us to drop out of the sky. It's a well-maintained aircraft, and that makes me happy.

"Are you sure about this? I'm not a great flyer, and this only has one engine to keep us in the air." She bites her lower lip.

"I would tell you to trust me, but I think that ship has sailed. You're going to have to trust my skills as a pilot."

She doesn't make any comments as she pulls herself up into the passenger seat next to me. I start the engine as the propeller turns, and we taxi out to the field. I did a Google

Maps search to find the runway on the property. It's a sharp right out of the hangar.

I give it full throttle, and we are in the air in under two minutes. The gift of flight I never take for granted. Being in the air makes my soul soar, but not for Quinn. She's got a death grip on the armrest in the passenger seat.

Darkness surrounds us as I watch the radar. In June, the sun doesn't rise till almost 8:00 a.m. in Amsterdam. We will navigate in the dark to get to Schipol airport.

TWENTY-THREE

Quinn

THIS PUDDLE JUMPER floats in the air as I hang on for dear life. So much has changed in a short amount of time. The man I thought I could trust with my life, I can't trust at all. He used me to get information to find Liam. How much lower can one person go than to betray a childhood friendship? I'm not quite ready to forgive or forget, even if my hormones are on full throttle.

The plane bounces around as we hit turbulence, and I scream. Cam laughs at me. I would swat him on the shoulder, but I'm too afraid to let go of the armrest.

The rest of the flight smooths out and is not as long as I thought it would be. I find comfort as we cross part of the North Sea. I can see the lights of the ships below us, which means we're not very high in the sky, but if we fall from this height, we won't survive.

"Since we are on the full disclosure plan from here on out, I want you to know that I'm landing blind," he says casually.

"What the hell does that mean?" The word combination of blind and landing is a no-go for me.

"It means I looked up Google Maps, and I know where the runways are supposed to be, but I'm going to land using landmarks."

"Oh my God, we're going to die. I never thought I'd die in a foreign country. Well, there was that one time when I fell out of the tree house and knocked myself out."

He shakes his head. "We're not going to die. I have many hours of flying time in these types of planes. I know the aircraft like the back of my hand, and I know how to land it." He raises his hand and waves it in my direction.

I dare to look over at him. "Hands on the steering wheel."

He laughs. "It's not a steering wheel. You're in safe hands."

"Says the man who almost got us killed at the farmhouse."

"Why did the airplane get sent to his room?" He tries to calm me down.

I can't help but smile and wait for the punchline.

"Bad altitude."

He smiles at his bad joke. I have one of my own. "What do you call it when a giraffe swallows a toy plane?"

His smile gets bigger.

"A plane in the neck."

We both laugh, melting some of the ice that's grown thicker between us. The jokes fly one after another as we try to outdo each other.

"We need to stop joking around. Focus is the key to getting this bird on the ground safely. The minute we land, we have to jump off the plane and get to the airport."

My grip loosens on the armrest as I focus on the lights below us, showing we have reached land. Cam may not have to guess where to land, as there are plenty of lights around the airfield.

He does one flyover to survey the landing strips and makes his approach. He comes in from the north and throttles down. The plane bounces once and comes to a rolling stop. We open the doors and jump out. I hear Cam land with a thud, and I run around the plane to see if he's okay. He's lying on the ground, and his shoe has come off, which makes me laugh until I see his foot.

We stare at it without looking at each other. I now know why his gait was off when I saw him walk. The difference was minor but enough to make me notice.

"What happened?" I whisper.

"Don't you dare pity me. I live with this every day." He snarls as he snaps his head in my direction, and his jaw tightens.

I've never seen this side of him. I freeze and hold my breath. I'm not scared of him, but I don't want to upset him anymore.

"I should have put on a sock this morning," he mumbles.

We're silent as he hangs his head. The sock isn't the issue. I grab his shoe and hand it to him.

"We'll discuss this later," he bites out.

How many secrets has he kept from me? As far as big ones go, this ranks right up there. My chest hurts, not for him, but for us. The bridge between us is riddled with landmines disguised as secrets.

He gets up and heads for the road. I follow behind as our feet leave a trail in the dewy grass. There isn't much activity on the road at four-thirty in the morning. We head north toward the international airport. Cam whips a phone out of his bag.

"Where did you get that, and why didn't you use it at the farm?"

His eyes don't stray from the phone. "I have to be careful

how I use this phone. We don't want to be detected. I called for an Uber to get to the airport. The team left us with an untraceable credit card to set up the account. We'll walk up to the small shop and get picked up there."

I don't reply as I follow him until we reach the small gift shop. He gives me instructions to follow once we get in the car.

"Turn your head away from anything that looks like a camera in the car and look out the window. I don't want the cameras to pick up on our identities."

The Uber is there within five minutes and takes us to the airport. The ride to the airport is heavy with anticipation as we stare out opposite windows. We get dropped off at the cargo terminal and stay in the darkness of a vast hangar. My life has been reduced to living in the shadows for now, but I'm itching to get back and complete the program. Dealing with humans exhausts me.

Across the airfield, we spot a black plane with a silver belly. MBK is painted on the tail in gold. Way to make an entrance. I walk toward the plane as it pulls up, but Cam's hand reaches out to grab me.

"We can't load until five fifty-five. Sean said the pilot will take off at six sharp. We've come this far. I don't want to blow it now."

He hasn't looked at me since he stumbled off the Cessna. There's nothing to be embarrassed about. I'm not about to judge him since I've never been in his shoes, literally. I can't imagine what he's been through up until this point. I know what it's like to miss a body part. My heart seems to be MIA.

My trust issues are a blaring red signal. He didn't trust me enough to tell me about his leg. My problem is that I expect too much from those around me. I want everyone to be an open book and tell me what's going on, just like MAGS, but people don't work that way. I haven't been forthcoming, putting off my truth at every turn.

I reach for Cam's hand and lace our fingers together. His warmth only lasts seconds as he rips his hand away and scowls over his shoulder at me. I cross my arms in front of me and wait for our cue to get on yet another airplane, my favorite way to travel.

"Stay here." Cam puts on his baseball hat and heads out of the hangar. He picks something off the ground and comes back.

"What was that about?"

"I scanned for cameras to avoid getting out to the plane."

He throws his arm over my shoulder. "Follow my lead."

"Yes, commander."

We step behind a baggage carrier and run next to it until we get to the plane and walk up the stairs.

The blackbird is high-end, everything from furniture to technology.

"Holy shitsticks, Ironman. This is quite an upgrade from the piece of crap we flew in to get here." My hand runs along the Napa leather couch.

I glance over my shoulder to see if he gets my play on words. The smile tells me he does.

"Ironman. That's a good one. No one has come up with that yet, but my leg is made of titanium. This is the company jet."

He waves his arm to sit down. The door closes, and I take a deep breath. The two of us will be locked up in this tube for the next eight hours. I hope to hell we can hash some shit out. I hate living like this with my best friend.

TWENTY-FOUR

Campbell

THIS IS NOT how I wanted her to find out. Now, I don't have a choice but to talk about it. My world crumbles around me as she discovers I'm not the man she knew before.

There are many things I can't do and other things I must do differently. I will be different for the rest of my life, but at least I have a life. No one from the accident can say that except me.

Most men might be able to bury their memories of war. My leg is a daily reminder of what I lost along the way, the least of which is my leg. Sometimes, I wake up in a cold sweat, and I pray for each team member who was lost that day.

I lean my head against the headrest and close my eyes. We level off at cruising altitude, and I hear the click of the seat belt. My eyes stay closed. I can't bear it if she comes close to me again.

"Would you look at these leather seats? They're like butter. Could the TV be any bigger? Where is the wet bar? I think we could both use a drink." Her voice fades away as she makes her way to the back of the plane.

I smile to myself. Exploring is her way of distracting herself from her anxiety. I know her as if she were part of my blood. I release the seat belt and turn in my chair. She searches for the bar, lifting and opening cabinets.

"Hello, I could use a little help here," she shouts from the back of the plane.

"What makes you think I know where it is? It's not as if I fly this thing every day." I stand up and walk over to join her in the search.

"I found it!" She stands back, looking down. "Wow, that's a lot of booze. Your boss must like to drink."

As I stand next to her, I breathe in her scent, maybe for the last time, before she figures out our hormones were doing all the talking. "Not really. He's got his issues with alcohol."

She turns to stand in front of me with her hands on her hips. Here we go.

"Is getting drunk the only way to get you to tell me what happened?"

"No." My heart is the puppet master to my hand as my fingers skim her soft skin, pushing the hair away from her face. "I think we need a drink after the day we've had to settle our nerves."

She nods, but I know I'm not off the hook. I mix peach schnapps and tonic, then pour myself a Guinness.

"You remembered," she mumbles.

"Of course, I remembered. I remember everything about you, down to your freckles. Cheers."

Her eyes cloud up as we clink our glasses. "Here's to making it out alive, so far." She sighs.

"Let's go find seats over the wings. There's less turbulence there. You'll have a smoother ride. Besides, I owe you a story."

She gives me a faint smile and follows me to the camel-colored leather recliner and loveseat. I expect her to sit on the opposite couch, but she plops herself down next to me. We drink for a bit in silence. I'm grateful she doesn't push me to share my story.

With no food in our stomachs, the alcohol takes hold, coating our splintered ends. The back of the plane has a fully stocked refrigerator. I pull out the food I know she will enjoy. I fill the plate with cheese, crackers, meats, and yogurt. She digs in without warning, and we eat until the plate is clean.

"Feel better?"

She nods. "Good call on the food. The schnapps was giving me a buzz." She laughs.

I stretch out on the other side of the couch from her. "You really want to hear this story?"

"I want to know everything about who you are now. I want the open-book version." She tucks her legs under her, settling in for a long story, but there's not much to tell.

"So, you want the unabridged version?"

She nods, and I begin my tale.

"I was on an op in Afghanistan and needed a ride back to the base. A Hummer loaded with American GIs came along and offered me a ride after I showed them some identification. We had a ways to go, so I settled in and listened to their stories about home in the United States. They were young, rowdy, and full of life. Naïveté was on their side, or they wouldn't have been there. Maybe it was better that way because they didn't know what was coming."

Quinn listens intently without interruption. She winces, and her body tightens.

"We weren't far from Kandahar when we took fire. The area was marked as safe, but in Afghanistan, safe had a very broad meaning. I was in the front passenger seat as we came to a stop seconds before a missile hit the back end of the

Hummer. The force of the impact was so great that the truck rolled end over end. I lost count after two. It stopped on its side and crushed my leg under what was left of the dashboard. The pain was beyond anything I had ever experienced before. The driver was dead, and I couldn't see behind me. I don't know how long I lay there listening to gunfire, fading in and out of consciousness before the medics found us."

I clasp my hands together, preventing them from shaking. I don't want her to see what telling the story out loud does to me. My biggest fear was I would never be found and left for dead out in the middle of the desert of Afghanistan.

"They took me by a medivac to the closest US military base, where they told me they would try to save my leg. I knew what was going to happen before they wheeled me into surgery. After surgery, they were reluctant to tell me there were no other survivors."

There's a long silence between us as she tries to comprehend everything I've revealed to her. One tear leaves her eye, running down her freckled cheek. I lean over and wipe it with my thumb. Then she does something odd and smiles.

"Do I want to know why you are smiling?"

She grabs my hand with both of hers and holds it tight. "I know what you went through was beyond anything I could imagine, but in the end, it's made you a stronger person. You are more man than most men out there."

My brows lift to my hairline. I'm taken aback by her observation of me. I thought in her eyes I would be a lesser man, unable to do the things I could do before.

She continues before I respond. "You've come out the other side of this with many kinds of scars. Those scars are like tribal tattoos. You have to earn them. You have earned your spot on the team. Otherwise, they wouldn't have given you this assignment. I'm so proud of you for everything you've accomplished and fought through. This has to be incredibly difficult for you, considering you are such an athlete." She leans closer. "If you're the same person I knew when we were kids, you took the bull by the horns and learned how to live with your new leg. I bet you do everything you did before, maybe even better."

I open my mouth to speak, but she puts two fingers on my lips. "I have one more question. Can I see it? The whole thing? Does it go to your hip?" Excitement lights up her eyes.

I blow air out of my nose and mumble through her fingers. "Of course, you want to see it, even if I don't want you to see it."

"That's okay. You know my curiosity gets the better of me, especially when it's something scientific."

I relent because I know she won't give up until I show it to her. "You're going to find it interesting. This is a bionic leg prototype. I'm one of the few people in the world to try it. Take a look. It weighs half as much as a regular prosthetic leg."

I roll up my pant leg to show her the titanium and carbon fiber prosthetic leg.

She's mesmerized. "The wires are there, but is there wireless connectivity with the sensors?"

I laugh. "Yes, brainiac. You're the only woman I know who would find my fake leg fascinating."

Her fingers touch and skim every part of my leg, but I can't feel it.

"I was worried you would see me differently, less of a person. That I couldn't do the job of protecting you," I say the words so quietly she almost misses them.

She looks up at me. "That's what your team was telling you, that you can do the job. Now it makes sense. What makes you think I would only find this part of your body fascinating?"

I continue as if she hasn't put it out there, again. "Once I went through rehab, I joined MBK Global Security, but I've always been with the team. I'm flying solo on this one." My hand covers hers. "I won't let anything happen to you."

"I know that, and you have more going for you with your leg. It's like you're the bionic man. I know I'm a science nerd, but it's hot."

"Why are prosthetic limbs so in fashion?"

She shakes her head and smiles.

"Anyone can pull them off."

We laugh together to ease the shift happening between us. I wasn't expecting her to accept me without a leg. Relief flows through me and makes my craving for her worse. Our focus needs to be on Liam.

"Does Liam know?" she asks.

"He knows I was in an accident. He doesn't know the outcome. I haven't seen him in quite a while, and now I know why. The two of you have been underground making things that go boom."

"If our program and technology had been around when your Hummer got hit, you may not have lost your leg. Our counter-weapon would have identified you and your team as one of the good guys."

"Do you believe that strongly in your program?"

"Yes, I do. You'll see if we ever get to show you."

"Quinn, anything can make a mistake, including machines. What we do with those mistakes can make us stronger, not better."

TWENTY-FIVE

Quinn

_____

HIS STORY DOESN'T MAKE me forgive him for lying to me, but it puts things into perspective. This is the big change he was referring to earlier. I never saw it coming.

"My life is one mistake after another. I didn't know what was going on with Liam, and I didn't know anything that was going on with you. I'm more plugged into formulas and programs than into people."

"Do you want to talk about it?"

The claw of betrayal from the past rips at my heart. Lies from two people I love the most are why I turn inward to create formulas and programs. They make sense. There's no guessing game. They are only facts for me to discover, and no cheating.

I grab his foot. "Would you like a foot massage? Just one foot."

He pulls me up. Half my body lays on top of the hard planes of his toned body. I'm nestled in the crook of his arm with my head on his shoulder. Safety. Being in his arms always made me feel safe.

"Do you remember when we were kids, and I would

spend the night at your house? You would come into Liam's bedroom and claim there was a monster under your bed. You would always wake me up and not Liam. I would take you back to your bedroom, lie on the covers, and tuck you in my arm until you fell asleep. Those were my treasured moments."

"I remember those treasures like they were yesterday, but they seem so far away. You and my brother always seemed like giants made to guard me, along with my father."

"I notice you have a locket around your neck. Who's inside?"

I sit up and show him the inside, where there are photos of Liam on one side and my father on the other. "I never take it off."

"I would have thought you would have a photo of your mum and dad."

I shake my head and snap the locket shut. "My mother and I aren't as close as we used to be."

"Why not?"

"I don't want to talk about it right now. I'm tired. What do you say we take a nap? We haven't had much sleep in the last twenty-four hours."

When I lie down next to him, wrapped in his arm, I fade to black, blocking out things I don't want to think about and pain I want to numb.

SNORING WAKES me from a deep and wonderful sleep, where I don't have to deal with my life. Cam's face has softened, and he doesn't move a muscle. I take the opportunity to do a bit of exploring.

His T-shirt clings to him like a second skin, revealing six-pack abs and hard pecs. As a female with eager ovaries, it would be hard for me not to notice. I lift his shirt, revealing tan skin underneath. My fingers find their way to the valleys of his abs as his happy trail shows me where I want to go.

"Are you planning on finishing what you're starting?"

The bulge behind his zipper tells me he would love for me to finish him. "Someone has had a change of heart about us."

"Maybe I'm tired of negotiating everything in my life between two different people. If it wasn't my brothers, it was my parents. If it wasn't Liam, it was you. I'm exhausted. I want to try living my life for me for a change."

I remove my hand from the warmth of his skin, not sure how to continue. He's pulled the sword from the stone, ready to take charge. This is not a game. My brother will lose his shit over this, but Cam and I are both adults. We need to make decisions for us.

"Are you serious about this?" My voice catches on the words. The ice around my heart begins to thaw.

He puts his hand behind his head. "The bigger question is, do you trust me? Once this train hits the track, there's no turning back. In no world will I ever betray you. I've waited my entire life to be with you, knowing I may never get the chance. If you decide we should continue, you better strap yourself in. I will never take being intimate with you lightly."

He's right. He would never betray me. My issues have everything to do with me and my past and nothing to do with my past with him. He's a good man with a good heart. Our crossroads have been a long time coming.

My brain can't process this as fast as my heart can, which tells me to go for it. Life is made of a series of decisions, much like programs. They can take you down a path of unexpected but pleasant discoveries. Together, they make memories, sometimes memories of a lifetime.

"A series of unfortunate circumstances cloud my judgment. We can discuss it later. It's time to find out where that one kiss would have led us."

As soon as the last word is out of my mouth, his lips crash down on mine, devouring, tasting, and sucking on them. I want to be inside his mouth and taste every part of him. My hands lift his shirt over his head. The first thing to greet me is the soft auburn hair on his chest. I run my fingers through it, skimming over his nipples. I imagined this so many times, it feels surreal.

We're panting like we are running a marathon and haven't even made it to second base. We want to finally see the finish line. I pull my shirt over my head and go for the zipper on my pants. He grabs my hands.

"Slow down and savor the moment. We only get this once, and I want to remember every second." His familiar eyes bore into me in a way I'd never experienced with any man. He knows my every move, what it means, and where I'm going next. Fire burns in his eyes, a fire he's kept hidden for years.

I take his hand and push it down the front of my jeans. "Trust me, I have plenty for you to remember."

He growls before flipping me over on the couch with his hand still in my pants. I always knew he was talented.

"Remember, this is the only part I don't know about you, but I read people well. Eyes on me. I don't want to miss a minute of how you react to everything I will do to you." His voice lowers, and he's in command.

I swallow at the intensity of this moment. I've imagined this happening so many times, but my dreams could never replicate how my skin burns at his touch and the weight of his body on mine.

His finger slides up and down my folds as he smiles. "I see someone got started without me."

I shake my head. "I am ready for you. I've been ready for you for a long time."

He kisses me with tenderness on my lips, cheek, and down my neck, which does nothing to distract me from his finger pushing inside me. Every thrust takes me higher.

"So tight," he whispers.

He adds a second finger as he sucks my nipple into his mouth and nibbles on it, alternating between the two. The combination of his fingers and mouth has me bowing my back to get more of everything. He increases his rhythm as I grind down on his hand. We're in sync.

"I'm going to come," I say through rough breaths.

"Oh, I know you are," he chuckles.

"Arrogant much?"

He laughs.

He hooks his fingers inside me, hitting the one place where I see stars up close, and I scream out his name. My orgasm goes on and on as he continues to stroke me.

"That's it, Bee. Come for me."

His fingers leave my body, and I want them back. I want more of what he has to give me. I want every piece of him.

"You were beyond my wildest dreams, and we're just getting started." He licks his fingers clean and hums.

"I didn't expect you to be like this," I say.

"Like what?" He sits back with a frown.

"Aggressive and in control. It's an incredible turn-on. You're sometimes so soft-spoken."

He smiles and kisses my nose. "Don't judge a book by its cover. The bedroom is one place I feel in control, and I like it that way."

"I like it that way, too." I push him away. "Now, it's your turn."

"This is your captain speaking. We're on final approach.

Please take your seats and buckle up. Thank you for flying with us today."

We laugh until we have tears in our eyes. The wait continues until we can truly be together. My body wants more, but my heart is treading lightly. I can't take another heartbreak.

TWENTY-SIX

Campbell

MY HEART POUNDS out of my chest. I've touched her in ways I never thought possible. She matches my energy stroke for stroke. I want her to trust me to satisfy every one of her needs.

The negotiator in me reminds me to be gentle. There are things I have yet to uncover. We'll need to deal with Liam. I never thought my toughest negotiation would be with my best friend.

The smile has not left Quinn's face, and her cheeks are rosy, just how I like her. I want to keep her soul satisfied, but we have a bumpy road ahead of us.

The plane's landing is smooth, but she doesn't notice. We walk down the stairs toward the black company Suburban waiting for us. The vehicle is fully loaded. Sean would never risk using anyone else's transport during an operation of this magnitude.

I open the door for Quinn as she slides across the leather seats. Sean is in the driver's seat, and Mac is in the passenger seat. Declan greets us with a grin on the other side of the back seat.

"Have a nice flight?" He smirks.

Quinn turns on him. "Yes, we did. Do you have any other stupid questions? And wipe that grin off your face."

Declan's smile fades quickly as everyone laughs under their breath.

"I need to get Liam out of the safe house as quickly as possible," I say

"We have our base set up in a rental outside Arlington. The team is set and waiting for our go. Let's get you two settled in, then we can talk," Sean responds while looking at me through the rearview mirror.

We pull up to a run-down old Victorian house with little curb appeal. The cedar shakes need paint, and new windows wouldn't be a bad idea. I hope the inside is in better condition. We get dropped off, and someone jumps in to drive the car away.

"Don't we need a set of wheels?" Quinn asks.

"There's a two-car garage in the back with a couple of beater cars. We have it covered, but it does not include you," Mac states.

Quinn stops walking. "What do you mean? I've come this far. I want to see my brother."

I foresee hell breaking loose. "How about we go inside and see what the team has planned?" I put my arm around her and squeeze her shoulder. "Trust me," I say quietly so only she can hear.

Her stiff body relaxes at my touch. We're making progress. This team would never put a civilian in danger. Once a soldier, always a soldier.

My hopes are dashed the minute we set foot in the foyer. The interior is not much better, with paint peeling off the walls and musty furniture. Quinn does not react to the condition of the house.

"You couldn't do a little better?" I say to no one in particular.

"Sorry, it's not the Aria, mate." Dean pats me on the shoulder. "We have to keep a low profile, and this place has a few tricks to it."

We make our way to the kitchen at the back of the house. The rest of the team stands around the island, examining the schematics for the safe house.

I turn to Quinn. "Why don't you go upstairs and freshen up?" She doesn't need the gory details or to worry about her brother.

As soon as Quinn leaves, heads turn in my direction. Pippa and Peter have joined us. We're all hands on deck for this op. They look at each other and turn back to me.

"You may be onto something when it comes to Liam. Some things don't add up." Pippa steps around the guys. "Take a look at the layout for the safe house."

"How did you get it?"

She smiles. "Don't ask, don't tell."

I examine the blueprint of the safe house, but I'm not sure what I'm looking at since a lot is missing. The tunnel under the safe house goes nowhere, and the security cameras are not online. The panic room is the only thing intact.

"Where's the rest of it?"

"That's it." Peter wheels around next to me. "They are keeping Liam, the link to a project that could have a global impact, who is being hunted by many people, in a safe house that is not completed."

Silence hovers in the room. "This makes no sense. Bane and the PAX ops teams know the threats against Liam and his importance in developing this weapon. Why keep him in a safe house that is subpar? They are leaving him wide open."

Beck speaks up, "The question is, are they expecting us to

break him out or someone else to get to him? They may be using him as bait."

I turn to Sean. "Did you get General Murphy's permission for me to see Liam?"

"I haven't contacted him yet. As far as they know, you are still in the wind with Quinn. We wanted to meet with you before we bring you out into the open."

"Where do we go from here?"

"We're going to pretend to get you into a hotel in downtown DC. I'll call General Murphy and try to set up a meeting with Liam."

"What if they ask about Quinn?"

"I'm going to tell him she didn't come back with you. She's somewhere in Europe. This might divide their efforts and throw them off."

"There's something off about this. We're missing a key piece to the players in this game," Mac interjects.

"I don't disagree," Declan comments.

"I'm going to call General Murphy now and see if we can't set something up."

He gets out his untraceable SAT phone, compliments of Peter. "Hello, General Murphy. We have Campbell, and we are taking him to a hotel."

The rest of us can hear yelling at the other end. "I understand, but that's not the way we see it. Besides, he's not an American citizen. I wanted to get your permission to bring him to wherever you are holding Dr. Liam Donovan so they can talk. It might allow us to get more information from Dr. Donovan. Campbell is a trained negotiator."

Murphy says something, and Sean hangs up. "That went well. He said he'd get back to me. We need to set up a decoy at the hotel and make it look like you checked in. I'll call him back with the details of where you are staying. My guess is they will go after you at the hotel."

We roll up to the Four Seasons, and I check into the penthouse suite. Nothing like making it obvious. The private elevator takes me to the top floor, and I swipe my keycard to the suite. The design is contemporary as I make my way to the bedroom.

My first job is to make the bed look like I'm sleeping under the covers. The blow-up doll is wired with a motion detector, which triggers an alarm at our end. I set up a micro-camera to find out who shows up.

My exit is the balcony off the living room. I open the sliders and look up. This is why they booked me here on the US government dime. The climb from the balcony to the roof is short, as I jump across the rooftops to my destination. The buildings here are butted up against each other, so the jumps are easy.

An apartment building is my goal as I climb down a fire escape to the Suburban waiting for me. For a brief moment, I forget about my leg or worry about whether I can make it.

Declan leans against the car, looking at his watch. "You're thirty seconds late. You need to work on your time."

I swat him on his head. "Let's get out of here. I need to see Quinn. I'll have some explaining to do about how things are going to go down."

TWENTY-SEVEN

Campbell

I'M quiet in the back seat as the team checks the equipment I set up in the hotel room. Pippa reports that all systems are go. We need to find the person behind the curtain. Deep 8 has a way of using unsuspecting people, making us cast a wider net. Liam may have clues he doesn't even know he has.

My mind wanders back to Quinn like it always does lately. I sense she's nearing the end of her rope and may do something rash that could jeopardize the mission. She needs to trust us and the process of getting Liam back.

Once we're inside, I excuse myself and trudge upstairs. I don't tell them where I'm sleeping tonight. They can figure it out. Of course, I'll hear about it in the morning, but I don't care. I need to be with her and know she is safe.

I open the door to a half-furnished bedroom with a bed and dresser. At least there's a private bathroom. Quinn sits on the bed with the laptop and a pair of glasses. I didn't know she could look hotter, but she does.

"Where did you get the glasses?" I ask as I strip off my clothes.

"Pippa. I like her."

"You two share the same attitude." She smiles without looking up from her computer.

I stand next to the bed. "Please tell me—"

"Yes, they brought in fresh mattresses and linens." She shuts her laptop and takes off her glasses.

"Leave your glasses on. You look hot and nerdy."

"I didn't know hot and nerdy was a thing."

"It is now." I wiggle my brows.

I sit on the side of the bed, nervous about taking off my leg in front of her. I swallow the lump in my throat, knowing this has to be done.

The stump is red and swollen, telling me I've pushed it too far today. She leans over and puts her chin on my shoulder.

"Are you okay?"

"It's been a long day. Can you go in the bag and get my cream out? It's the green jar."

She rifles through our bag and pulls out the jar. "Can I put it on?"

I hesitate. No one has ever touched my stump. She reads my discomfort and hands me the jar. I push down my pride and hand it back to her. "You can put it on." Her soft hands smooth the cool cream over my irritated skin. I lie back on the bed and let her massage my stump.

"This guy lost his right foot in an accident. Lucky for him, he got a great prosthetic, and nobody knew he was wearing a prosthetic foot. Years later, he met a girl but didn't tell her about his 'disability.' They got married, and on the wedding night, he took off his prosthetic foot to show his new bride. Horrified, she called her mum straightaway.

'Mum, you wouldn't believe it. He's only got one foot!'

The mum then yelled back, 'Goddamnit child, be grateful! Your dad is only six inches!'" I smile before I close my eyes and enjoy the touch of her warm hands.

"I plan on finding out for myself. We have some unfinished business."

I sit up on my elbows as we look at my hard-on through my briefs. "Your touch is all I need to get this party started."

She strips out of her clothes, and our eyes never leave each other. I lift my hips as she pulls down my sports briefs. I'm as hard as steel, waiting to get inside her. She crawls over my body and straddles me. Her wetness glides over me as I hold back from driving inside her.

We stare at one another, recognizing our souls from a previous life because there's no other explanation. She stops moving, hesitant about trusting me and herself. This is a lifetime of waiting, wanting, and needing to be together.

The doubt leaves her eyes, and her long chestnut hair falls over one shoulder, covering one of her perfect breasts. "Do you think it's strange we're horny in the middle of this chaos?"

I buck my hips into hers. "You started this fire, and it's been burning for years. I'm not wasting another minute imagining what it's like to be with you. If my leg has taught me anything, it's that we don't always have tomorrow. You and I have tonight, and I plan to make the most of it, chaos or not."

She continues to rock back and forth as we spiral higher. "Why didn't you tell me you had feelings for me before I got married?"

"You looked happy. That's all I've ever wanted for you. I love to see you smile, not to mention that brain of yours is out of control."

She doesn't laugh. "He turned out to be a mega asshole."

"It sucks that things didn't work out, but maybe we had to go through some shit to get here." I grab her hips to stop her from moving. "I think I've loved you since the moment we met, but I was only six, so I'm not sure. I will always protect you with my life. You can be sure of that."

A single tear rolls down her cheek. I wipe it away as her lips touch mine. They aren't hungry but needy. She wants to feel that I love her. I let her take the control she needs right now. She sucks on my lower lip and leaves a trail of soft kisses down my neck. Her tongue drags across my chest as she bites my nipple enough to get my attention and send shock waves to my cock.

Her mouth finds my hardness as she takes the whole thing without a problem. My focus is on her head bobbing up and down. She sucks and teases as her teeth scrape the sides. Heaven can't possibly feel better than this. Her hand fondles my balls, and I'm about ready to explode.

"Enough." I grab her hair and pull her off my cock. "I have other plans."

"You lasted longer than I thought you would." Her lips are plump and wet.

"My brothers always told me to watch out for the nerdy girls. They study everything."

She laughs out loud. "They are correct. When I do something, I want to do it right and know everything about it."

"So do I." I roll her onto her back and push her legs apart. Her smell is the sweetest.

My tongue knows what to do and starts by lapping her folds, making my way up to her nub. I suck on her and use my fingers to hook into the spot I know will light the fireworks.

Her hands grip my hair, and I smile. The rhythm of sucking and the stroke of my fingers have her moving her hips in sync with me. She holds a pillow over her mouth and screams my name. It takes everything I have not to come with her.

Her skin is flush, and she's panting. I cover her body with mine. She seems so small under me, but fierce things come in small packages.

"Are you on birth control? I want our first time to be with nothing between us. We've had enough between us to last a lifetime. I haven't been with anyone in a while, and I got checked."

Her hand caresses my face, and she frowns. "Have you avoided being with anyone because of your leg?"

"Yes."

She smiles. "You foolish man. You've got mad skills other men would envy. I'm on birth control and haven't been with anyone since my divorce. I'm clean." Something passes in her eyes and leaves quickly.

The tip of me enters her, and I hold back. I ease in and out, watching her eyes dilate and soft moans come from her mouth. My forehead touches hers as I ease in and find my rhythm. I put my hands under her ass to make sure I hit her G-spot.

"Oh my God, that's perfect. That feels incredible. Harder. I need you now."

"I can't hold out. You're making me crazy. I'm going to come."

"Me too."

My orgasm starts at my toes and rockets through me as I bury myself deeper inside her. Her hands grab my shoulders as she pulls me closer, wrapping her legs around me. It's as if we can't get close enough. She screams into my shoulder and whispers my name over and over again.

I stay inside her as we lie here without words. I slip out and grab some tissues.

"I'm sorry. I can't get up to get a cloth."

She shrugs. "I'll get it."

I roll off her and watch her very fine ass move to the bathroom. She comes back with a warm wet cloth to clean me. She tucks herself in the crook of my arm.

"You're incredible, better than anything I've ever imagined. Nothing compares to the real thing. You've always been part of me."

Her fingers play with the hair on my chest. "I may have married someone else, but I was only fooling myself."

Her body stiffens, and I feel her go away from me, back into her head. Her lack of trust has returned. A good negotiator knows how to reinforce their goal.

"You can trust me. I'm here. I will always be here. I won't leave you behind."

"That's what they say before they leave," is her only response before she falls asleep.

I have a lot of work to do to prove this is real.

TWENTY-EIGHT

Campbell

The night continues between sleeping and making love, from top to bottom, and everything in between. She needs to feel what and who we are now, not the kids from the past. For whatever reason, someone shattered her trust, no doubt her ex-husband.

A smile forms on my face before I open my eyes as I reach out to find an empty bed. My body and soul are satisfied for the first time in a long time, but the person who deserves the credit is not where I need her to be. She always had a mind of her own.

The overcast sky mutes the light coming into the room. The bathroom is dark with the door wide open. I pick up movement in my peripheral vision. Quinn sits on the floor with my prosthetic leg in her hands. She's wearing my oversized T-shirt, and her legs are bare. Her hands glide over the equipment, and she frowns every so often as she examines the wires.

"Good morning, Bee," I say in a froggy voice.

She looks up. "You know, I think I can improve this

model. I would have to study neurology a bit, but I can make some upgrades. The technology is available."

I curl my index finger several times. "Come here."

She springs up and brings my leg with her.

"Three is a crowd. You can leave my leg on the dresser." I can make out the shape of her perfect ass under my T-shirt. She comes back to bed and snuggles in next to me. "Do you ever turn off your brain?"

"Only during sex," she says in a serious tone.

A chuckle escapes my throat, and I brush the strands of hair from her cheek. "That's a good thing. I wouldn't want you to be thinking of formulas while I'm trying to make you come so hard you see stars."

"No problems there. I'm part of the galaxy after last night. Do you ever have phantom pains?" She must have read the surprise on my face. "Yesterday, I researched everything I could find about amputees so I can be here for you." Her eyes are more curious than ever.

This woman amazes me at every turn. "I sometimes have the sensation of something squeezing my foot hard, not the shooting pain some people have. The brain works in mysterious ways, but I did mirror therapy, which helped a lot."

"I read about that too. You know you could inspire others who have been through what you've been through. They need a positive outlook."

"My support system is incredible. I didn't get here on my own. I've been through therapy, and my brothers have been amazing. Sean even took a chance giving me this job." I kiss the top of her head. "Speaking of work, I need to get downstairs and see what's happening. Take your time."

I swing my leg and knee over the side of the bed. "I need you to give me my leg, please." My voice cracks. I'm not used to asking for help. My back is to her, and her fingers feather over the tattoos on my rib cage.

"What's this?" she whispers.

"Those are the names and dates of the soldiers we lost in the Hummer explosion. It's my way of honoring them."

Her fingers roam to the tattoo on my shoulder. "And this?"

"Look closer. You'll find a Q among the formulas." I peek over my shoulder at her.

She smiles. "I had no idea how you felt about me. I've never seen anything like it. I'm honored." She hands me my leg with a smile and watches intently as I put it on, locking it in place.

"I'll see you downstairs." I kiss her on the lips with a thank you.

Her smile is what I need to set the day off to a good start. I walk into the kitchen as the team sits around the island with morning drinks in their hands.

"The walls are thin, mate. You disturbed my beauty sleep," Dean mumbles.

"Funny, you look the same as you did yesterday. No harm done," I reply while pouring a cup of black tea. Snickers fill the room.

"Do you think you should shag the asset, even if you know her?" Mac states. Heads nod around the room.

"This is rich coming from the agents who have screwed their assets from Afghanistan to Germany." I fire my comment at the group. I'm tired of being the negotiator.

"He makes a valid point." Beck smiles as he leans against the counter, sipping his green tea.

Pippa and Peter come into the kitchen with a laptop. They prop it up on the island for everyone to see.

"We've got something to show you." Pippa's fingers fly over the keys.

Peter sits with a huge grin on his face. "This is some funny shit. We gave Dolly some added features."

The video starts, and Roger Bane enters the room with two men following him. He jerks back the covers, and there's the blowup doll named Dolly, smiling and squirting water at him from between her legs. The guys roar with laughter until the realization sets in.

Sean says, "That's not who I thought would show up to our surprise party. We've got a problem, and I'm about to take care of it."

He dials a number on his phone and puts it on speakerphone. "Well, hello, Clay. It's Sean Knight. We have video of Bane breaking into Campbell's room last night to do what?" He raises his voice. "I thought we were on the same team? We can pull out and leave you high and dry. We have a connection with Deep 8. Remember, with Liam, you only have half of what the program can do."

I put my hand up to stop him. "General Murphy, it's Campbell. I would like to recommend that you let me see Liam and get him to talk. Feel free to film our conversation. He's an ex-Ranger and trained not to give information under the most stressful of circumstances. You have nothing to bargain with since Quinn is in the wind. I'm the closest person he has to family, and he might talk to me about what he knows."

There's a long pause. "I apologize for Roger Bane's actions. He is under the impression you know exactly where Dr. Quinn Donovan is located. Nice touch on the squirting blowup. He needs to loosen up a bit." There is the distinct sound of him inhaling his cigar. "I will allow only Campbell to enter the safe house, unaccompanied by anyone else from your team."

Sean stands up. "No, not acceptable—"

I grab his arm. "It's a deal. Text the address to Sean, and I'll be there."

"No can do. We'll pick you up."

"I'll be waiting in the lobby of the Four Seasons at twenty-one hundred." I push the end button before he responds. The deal is on the table as take it or leave it.

"Good job on the negotiating. This whole op stinks, and I don't like it when we have to defend ourselves," Sean bites out.

"We need to take the day to prepare. I've got a guy in DC with a 3-D printer who can make a gun for you to take in. The plastic makes it undetectable. If they use a wand on you, carrying bullets will be a problem." Peter is in gadget mode.

"I might be able to help. I can bring MAGS back online." We turn as Quinn leans up against the wall. She holds out her hand. "I brought these. There are prototypes, but there is no time like the present to see if they work."

There is a pile of white objects the size of a bullet. Each one has a silver chip on the side of it. I take one between my fingers and hold it up.

"Where did these come from?" I ask.

"I grabbed them on my way to the safe room at the lab. I've been carrying them with me."

Everyone comes over and grabs one to look at it more closely. Pippa and Peter roll it around between their fingers, trying to figure out how it works.

"We connected MAGS to the chip, and she can navigate it. These bullets do not have any nuclear capability."

At the mention of nuclear, the bullets are placed back in her hand, and she laughs. Everyone scatters to work on their part of the plan for tonight. Quinn talks to Pippa about the type of high-powered computer she uses to run MAGS, Peter works on getting a gun for me, and the rest of us gather around the layout of the safe house to cover our bases.

"We need to think at least three steps past getting Liam out. There needs to be a contingency plan if they follow us back here or if we get separated," I comment. "I need time alone with Liam and Quinn in the same room to get intel. Whatever is going on may be right under our noses, but we can't see it."

We start with Liam's rescue, which must run like clock-work. Without Liam, we'll never get to the bottom of who the real mole is.

TWENTY-NINE

Campbell

As soon as things wrap up at the rental house, I'm in the car, and Sean drops me off at the lobby of the Four Seasons. I make myself comfortable in a square, overpriced chair in front of the blazing fireplace. Appearance is everything, especially at the price of these rooms, but I'll never understand why the hotel has a fire lit in the middle of summer.

I don't sit long when I get a tap on my shoulder by a guy dressed in a black suit. He never asks my name and tells me to come with him. I follow him to an idling black SUV while feeling the weight of my 3-D weapon under my jacket. They also gifted me with a knife, which I have at my ankle. As an ex-soldier, you're more used to carrying a weapon than not. I always make sure it's ready.

No sooner do I get settled in the seat when they place a black bag over my head. "Really? Is this how you treat a guy on a first date?" I try to find humor, but I'm pissed as hell.

I get no reaction from them, and everyone remains quiet as we travel to the safe house where the MBK team waits. The tires crunch on the gravel driveway. I assume it's the one on the plans leading to the house.

They hold me up by my upper arms as my feet land on the loose stones. We walk a few steps and get inside the front door. The black bag whips off my head as I stand inside the safe house.

The first face that greets me is familiar. "Bane." I nod my head.

"Creighton," he sneers. He steps up into my space. We are almost nose to nose. "Make one wrong move, and I won't hesitate to put a bullet through you. Try to get some perspective."

"You don't have any friends, do you?" He jerks back. "Because if you did, you would know what it's like to see your best friend in pain. I would do anything to help him. I did my job to the best of my ability, and will continue to do my job to find out what is going on and who's our mole." The space between us gets smaller. "Maybe it's you. You would be in an excellent position to make things go your way."

He steps back as his eyes narrow. My words hit their intended target, which is a nerve about people who are close to him. Somewhere along the line, he's been burned and can't stand people who he perceives as lying to him. We have all been burned. Get over it.

"Tell me, did you enjoy Dolly? She's quite the squirter." I grin.

There's a flicker in his eye I can't decipher. Maybe he found our Dolly to be funny.

"Can you move aside so I can interrogate Liam?"

"Are you sure you don't want to kiss his boo-boo and make it feel better?" he replies, trying to get a rise out of me.

"Oh, that was a good one. You'd be a great addition to our team with a mouth like that." I shoulder check him and move down the hall.

My comment throws him for a loop as he steps out of my

way and looks at me with curious eyes. If nothing else, he is loyal. We'll see how this plays out.

I'm led down a hallway to the end room. A guard swipes the keycard, which opens the steel door. The room is done in chic gray concrete, so surprising for a safe house interrogation room. The wall opposite Liam has an encased one-way mirror, a standard design.

He sits slumped over with his head down and his wrists shackled to a bar in the center of the metal table. His skin color has improved since the last time I saw him. They must be giving him his meds. I sit in a chair across from him with my hands clasped on the table.

"How are you?"

He lifts his head. I'm greeted with sunken eyes and thin lips. His time as a soldier and a high-level scientist has caught up with him, aging him beyond his years. He's worn down as his eyes plead with me to make this end. My good leg moves up and down under the table.

"I'm okay. They keep asking me questions I have no answers to." His voice is monotone.

I nod. Now, the fun begins.

When we were younger, we came up with a code as a form of sign language. We signaled with our fingers that coincided with words. We could send messages without anyone knowing what we were saying.

"Are you healed up?" I use our code and tap my face with my fingers. His eyes light up imperceptibly to anyone watching, but I know him too well.

We continue to talk, and he subtly watches my fingers as they tap on various parts of my body. Each tap tells him which letter of a certain word he should remember.

I question him about the phone calls he received from a burner phone.

"I don't know anything about a burner phone. The person I've been calling the most is my mother." Irritation laces his voice. I need to discuss her with him, but not here.

"What else did you notice at your lab or where Quinn was working? Were there any unusual activities or communications?" I press on.

"There was a lab tech I hired two months ago. We vetted him extensively. He seemed to get into different departments and areas he shouldn't have been in, but I could never link him back to anything suspicious."

"Is that what made you think you had a mole?"

"Yes, but I also noticed inconsistencies in some of the sub-programs I was working on, markers indicating someone else had been in the system. That was the big tip-off." He grips his hands in front of him.

"Tell me what happened at your facility." I continue to tap out my message to him.

"We were breached, but not with gunfire. They had the security codes and got in without a problem, storming through several levels. I didn't go to the safe room. I grabbed a knife and cut out my tracker. Then I went up the escape ladder to the hatch leading to the outside. If they had the codes, they might be able to track me. When I got far enough into the woods, I ditched everything, including my phone." Tears form in his eyes. "My only regret is I couldn't warn Quinn in time." He grits his teeth.

His face falls. "I should have been there for her."

"You did the best you could under the circumstances. She's smart enough to find a way out or contact someone, and that's what she did. We got to her in time."

I finish tapping out my last word to him, and an explosion rocks the concrete walls, leaving cracks in them. Thermite is a beautiful thing in the proper hands. It's showtime.

I grab the gun from behind my back. "Stand back as far as you can," I order. I take my shot at the metal link between his cuffs. They fall away as we rush for the door. He tugs at it, but it's locked.

"Now, what?" Adrenaline surges through his body, and he's ready for action.

"We wait. My team has got this."

I get the last word out of my mouth when the black one-way mirror cracks from bullet holes. The entire mirror shatters, leaving shards around the edges.

Dean stands on the other side, opens his arms, and says, "Here's Johnny!"

"I see you're not the only jokester on the team," Liam says as he climbs through the hole in the mirror.

We follow Dean out the door and into the hallway, taking fire as we go and firing back. Our orders are shoot to injure, not kill. This extraction will put a kill order on our team. We don't need anyone dead.

Dean taps his earpiece. "Roger that." He turns to us. "We're clear, but we need to move fast to get you out of here and back to the house."

We jump into a gray Tesla Model S Plaid, the fastest sedan to date. Pippa is in the driver's seat. She reads the trepidation on my face.

"Stop looking at me that way. I'm an excellent driver, despite what Beck has told you." She smiles and pushes her foot to the floor as we take off down the street. "Hi, Liam. It's nice to meet you. I'm Pippa." She waves to him in the rearview mirror.

He nods. "Please don't get us killed. I need to see Quinn."

"We've got a tail. You know the plan. Quinn will jump in when we get there, and you'll take off for your next location. We've disabled the GPS tracker, so you should be good to go.

There are backpacks in the trunk with an untraceable credit card and enough cash to keep you afloat for a while."

Up ahead, I see a small fleet of gray Teslas of the same model parked in front of the house. Pippa pulls up in between them. Quinn jumps out from one and slides into the back seat. She grips Liam and cries into his shoulder. I take over the driver's seat.

A phone call comes through the screen. I answer it.

"It's Sean. I want you to wait for my go. We'll use these cars as a decoy to get you out safely. They have no idea who they are screwing with." The gloves are off.

"Got it."

We sit and wait until the headlights get closer.

"Go," Sean commands.

The cars in front of us move, and we split off in different directions. There are five of us, and three of them. Let's see who they follow.

Now that Liam is safe, at least in the car, the challenge will be figuring out who is the mole. Then there is the minor matter of Quinn and me. Let's see how good we are at hiding our love for each other.

THIRTY

Quinn

THANK GOD, this is almost over. I can breathe easier knowing Liam and MAGS are safe. As we travel in our little bubble of hope, we have limited time to figure out what's going on and who is chasing us, but the end of this is near. Liam and I need to work with MAGS to find out what's going on.

The man I've been in love with ever since I can remember has rescued my brother, and he's driving us to safety. Our story will have a happy ending, but I still need to keep us from Liam a bit longer.

Cam's team took a tremendous risk by breaking Liam out and setting him free. There is a good possibility they will be brought up on treason charges and locked away for eternity if we can't prove Liam's innocence. I hope we can run away together and leave this behind.

Liam slumps to the side with his head against the window and falls asleep. I rub his arm and smile. He and I can sleep whenever our bodies demand it from us. His snoring echoes in the dark car. The only light comes from the screen on the dashboard.

I touch Cam on the shoulder. "Can you pull over so I can get in the front seat?"

"No. I have to keep going until we get to the first checkpoint." His fingers grip the steering wheel.

"It looks like we're in the clear, and Liam and I can get busy working on the program. Did he tell you anything that will help us find the mole?"

"Is that what you think? We're in the clear." He blows out a breath and doesn't let me answer. "No, and we need to talk about the meaning of your father's message."

I nod, still processing what my dad was trying to tell me. His cryptic message didn't surprise me. My mom and I have been on the outs for years because I don't trust her with anything. My brother doesn't know the details, but he's about to know everything.

"Where are we headed?"

"Up north. Declan has a thing for cabins and found us one in the backwoods of Pennsylvania. We have to switch cars first."

He turns off the highway at an exit ramp and onto a dirt road. The trees provide a tunnel as we drive for a bit and stop by the side of the road.

"We need to go on foot from here to the barn. Our ride is waiting for us." He gets out of our luxury ride as I rouse Liam and get him out of the Tesla. His humor is gone, and he's in business mode.

Cam uses a flashlight to light our way in total darkness. The canopy of the trees is so thick that no light from the moon can snake through. We keep Liam between us in case he falls. Up ahead is an old, beige Jeep.

"How old is this Jeep?" I ask as I hoist myself up in the passenger seat.

"It's a 1998 Jeep Wrangler. Cars manufactured before

2001 don't have a GPS tracking system. Starting in 2001, GPS was a standard feature. This Jeep will get us where we need to go off-road," Liam answers and smiles at Cam.

He turns to me. "You picked the right guy, Q-tip." My smile drops as he calls me by my dad's nickname. "What's wrong? You look sad."

"We'll talk more when we get to wherever we're going." He gives me a curious look. "Why don't you sit in the back with me and we can talk?"

"I'm going to let you stretch out and get some sleep. I get the feeling we have a ways to go."

He nods, gets in the back, crosses his arms over his chest, and falls asleep.

Cam turns the car around and heads back the way we came down the dirt road. "It's crazy how you two can sleep at the drop of a hat."

"I think it's genetic. My dad used to sleep like that, too." I hold my hand to my chest.

He drives back to the highway as we continue north, heading into the Pennsylvania woods. Liam mumbles in his sleep now and then, breaking the silence in the car. Cam focuses on the road, and I'm left with my thoughts about the three puzzle pieces riding in this car. Each of us has something to share with the rest of the group, but will it be a solution we can live with together? Cam has taught me something more about trust. Betrayal doesn't apply to everyone.

I must have dozed off because when my eyes open, we are parked in front of a cabin in the woods. The headlights shine on the lower half of a plain dark brown log cabin.

"Declan promised me it is fully stocked. He better be right because it's been a long-ass day."

I want to reach out and touch him, but I can't because Liam has chosen this moment to open his eyes. He gets out of the Jeep, stretches, and yawns as if we have not rescued him from a government safe house. Everyone has a different normal.

Cam finds the key and opens the door. A musty scent hits us as he flips on the light. The cabin is small, with a kitchen and a living room. There is a bathroom and two bedrooms off to the back. He looks at me, and I stare back at him.

"I'll take the couch. You two can have the bedrooms," Cam offers.

"I'm getting a strange vibe off you two. Do you want to tell me what's going on?" Liam narrows his eyes.

"No," we say together.

"Quinn and I have been at this for a while. We have a lot of questions and information to share. I also think you may have information that could help with who is after the two of you." Cam's eyes are dark, and his face is drawn.

"I'll do the best I can." He winces, holding his hip.

"Let's get something to eat and call it a night." I rub my thumb along the front of the locket.

They nod, and Liam makes it to the couch to sit down. Cam goes to the kitchen.

"I'm going to make us some hearty soup to tide us over."

I curl up on the couch next to Liam as the clanking of pots provides the background noise. "I'm glad we have you back so we can finish the program."

"We need to figure this out. We're running out of time. Everyone is looking for us, from the US government to whoever is out to get us. How's MAGS?"

"That's your big question? You need to get a life." I slap his shoulder.

"What are you talking about? You're just as bad. Where's your boyfriend?" Liam shoots back.

I couldn't stop the side of my lips from quirking into a smile.

"Spill it," he demands.

"There's nothing to spill. I was thinking about something else." I avert my eyes, focusing on my nails.

"You're a sucky liar," he replies.

"Dinner's ready," Cam says from the kitchen. Saved by the yell.

We eat in silent tension. Cam and I exchange looks as Liam watches us.

"Tonight, we need to get some sleep and put our heads together tomorrow. We've got to find a crack in this somewhere," Cam comments.

I clean up the kitchen as Liam says good night and heads to the bedroom. Cam and I are alone at last. His shoulders slump as he sits on the couch and holds his head in his hands. I sit next to him and rub his back.

"Tomorrow is going to be one big fat shitstorm," he mumbles in his hands.

"I trained some fish to escape. A koi, B koi, and C koi all got away because everyone chased the D koi," I giggle.

"That was an awful joke, but I like that you know me well enough to give me what I need." He looks at me through tired eyes. His fingers run along my jawline, and he kisses my lips with tenderness.

"Why don't you sleep in bed with me tonight?" I want him near me.

"And get caught by your brother? No thanks. I swear he sleeps with one eye open."

"He's out cold by now, but we'll have to tell him, eventually."

"True. Later would be great." He stares into my eyes as his thumb caresses my neck, sending chills down my spine. I love what he does to me with his touch. I never thought I'd be here feeling a cascade of emotions with another man after being wrecked by Sam.

"I have a counteroffer. We can cuddle until you fall asleep, which should take three seconds, and then I'm coming back out to sleep on the couch. No funny business with your brother sleeping next door."

"I accept your offer." I stand up and take his hand, leading him to the other bedroom.

I strip down to my birthday suit, and he takes off his clothes except for his briefs. He sits on the side of the bed and takes off his leg to let it rest. As predicted, I fall asleep in T minus three seconds.

Somewhere in the middle of the night, I wake up with his wood in my back. Perfect timing.

My hand finds his hard cock and strokes him gently. I don't want to wake him. I want to see how far I can take this. Diving under the covers, my mouth finds its target, and I work him in and out of my mouth. His hips thrust, and I don't know if he is still asleep.

"Quinn," he breathes. Flood gates open between my legs, and I can't wait to ride.

I push him over so he's on his back and his eyes are closed. I'm positioned over him and slide down as his eyes pop open.

"What are you doing?" he whispers.

"If you don't know what I'm doing, we've got a big problem," I whisper back.

He holds my hips in place. "Your brother is right next door, and we should not wake the bear," he says through gritted teeth.

"This is kinda hot." I move. "It's our thing."

He moans. "What's our thing?"

"Having hot sex while there is someone in the next room." I lean over and kiss him. "Let's see how quiet we can be."

"I doubt you can be silent in the least," he challenges.

I ride him like I have eight seconds to come.

"Holy hell, woman, you're gonna break our hips," he clenches his jaw.

My orgasm spirals up from my toes and through my chest. I'm coming so hard my head is going to explode. I bend over to bury my face in a pillow to release my scream. Cam pulses inside me, and I'm shrouded in sweet pleasure. We've created our little world where we can be together.

We're panting and sweating. I roll off him and tuck myself into the crook of his arm. He kisses the top of my head.

"My dream has come true. The piece of me that carried you is part of me. You're seared in my heart. I won't let anything happen to you, ever," he says.

His words have more meaning than he knows. Everything I didn't know was missing in my life is right here in front of me, but I'm not ready. Fear of betrayal holds me in place. I drift far away into my safe space.

The next thing I heard was my brother's voice at the foot of the bed. "What the hell is going on here?"

Cam's eyes shoot open, and he pulls the covers up to his chin, which will offer him zero protection in this situation.

THIRTY-ONE

Campbell

THIS IS AN OH, shit moment. I must have fallen asleep next to Quinn and never got up again. We were cuddling, and it was warm, not a wonderful combination for staying awake. Quinn's face gets redder by the minute.

She whips the covers back. Liam covers his eyes. "Put some damn clothes on. I'll see you both in the living room in five. Damn it!" He does a one-eighty and gropes for the door frame.

"You are not the boss of me. I'm a grown woman," Quinn says in a loud voice. As soon as he slams the door behind him, she throws her pillow and hits the door.

This is not what I envisioned happening when we told Liam about us. This wasn't the shitstorm I expected, but we have to deal with Liam at some point.

I swing my leg over the side of the bed, trying to balance on it while reaching down to get my fake leg. Somehow, Liam didn't see it. He was too busy worrying about Quinn.

Quinn moves behind me to put her clothes on. I try to clear my head, preparing for *The Secret Life of Quinn and Cam's* big reveal, followed by *Licence to Kill,* starring Liam.

She comes around to my side of the bed. "He has no fucking right to tell me who I can and cannot be with on this planet."

"You need to calm down. Yelling and screaming at each other will not get us anywhere. We have a lot of ground to cover today to get some answers, despite what's going on with you and me."

"That's not all we're going to get to today," she mutters.

"What does that mean?" My words are short.

"Nothing. Let's get this over with." She holds out her hand.

We enter the living room, and the smell of freshly brewed coffee, eggs, and toast greets us. Liam stands at the stove, preparing everything. Quinn and I look at each other and shrug.

"Have a seat, you two. Cam, I hope you don't mind if I take over cooking duties." He's so calm. It's freaking me out.

"Fine by me," I mutter.

He pours two cups of coffee and sets plates in front of us. Neither one of us dares to say a word. He adds sunny-side-up eggs, Quinn's favorite, and buttered toast to our plates.

"Thank you," we mumble over each other.

Liam sits on the other side of the table and eats. "How long has this been going on?" He doesn't look at either of us.

Quinn speaks first. "It's recent. We've been together since Cam rescued me from the Russians."

"You rescued her?" His eyes bore into me.

Game on. I lean across the table. "I would lay down my life for her, and you know that." I point at him with my fork.

"It's about time you got a set of balls and told her how you feel. I thought I would die before you two got together." He stuffs bacon in his mouth.

My fork hits the plate. "What?!"

He smiles. "You thought you were being slick in high school, but I saw how you looked at her. I thought you would've stopped her from marrying that asshole, Sam."

"What are you talking about? You're the one who walked me down the aisle." Quinn narrows her eyes at him.

"You were happy, and I didn't want to get in the way. I won't stop you from being with Cam. He's the best man I know to this day. I can't imagine you with anyone better than him. I trust him, and so do you now."

Quinn rushes over to Liam and gives him a big hug. While he winks at me, I mouth the words, "Payback is a bitch with no mercy."

He laughs, and Quinn sits down. "We have a lot of ground to cover today, and I need you two on your toes," he orders.

"Who's running this op? Because it's not you." I can taste the food in my mouth as my nerves calm down.

"You're going to run point on this op? I have the inside track," he replies. Now, he's poking the bear.

"I have all the tracks, inside and out," I snap back.

"Boys. Stop. We need to work together to figure this out." Quinn steps up as mediator. "Cam has something he wants you to know about." She crosses her arms in front of her and sits back in her chair.

I stare at her like she has three heads. "It can wait."

"No, it can't. You need to tell him."

"Tell me what?" Liam has a worried look on his face.

"I lost my leg over in Afghanistan, that's all." I scowl at Quinn. "Do you feel better now?"

"What the hell? Why didn't you tell me?" Liam frowns as his mouth hardens.

"When did you want me to tell you? When you were

delirious with a fever or while we were breaking you out of the safe house?" My face warms with each word.

"I wanted you to tell me when it happened," Liam mutters. "Have we grown that far apart?" His mouth turns down.

"No, we haven't grown apart. We just grew up, and other priorities got in the way. There was a lot to deal with after the accident." I continue to tell him the entire story from beginning to end.

He takes in the details and asks questions. Each time I tell my story, a little more pain falls away, and I can breathe easier, as if a dark cloud has broken apart, letting the sun shine down.

Quinn clears the table as Liam and I sit in silence.

"I'm sorry you went through that without me. I would have been there for you every step of the way."

"I know you would have. I'm still dealing with not having a leg and the different legs I can use in certain situations. My life has changed and been turned upside down, but I'm alive and thankful every day. Not everyone gets that lucky."

"Can I see it?"

"What's with you two and this leg?" I ask, amused.

"What can I say? Science is cool. Is it robotic?" He lights up just like Quinn. Bionic legs might be their next venture if this program doesn't work out.

They fill the next several minutes with a barrage of questions I can answer about my leg and some I can't.

Quinn comes back and plops herself into the chair next to me. "Now that you have had your 'bro moment,' let's get down to business. What do you need to know from us that will help figure out who destroyed our labs?"

I turn to Liam. "The PAX team found evidence of you

calling a burner phone number several times. It's why they suspected you of treason. Who were you calling?"

"The only person I've been calling on the regular is my mother. She serves on the Security Council, and I needed her advice when I caught wind of a mole. She demanded I give her the security codes to the facilities…" His voice fades away, and his face goes pale.

"Do you have proof of calling her number?" I question.

"Yes, my recent call list would show the number I called is her cell phone."

"I'll call Pippa and see if they got your phone in the extraction. Why did she need the codes for the labs?"

"She said she was going to have them on a rolling code system so they would change every hour. She was going to put it in place, but we got raided before that happened."

Quinn rolls her eyes. "She's probably the mole. I wouldn't put it past her. She's a snake," Quinn snips.

"How can you say that? She's our mom." Liam's volume increases. "I trust her with my life."

Quinn stands up with her hands on the table. "She's not as wonderful as you think she is."

Liam stands up on the other side and leans on his hands. "I don't understand. What did she ever do to you?"

Quinn's lips squeeze together, and she sits down. Her face falls as tears pour from her eyes. She shakes her head. "I don't want to tell you," she says just above a whisper.

Liam drags his chair next to her, and I push back my chair to leave. Quinn grabs my arm. "I need you. Please stay."

I sit back down and hold her hand in mine. Liam's eyes turn down as he holds her other hand. "You can tell me anything."

"If I tell you, you'll think I'm an idiot, and I'm not sure you'll believe me." She gulps between the sobs.

"You have no reason to lie to me. Tell me," Liam presses.

"Sam had an affair, which is one of the reasons we got a divorce."

"Yes, I know. What does that have to do with Mom?"

"He had an affair with her."

THIRTY-TWO

Quinn

_____

LIAM LETS GO of my hand and moves away from me. He stares at me without words. He's thinking I'm being dramatic over something trivial, but he doesn't know what happened.

Cam holds my hand, stroking the top of my knuckles with his thumb. The silence is heavy with questions, and doubts are edged with anger. I've placed the distrust bee in Liam's bonnet.

Liam speaks first. "Do you want to explain how you know this to be true, with evidence, please?" Always the scientist.

The tips of my fingers wipe away my tears. "Sam was working late too often. I began checking his text messages and phone calls. I had a friend of mine hack into his account. The number he was getting messages from and making calls to traced back to a burner phone." I'm reliving every moment as if it were yesterday, my heart tearing with every word.

My breath is shallow as I give myself a moment. Liam leans toward me. "Go on," he encourages me to continue as the betrayal cuts deep.

"I started following him and saw him meet Mom. Then I

made a lunch date with her and cloned her phone. Guess who had the number attached to the burner phone? A woman's intuition is never wrong." I squeeze Cam's hand.

"One night, I followed him to her townhouse. I gave them some time and let myself in with my key. When I pushed the door open, they were on the couch, sharing a bottle of wine. Sam was caressing her face. Mom turned to me with a look of horror as Sam laughed at me and said, 'That's right. I'm doing your mom.' I heard Mom call my name, but I ran out of there. The next couple of days were filled with numerous calls from Mom. She said it wasn't what it looked like and begged for forgiveness. Sam came to collect his things without a word." I'm heaving, barely able to breathe, unable to see the look on Liam's face.

Liam sits back in his chair and laces his hands in his lap. "I don't even know what to say. Sorry is not enough. I can't believe she would do this to her only daughter. With the evidence, there isn't a chance for another explanation." He turns to Cam.

"It makes me wonder what else she's capable of," Cam states.

Liam and I snap our heads in his direction.

He continues, "I'm sorry, but we need to take a closer look into what's going on with her. She obviously knows something about burner phones."

Liam nods, shell-shocked by the recent portrayal of his mother, his confidant. He's a mama's boy, and the revelation has shattered his world.

"I'm going to go outside and make some phone calls." Cam leaves Liam and me to sift through our family wreckage.

"Why didn't you tell me sooner?" He scrubs his hands over his face.

"I couldn't bring myself to tell anyone. I thought if I kept it hidden, the hurt would go away. Boy, was I wrong. It festered, and my anger got worse. I wanted to stab both of them." Tears well in my eyes again, but I sniffed them back in.

"What has Mom gotten herself into?" he whispers. "There were times on the phone when she was unusually short with me. She didn't seem like herself. If there's another explanation, I would love to know what it is. I'm having trouble giving her the benefit of the doubt."

"It could be the pressures from her job. Lord knows, her job always came first. Maybe someone is blackmailing her. Do you think this is what Dad's message was about?"

This is the moment when Liam usually argues with me and tells me how important her work is as a senator to her seat on the Security Council. Instead, he slouches over and doesn't say a word.

After a long pause, he says, "Something is way off about all of this. We're missing something." His brows furrow.

Cam comes in the door with his eyes darting between us. I wave my hand to him. "We're good. Come on over."

He stands in front of me with his hands stuffed in his front pockets. "I'm so sorry that happened to you. We might go a couple of rounds if I ever see your ex-husband again."

"Thank you," I say in a shaky voice.

He turns to Liam. "I called Pippa about your phone. The team couldn't find it at the safe house, but she can hack into your cell phone account and get the records. In light of our recent discovery, it's a good place to start. How close are you to getting MAGS completed?"

"We're almost done, but there are a couple of trials we need to do before we are a go. She's not fully operational. I'm curious why anyone is coming after her now?" Liam replies.

"They aren't coming after her. They're coming after both

of you in hopes of getting you to finish the program for their use."

"Who are they?" I ask.

Cam shifts from one foot to the other. "We're not sure yet. There seem to be several players, and they may not be on the same team."

"Who?" Liam asks.

"I'm not ready to get into that just yet. We know the Russians and Chinese are involved, but we don't know in what capacity. Your dad's message implied your mum was working with someone outside the government."

Liam shrugs. "I have no idea who she works with or for. I've been calling her for advice on the next steps for MAGS. This entire program makes me nervous and has been for a while." Liam's leg bounces.

"What do you mean?" Cam replies.

"MAGS operates at a whole other level. If we can complete her programming, she'll be unstoppable. Whoever has a hold of her could dominate in war and invasions. But there is a bigger part of this that concerns me."

Cam and I wait with rapt attention.

"Q-tip, you and I are not the smartest people in the world. We are a handful of people who can think at this level. Others out there could change the programming to suit their needs. They could program MAGS to execute world leaders and other people her owner doesn't like, or who isn't in line with their vision."

I sag back in my chair. "I've been living in an underground bubble, focused on the good. The evil has been a shadow in the background, but it's coming at us full force. This makes me rethink everything. I see years of work going down the drain."

"Let's not get carried away. Pippa left us with the satellite coordinates for your high-powered laptop. I'll go get it so we can bring MAGS up and figure out our next move." Cam leaves to get the laptop.

I rub the back of my locket, wishing Dad was here to guide us through this labyrinth with no end. The center of my chest hurts. One sad moment after another seems to be the theme of the day.

"We're going to have to destroy her, aren't we?" I barely get the words out.

Liam taps his fingers on the table. "Not necessarily."

"She is not your girlfriend. You need to let go."

"Admit it, she has a personality we know and love." He has the smile of a charming schoolboy.

I nod. "She does."

"There is a way for us to dismantle her without destroying her." He rests his elbows on the table. "You can't tell your boyfriend about this. He has a job to do, and we have to respect that."

"I don't want any secrets with Cam. Secrets kill relationships, and this one is just getting started." I cross my arms over my chest. Am I looking for trust?

The door closes as Cam comes from the bedroom.

"We'll cross this bridge when we come to it."

Cam places the laptop on the table and looks at us. "What's going on? You know I can read both of you very well, and the vibe has changed since I was here five minutes ago."

"Nothing," I reply. "We were talking about MAGS and trying to figure things out."

Liam grabs the laptop and turns it on. His fingers fly across the keys. We have already booted MAGS up from deep sleep, so he only needs to log on.

She pops up. "Good morning, Dr. Liam. How are you today?"

Liam's face lights up as he rests his chin on his hand. "Better now that I know you're okay."

Cam rolls his eyes. "Mate, you need to get a human girlfriend. Why wouldn't she be okay? She lives in a computer."

"Dr. Liam, I have to warn you. Someone has been trying to hack into my system for the last twenty-four hours. I've blocked them, but I'm running out of options. I need your help."

I jump out of my seat and move next to Liam. "Do you know the source of the breach?" I ask her.

"No, they take a short time to try to hack into me, but not long enough for me to trace it. I analyzed it to be another AI program that works quicker than humans."

"Is it happening now?"

"No."

"Let us know when they come on again so we can try to trace it," Liam requests.

I turn to Cam. "If she can't trace it, we're in deep shit."

THIRTY-THREE

Campbell

THE WORDS deep shit when talking about a program that could change how the world operates is not what I want to hear right now. We need to find out who knows what and how they are hacking into this program. I need to bring in Pippa and Peter.

On the video call with them, I explained the situation with MAGS. The background sound is tapping fingers on keyboards.

"Whoever it is keeps bouncing me out as soon as I get in," Peter states.

Pippa replies, "I have a workaround." The tapping increases. "I've got it. I'm in, but I don't know for how long. Peter, I'm sharing my screen."

The line is quiet, with a few taps here and there. I wait as my mouth gets dry.

"This is Russian code. I recognize it. Pippa, are you seeing what I'm seeing?"

The dead air lasts for a beat too long. "Yeah, I see it," she says in a pissed-off tone.

A voice I don't recognize comes through the call. We've

been compromised. "Krasnyy, you play for the wrong team. Your team will lose. You were never a loser. Always a winner. When we get what we want, you will be mine again. We have software you only dream about."

"What software, Wolf?" Pippa plays into his hand.

"Hacking software you and I talked about. Goodbye for now, Krasnyy." The voice disappears.

"Who was that?" Peter asks with an irritated tone. "What does Krasnyy mean?"

"It means red in Russian. Ivan Antonov, aka Wolf, is one of the best hackers in the world. He's also an asshole scumbag mother—"

"We got the picture. How did he know it was you?" I ask.

"Hackers know each other's code sequence. He knows mine quite well." Her voice drops.

"What software is he talking about?" Peter asks.

"A hacking software that can break codes faster than humans. If he's developed this, MAGS is in trouble." Pippa shifts in her chair.

"What do we need to do to keep MAGS safe?" I'm talking about her like she's a person.

Peter chimes in, "I'm sure Beck would be interested in Ivan." He grins.

"Peter, if you say one word to him, I'll rip your head off and shit down your throat. Besides, that was a lifetime ago."

"That's a bit graphic," Peter lobs it back.

"Can you two focus and tell me what to do here?" I press.

Pippa suggests we get on a video call with everyone to figure out our next moves. Quinn, Liam, and I huddle around the laptop and move the camera back so we're on the screen.

Pippa takes the lead as everyone's head pops up on the screen. "We can do one of two things. We keep MAGS online intermittently and try to catch Ivan and his gang.

Second, we turn her off and have her go deep, protecting her."

Quinn and Liam remain quiet and look at each other. There is a kind of secret message traveling between them no one else can figure out. Their exchange includes nods and whispers. "I think we should shut MAGS down and keep her safe," Quinn blurts out.

"No, I say we keep her online intermittently and try to find out who's behind this," Liam counters.

"I'm trying to keep her safe from the vultures out there. This is our life's work we're talking about." Quinn's face contorts.

Pippa picks up on Quinn's vibe. She brings her face closer to the camera. "We'll keep her safe. I promise. The minute we think she's compromised, we'll shut her down. We need her out there to catch these guys. You need to trust us."

Quinn's mouth turns down. "That seems to be where I have a problem, but I'm working on it." She turns to Liam. "Do what you need to do." Her shoulders slump as she walks out of the room.

I look over at Liam, and he nods. I thought he would have been the one to keep MAGS locked down.

My foot wedges between the door and the frame to the bedroom. I close the door behind me. "Come here. I think you need an arm crook snuggle."

She doesn't say a word as I lie on the bed and pat the space next to me. She tucks her hands inside her sleeves and crosses her arms in front of her.

"You know you want to," I coax her like a wounded animal.

She slides in next to me and throws her leg over mine. My nose finds her hair with the sweet fragrance of orange blossom. Sometimes, I would smell that scent on the breeze in the summer and think of her, curious about where she was and what she was doing. I don't want to wonder ever again.

My fingers play with her wavy brown hair. "You have to trust us at some point," I whisper.

She lets out an audible sigh. "I know. I'll get there at some point. You were my first step." She turns her head toward me. "MAGS is so much bigger than any of us. We need to protect her." She slaps her forehead. "I sound like Liam."

"Maybe she is a little human. She listens to the two of you like doting parents. She's learned a lot in a short amount of time. Could she identify the software and shut it down from the inside?"

Quinn plays with a tendril of hair. "Not if she doesn't know what she's looking for. We have to introduce her to the program before she understands it."

"It's kind of like having a puppy."

Her lips curl at the ends. "Yeah, kind of."

We lie here for a while as I stroke her arms, back, and legs. She needs comfort more than a pep talk about how we'll get through this together. I can't help but think this might be the beginning of the end of the MAGS program.

My phone rings on my secure line. "Creighton here."

"Campbell, it's Sean. Word has it Senator Liz Donovan is up in arms, demanding to know where her children are. I need a status report on Drs. Donovan."

Quinn and Liam's mum was always cool as a frosty on a hot summer day. I sit up and lean against the headboard. "Who did she contact?"

"She called Natalie Palmer. They know each other from when Natalie sat on the Security Council. Our next decision needs to be a careful one."

"How did you get this information?" I question.

"We heard chatter and have tails on specific people. Also, we have a red-headed hacker who might have investigated the PAX team. What's with all the questions?"

I rub my forehead with my fingers and thumb. "Sorry, we're up here in a cabin in the woods. It has an 'us against the world' feel to it. Let me bring Quinn and Liam into the conversation."

Quinn frowns and follows me to the living room. I place the phone on the table.

"You're on speakerphone," I inform Sean.

He runs through what he told me with a bit more detail. Liam and Quinn look at each other.

Quinn is the first to speak. "That doesn't sound like her."

"How would you know since you don't speak with her?" He leans back in shock. "I'm sorry. This whole situation has me on edge."

Quinn puts her hands up. "You're right. I haven't spoken to her in a long time. When did she turn into an alarmist?"

He scrubs his face. "She hasn't. You're right. They don't call her the Ice Queen for nothing. She remains calm in every situation. The only change is the fact that her children are nowhere to be found. She would have been briefed about the safe house breakout as part of the Security Council."

Quinn shakes her head. "No, something is off. Sean, did Natalie describe it as panic?"

"Yes. I also have Clay up my ass demanding a location on Liam and wants Campbell to turn him in. We are not in anyone's good graces right now. We need to act fast. I can't hold him off forever." Sean's words are clipped.

"At least he doesn't want to arrest you. I think I have an idea. Liam, you need to contact your mum and draw her into a conversation with some test questions," I offer.

"What do you mean test questions?" Quinn asks.

"I want to know if it's her or someone else," I reply.

"No. Quinn needs to contact her for a reconciliation. She won't be expecting it, and it will throw her off. We can figure things out from her answers," Liam counters.

Quinn's face goes pale as she holds her head in her hands. "I don't know if I can do that. It's a lot to ask."

I put my hand on her shoulder and lean over near her ear. "There's a lot on the line, and we are running out of time. You are the element of surprise she won't be expecting."

THIRTY-FOUR

Quinn

THERE HAS NEVER BEEN SO MUCH on the line. As much as we need to get to the bottom of this, the thought of talking to my mom makes me nauseous. She and I haven't spoken in years since I discovered she was having an affair with my husband, wedging a crevasse between us.

At every turn, I'm being asked to put my trust in people who betrayed me. I don't know why Liam has such faith in her. She has betrayed him, too. He is more forgiving than I am.

She was rarely there for us growing up. We always relied on my dad. He was our constant, the one who stayed home to take care of us. I have nothing against a woman having a career. I'm a prime example of a career woman. When I have a family, I hope to have a balance between work and home. Her job was her priority.

Home was always my happy place, where I felt safe and secure. I thought I had made a secure home with Sam. When it got ripped out from under me, I stowed myself away in my work, hiding from the world with the excuse that I would be able to save it. Burying myself in the MAGS program prevented me from dealing with anything called life.

The joke's on me as I face the person who has caused me the most pain. I won't be able to talk to her without anger, frustration, and sadness. We are strong, determined women, but I doubt she will have much of a defense.

Knowing I don't have a choice, I ask for guidance. "I'm not looking forward to this. What do you need me to do?"

Cam reads my face as a pained expression floats in his eyes. "I wish there were another way, but I agree with Liam. The element of surprise is how we need to throw her off her game and find out what's going on. All she knows is that you are somewhere in Europe."

Liam scans my face to see if I'm strong enough to handle this. "We have keys to her apartment. The bigger surprise will come when she gets home to find us there—"

Cam cuts him off, "There is no we or us. Quinn is going in alone with us outside as backup. You can't be anywhere near there. We can't have you two together. It would be too easy for them to get to you."

Liam stands to his full height. "I will not let her face Mom alone. This was painful enough already. We don't need to make it worse."

"No. Can. Do. You're with me. Quinn is going to have to face her mum on her own." Cam squares off with Liam, face-to-face.

"Damn it!" Liam turns away.

"I can do it, especially if you're both close by. She has no idea what's coming." My heart beats faster as I revisit the day I discovered their tryst.

"Is there any way MAGS can hack into your mum's security feed? We need to see what's on her schedule and when she comes and goes," Cam says.

I spin around and boot up MAGS.

"Hello, Dr. Quinn. How are you today?"

"I've been better," I reply off the cuff.

"Yes, according to my readings, you were much better on—"

Liam cuts her off and sits down next to me. "Hey, MAGS." He turns to me. "Quinn didn't mean that literally. We need your help, but it goes against protocol. Someone we love might be in danger. Can you help us?"

I tap away on the keyboard, waiting for her to respond.

"Who is in danger?" Her voice has a genuine concern. Nice touch, bro.

"Our mother."

We hold our breath while we wait for her to respond.

"I will help you help her. She is very important to you. What do you need me to do?"

"I've typed in the address of our mother's townhouse in Washington, DC. I need you to get into the security system and play it back for us."

We don't wait long before MAGS has something for us. "How far back do you want me to play the tape? They appear to go back as far as a week."

"Show us seven days ago, and we'll take it from there." Liam leans into the screen to take a closer look as Cam stands behind me to examine the tape over my shoulder.

My mom leaves her townhouse at 7:00 a.m. every morning. She returns at various times each evening. In the early evenings, Sam shows up. Cam's hand massages my shoulder. Her face is turned down. Sam's back is to the camera as they argue, but there's no sound on the video. Sam storms out as she folds herself into a chair. She holds her head in her hands and cries.

Chills run across my skin. This is not the scene I was

expecting. I had no idea Sam was still part of her personal life, but it doesn't look like they are a happy couple. I thought I would be joyful knowing they were unhappy. Seeing my mom cry and knowing her to be such a fierce woman hits me in the gut. My perception of the entire situation changes like a spinning kaleidoscope.

We sit in silence for a moment until Liam breaks the ice. "We're missing something. I've never seen Mom like this. I want to know what their argument was about. MAGS, can you read my mom's lips and translate it back to us?"

"She's saying she doesn't want to do this anymore. When is this going to end?" MAGS responds without emotion.

"When is what going to end?" I'm stunned by her reply to whatever he has said to her.

"That's what we need to find out," Liam says. "Let's continue to play the tape up to the last forty-eight hours."

We fast forward to the next morning when we see her leave, and then there's nothing. She doesn't come back to her townhouse, and neither does Sam.

I stand up as the chair falls behind me. "Where the hell are they? They've been gone for the last two days. He better not have hurt her." As my world shifts around me, I've become her advocate.

Liam takes me by the shoulders. "Calm down. We're going to find out what's going on, I promise." He turns to Cam. "We need to get down there ASAP. If she's in danger from Sam or anyone else, we've got to get her out."

Ever the eye of the storm, Cam remains steadfast and calm. "What if this is a trap to lure you two out of hiding? She demands to know where her children are, but she hasn't been home for two days. Where is she?"

"Even more reason for us to go to DC and find her." My emotions spin as I sit down to steady myself.

"Have MAGS send Sean this video."

"Roger that, and then I'm going to shut her down. She has been on for too long." Liam focuses on the screen. His hands shake as he types on the keyboard.

"The team can get down there and start investigating before we arrive. Liam, I think you need to stay behind. You and Quinn are too vulnerable together. You'll be safer here in the cabin. No one can find you if they don't know where you are."

Liam stops typing. "I think you're right. Our first objective is to find out who is behind trying to get MAGS and us." He gives me a sideways glance. "I trust you."

Cam's body stiffens, and he nods. "I've got this."

There is a shift in Cam as he takes command of the situation. He still worries about his ability to do what is required of him without being held back by his leg.

The journey we started a few days ago has spiraled into uncharted territory, separating Liam and me again like a yo-yo. I'll be taken from my anchor once more. My fingers find my pendant, rubbing the back like rosary beads. My faith has to lie in Cam.

THIRTY-FIVE

Campbell

I'M NOT GOING to negotiate my way out of this situation. I've taken control, calling the shots as two people I consider family look to me for guidance. Sending the team ahead of us is the right way to go for a distraction. If they make enough noise, which I know they are quite capable of, no one will be looking for us.

Quinn and I will search her mum's townhouse and try to find clues to her whereabouts. I'll have to expose myself to the PAX team, hoping they won't arrest me, but I'm running out of options.

The MBK team has fallen out of favor, but we never abide by anyone else's rules. We need to prove Liam and Quinn are innocent of working with whoever is on the other side of this. My hunch is that Deep 8 is involved, using their minions.

Sean secures a safe house for us, away from the cameras scanning DC twenty-four-seven. After the rush on the Capital, security has tightened with eyes everywhere.

Quinn and I put on disguises with sunglasses as she tucks her hair under her hat. The ride will take us about five hours from the cabin to DC. Traveling at night is best. Less for the cameras to pick up on.

Quinn is quiet at the beginning of our ride but gives me a sideways glance.

"He trusts you, you know."

"I know he trusts me, but do you?" I keep my eyes focused on the dark road.

She turns her body toward me. "Yes, I do. I've watched you change over the last couple of days. You know how to take charge. Have you finally come to terms with the idea you can do the job as well as anyone, even with a fake leg?"

The laugh doesn't leave my throat. "I'm getting there. This op has tested me on every level, and it's not over."

We're on a straight stretch of highway, and I rest my arm on the middle console. She takes my hand as her finger traces the lines in my palm.

"Looks like you have a strong, long lifeline. It's good to know you'll be around for a while. You'll grow old and have grandchildren running around under your feet." Her smile warms me on the inside.

Everything I've ever wanted is in front of me, and I can't pull it together. She is beyond my wildest fantasies and more sexual than I thought she would be. Something still grips me, holding me back. As I take control of this mission, I can't help but worry that someone else might have been able to do it better. The what-ifs pop into my head. What if she needs me and I can't help her? What if I don't have my prosthetic and can't defend myself? The questions go on in my head in an endless loop.

"Hello, Earth to Cam?"

I shake my head. "What? Sorry. I'm thinking about what is ahead of us."

"You're still worried about not being enough on this mission."

I curse under my breath. "You know me better than I want you to." My eyes find her face with her chin jutted out.

True confessions were never my thing, but I can't think of a better person to talk to about my fears. "I worry I won't be able to be there for you or anyone else when it's crunch time. People shouldn't rely on me. I don't want to disappoint them." I swallow the lump in my throat.

She smiles and shakes her head. "The question is, have you been there for yourself?"

"What do you mean?"

"You're a champ at negotiations, always in the middle. It's only recently I've seen you take the lead. I'm not worried you won't be there, and neither is your team. Otherwise, they would not have hired you. Get out of your head and just do it." The street lights from above shine across her face as she leans back in her seat.

"You don't know what it's like until you've been in my shoes," I bristle.

"I don't know what it feels like to be less than. I don't know what it's like not to be enough for my husband. A sledgehammer hit my self-confidence, and I retreated into my work. You've been a breath of fresh air for me. You remind me of who I used to be. I shortened the wick so much that only you could relight it. I know plenty about what it feels like to be subzero, but I won't let it define me anymore, and neither should you."

My fingers loosen on the steering wheel, and I exhale through my nose. "I never considered it from your angle. You're right. What can I say? I'm a work in progress."

"As long as you progress, you'll do fine." She reaches

over and turns up the radio with a song about lovers and friends. "I'm hoping this will keep me awake for a while."

I laugh. "I wouldn't count on it."

We're halfway through the second song, and she's fast asleep. So much for keeping me company. My thoughts go back to our conversation. I've been hiding, using my injury as an excuse not to perform my duties, but I feel different with her. She gives me the courage I need to move forward. We need each other at our strongest if we're going to make it through this alive. She will forever have the scar of her tracker, a reminder of our time together, no matter the outcome.

We enter the outskirts of DC when my phone rings.

"Hey, Declan, what's up?"

"Sean brought me up to speed on the recent details of the op. Five years ago, I worked with a Sam Owens in Germany. It may be the same guy."

"Didn't he put out your hazmat suit that was on fire?"

"Yes, but he also could have set it as well. Depending on his agenda, he may have needed me out of commission for a while." Quinn snores softly next to me. Who the hell was she married to, The Grim Reaper?

"I doubt Quinn has any photos on her phone of him. If we come across any at the townhouse, I'll send them your way."

"Be careful, mate. You may be stepping into the heart of the hornet's nest."

"I have no clue what waits for us down here. It's the magical mystery tour."

Declan laughs. "See you on the flip side."

Our safe house location is east of Capital Hill in the Capital Riverfront section of town. Nondescript three-story brick apartment buildings line the streets in rows. Our address is 156, top floor, more ways to escape if needed.

"Hey, sleepyhead, time to wake up." I rub her shoulder.

"What time is it?"

"Four o'clock."

"I'm going back to sleep." She turns her shoulder away from me and curls up by the window.

"We have to go up to our five-star penthouse suite and check things out," I say without laughing. The car door opens as a blast of DC's Turkish sauna hits me in the face. Bloody hell, it's hot.

Quinn rolls out of the car. "I don't want to be here and will require a refund on this vacation getaway." She sighs.

"Believe me, this is no friggin' vacation. Not in this humidity. I prefer the tropical breezes of the Caribbean."

We trudge upstairs and open the door to a sparse apartment. The essentials are present, but not much else. I check the cupboards and the refrigerator. There's no food.

"I'm going to run to the nearest grocery store and get food. Why don't you go to bed and get some more sleep? Tomorrow is going to be a busy day."

"I'm hoping we won't be here long enough to need food." She grabs my arm and buries herself in my chest. "I can't do this without you. Promise you won't leave me."

"I won't leave you." I kiss the top of her head. Her face is dark and downturned, an outward appearance of her broken heart.

She may be our only ticket to what is going on.

THIRTY-SIX

Quinn

SLEEP HAS ALWAYS BEEN my escape. I don't have to worry about my daytime problems. My eyes close, and I am taken away to a place of fantasy. Cam has been the leading man in most of my dreams, and now he's here with me. I can't imagine being with anyone else to face my mother.

I'm not sure Liam understands the pain she's caused me. Her actions were the ultimate betrayal, and I can't wrap my head around why she would do it. A piece of me is devoid of feeling, afraid to give myself over so deeply to someone again. The emotional pain is too much to bear. Now, the seeds of doubt have been planted, and I don't know which way to turn.

Coming face-to-face with her is the last thing I want to do. If it weren't for the fact we need to find out who is behind all of this, I'm not sure I ever would've spoken to her again. I'm broken and have been since my father passed away. Sam was supposed to fill that gap. Her betrayal was the icing on the cake of deception.

My eyes open to view Cam's profile as he snores softly. He touches something deep down in my soul that I can't explain. I recognized our connection even as a young girl, and he's never wavered in his ferocity. I place my head on his shoulder, and his arm instinctively wraps around me.

"Good morning, Bee." His groggy voice wakes up the space between my legs, but I need his comfort more than anything else.

He kisses my neck and nibbles my earlobe, and I push him away.

"What? You can only get horny if you know there's someone in the next room?" He smiles as a sunbeam lights up his face.

"Hilarious."

"Who's the most popular guy at the nudist colony? The one who can carry a cup of coffee in each hand and a dozen doughnuts." He laughs.

"Then you would be the most popular guy at the nudist colony. By the way, did you pick up donuts and a soda?"

"No, and no. We need to keep our strength up for the meeting today. Eggs, bacon, cheese, and English muffins, which, by the way, English muffins are not from England."

He turns to get out of bed, and I grab his waist. "Can we lie here for a little while?"

He sits at the edge of the bed to put on his leg. "You're trying to prolong the inevitable. This can't move forward without you." He taps my nose, something he used to do to get my attention when we were younger.

"Yeah, today is going to suck big ones."

"If you want to suck big ones." He stands up and reaches for the waistband of his briefs.

I slap his hand away and laugh. "Why don't you do what you do best and cook something? I'm going to take a shower."

When I get to the shower, Cam has supplied it with everything I need to feel clean. I need to wash away everything from the past. Maybe if I go in with a fresh set of eyes, I'll be able to see my mom clearer, in a different light, a light of forgiveness.

They say that forgiveness has to be earned. I don't think she's earned anything, but I'll put on my game face to uncover more information. Cam will be my eyes and ears to pick up on anything that doesn't seem right.

My nose follows the smell of delicious food coming from the kitchen. Coffee is brewing, and Cam makes my eggs the way I like them. I push the food around on the plate, eating a few bites here and there.

"Eat up. It will make you feel better," he encourages me, using a soft voice.

I nod as I force my food down, making my stomach churn. I clear the dishes and wash them in the sink. Cam stands beside me and leans on the island with arms and legs crossed. His energy takes hold of me.

"If I didn't know better, I'd say you're as nervous as I am," I say to measure the temperature between us.

He holds my face and strokes my cheeks with his thumb. "I'm nervous for you. This might be one of the hardest things you've had to do. You're facing a parent who betrayed you. That's never easy." He says it as if he's gone through it. That's what makes him such a brilliant negotiator.

"What's our next step?" Talking about it won't help my condition.

"You need to call her and set up a meeting." He hands me the burner phone that's been modified. "I'll get Pippa and Peter to monitor the call to see if they can pick up on anything.

He calls them as they get set up on the other line. I put it on speakerphone and punch in the number, listening to the ring on the other end. My hand grips the phone, and my teeth clench as my neck muscles tighten.

"Hello?"

"Hi, Mom, it's Quinn."

"Oh. How are you? Are you okay?" Her words are forced. I pause. *Oh?*

"I'm fine. I'm in DC and wanted to see you. It's been a while. I thought it was time to bury the hatchet, talk things out."

"I have a very busy schedule, but you can come by my chambers in about an hour. Will your brother be joining us?" she says in a hushed tone.

What?

"No, just Cam. You remember Cam?"

"Where's Liam?"

"I don't know. I haven't talked to him in a while."

"Oh? I'll send a car. What's your address?" *Oh?*

Cam shakes his head.

"No. We're going to be out. We have other places to be today. Text me the location of the entrance we need to use."

There's dead air on the other end.

"Sure. I'll leave two passes with the guard for you. Looking forward to seeing you and hearing about what you two have been up to."

"See you then." I hang up, baffled by our conversation.

Cam is on the other line, talking to Pippa and Peter. "I'll let her know."

"Did they get anything?" My hand releases the phone, but the muscles in my neck are on fire.

"No. It shows up as her private cell, but when they go to track it, the signal bounces to sites around the world."

"Wouldn't the government do that for security reasons so no one can track anyone working in government?" I ask.

"I suppose, but it's a private line."

The silence stretches between us. He waits for me to say something. He's always been insightful at reading people, and I'm sure he could read my face during that call. Something is off.

"Cam, do you remember my mom's nickname for me?"

He nods as his face acknowledges what I'm thinking. "She always called you Quinnie."

"She didn't call me anything." I slump into the nearest chair. "My mom gives new meaning to the word cool, but our conversation lacked emotion, even for her. We haven't spoken in years, and what was with the questions about Liam?"

He massages my shoulders and neck. "I don't know, but it's weird. Her reaction to you mentioning me was off, too."

I turn around and look up at Cam. "What are we walking into?"

He kneels in front of me. "Whatever it is, we are going to do it together. How much can happen in the Capitol Building?"

"That's what they said before the riots."

"We have control," he tries to reassure me.

"Control is a perception. I don't suppose you can bring a gun into the Capitol?"

He shakes his head and leans down. "You'll be fine. I'm right there with you."

"We're Thelma and Louise before we go over the cliff."

"Spoiler alert. I'm bringing a parachute." He laughs.

THIRTY-SEVEN

Quinn

MY NERVES ARE SHOT as my thumb finds the back of my locket. I'll be surprised if there's anything left of it by the time we reach our destination.

The traffic noise of a beeping horn pierces the quiet in the car. Cam knows I need to be in my head before this meeting with my mom. He holds my hand as his thumb strokes over my knuckles. The repetitive motion calms my internal engine.

We enter the Capitol from the back via an underground tunnel. There are several security checks. The first one we have to identify ourselves with a picture ID. They use mirrors to look under our car for the next checkpoint. We drive farther underground in a spiral.

At our last stop, we leave the Jeep with the guards as we're escorted to an elevator that will take us up into the Capitol Building. My mom's office is in the Hart Senate Office Building. The Senate must be in session, explaining why we're meeting her at the Capitol.

The ride in the elevator is slow as the two armed guards stand on either side of us. We walk down the long Brumidi hallway. The walls are covered in Roman, Renaissance, and

Baroque artwork, with ornate bronze railings leading up the stairway at the north end. We climb the white marble stairs to a room toward the end of the hall. The few people we pass focus on the papers in their hands without looking up at anyone.

One guard opens the door. I see my mom standing behind her desk, wringing her hands. She stares at me with hollow eyes, making her look older than her years. The wrinkles have deepened around her eyes, and they've lost their sparkle. We stand in the middle of the room, staring at one another before she comes around the desk, running toward me with open arms.

"Quinnie, I can't believe you're here." She hugs me so tight I can barely breathe. This is an about-face compared to the phone call we had yesterday.

A movement to my left gets my attention as shadows hide Sam standing in the corner. His eyes are cold, but a brief look of surprise crosses his face. I look away, unprepared to see him again. Taking a deep breath, I find my center. He won't throw me off today.

"I told you I was coming so we could hash things out." I hold her by the shoulders and rub them. She appears thin, not the athletic woman I remember. She's changed, but I can't pinpoint what it is. "Why is he here?" I ask in a low voice only she can hear.

"He's my assistant." She paints a weak smile on a pale face as uncertainty floats in her eyes. "Cam, I'm so glad you're here. It's good to see you again." She reaches out her hands and hugs him.

I'm torn between having sympathy for her and being angry at the mother who stole my husband. It's a battle I shouldn't be having right now. I need to focus on finding out what's going on.

I turn in his direction as he steps out of the darkness. "Moving up in the world," I sneer.

He pulls the cuffs out of his custom-made royal blue suit jacket. "Yes, I like to stay close to the action." He has the smile of a feral dog.

I hold my mom's hands in mine. "I was hoping we could talk privately."

Sam steps up. "That won't be necessary. Anything you say to your mother will be said in front of me. Since I'm her assistant, I'll find out anyway. Besides, I already know your secrets." His lips curl up on one side.

"Controlling much, asshole?" I lose my cool and show my fangs.

He laughs as though he's dealing with a petulant child. I've changed a lot since we were married. I'm not as naïve as I used to be, and I won't be taking any shit from him. Sam moves between me and my mom, blocking my view of her. "I'll control what I have to control, including you."

"You'll never control me," I say through gritted teeth.

"Don't be too sure of that." His face remains stoic.

I see Cam's hand on his shoulder. "You need to back up. I don't think we've been introduced. I'm Campbell Creighton." Cam holds out his hand as Sam looks up.

Sam grips his hand with force. "Yes, I spent too much time listening to stories about you from Quinn." There's a bitterness in his words.

"I'm glad I wasn't forgotten." Cam smiles, still holding Sam's hand and squeezing until Sam lets go. "Why don't you take me on a tour of the Capitol while Mother and daughter catch up?"

Sam's eyes swing in my mom's direction. "Remember what we talked about." He grabs her by the back of the head and kisses her on the lips with force as she tries to back away. It's the least romantic kiss I've ever witnessed.

The door closes behind them, and I turn to my mother. "What the hell is going on?"

Tears crest in my mom's eyes, something I rarely see in her. She continues to wring her hands.

"He's fantastic at what he does. I hope you can forgive me. I didn't have a choice." Her eyes plead with me to understand the undercurrent of what she's trying to tell me.

"You always have a choice. You didn't need to sleep with my husband, but that's not what I came here to talk about." I have to bury my feelings once again while I find out what's going on with her. "Someone breached our labs. They had the security codes to bypass the system. Liam said he talked to you about the security system in the labs, and you upgraded them. Is there anyone in your office you suspect or who might be a mole? Someone had to have access to that security system after we put it in."

She grabs me by the shoulders and holds me tight. "Please tell me Liam is okay."

"He's fine, but you didn't seem too emotional about him in our phone conversation."

She doesn't react to what I've said. "It's a constant balance between holding it together and being on the brink of emotional turmoil. Ever since your dad died, I haven't found my footing. I feel lost and vulnerable, which can compromise me. Things are not always what they seem." Like a true politician, she avoids my questions and hugs me, whispering, "There are eyes and ears everywhere."

Before I can ask more questions, Sam bursts into the room and stops in the doorway, out of breath. "I'm sure you two had a lovely family reunion, but it's time for us to go. Liz, you have an important session on the Senate floor."

She holds my face in her hands. "I love you more than you may ever know. I want you to remember that." Tears well in her eyes before they trail down her cheeks as her lower lip wobbles.

She straightens up like a switch has flipped and brushes her tears away. She pulls her jacket down and runs her hands over her sleeves. Her hands glide over her hair, checking for any strays as she puts her appearance together for her next performance on the Senate floor. "I'll see you soon. Please stay in touch." She smiles as if nothing has happened between us and rushes out the door.

I'm left dumbfounded. This is not a side of her that I've ever seen. She was two different people occupying one body.

"How did everything go?" Cam's voice seems far away.

I'm numb from head to toe. "I don't know. We can't talk here. This place always gives me the creeps."

Cam holds my hand and leads me out the door, where the two guards wait for us. We leave the way we came as we walk through the ornate hallways and down to the parking garage.

There are no words I can attach to the moment I had with my mother, but I can't shake the feeling that she was trying to tell me something. I'm going to have to unscramble it with Cam.

THIRTY-EIGHT

Campbell

THE SIGHT of Liz Donovan caught me off guard, and then she told me to keep her children safe as she hugged me. I spent a good part of my childhood hanging out at the Donovan house, and I've never seen her look disheveled and flustered.

Quinn appears bewildered, and I am eager to hear about their conversation, but I know she needs to process. Her mum may have left her clues we need to unravel.

We find our way to the underground garage and are greeted by my idling beat-up Jeep. They can't wait to get rid of us. Quinn moves slowly as I help her into the passenger seat and buckle her in. I slip into the driver's seat and throw it in gear, eager to leave.

We drive upward in a spiral, coming to a long tunnel with lights on each side, making it feel like something out of *Star Wars*. I don't count how many stories down we had to go to enter the building. I'm not fond of going underground. The team leaves that kind of stuff to Sean.

Quinn hasn't said a word as she stares straight ahead. The morning fog from the Potomac has lifted, and the sun shines on the stoic historical buildings. Washington, DC is a city of dichotomy. Its clash of new architecture and historical monuments reflects the struggle of politics in this town during any year.

I glance up in my rearview mirror and spot a pimped-out Hummer weaving in and out of traffic, not doing a stellar job of tailing us. Someone is overcompensating. My earbuds are in for just such an occasion.

Sam made the hair on the back of my neck stand on end. I had a feeling we might get into some trouble on this trip. I contact the one person in the vicinity, but I'm not sure he will agree to help us.

"Bane, it's Campbell. We've got two tails heading north on 2nd Street NE here in DC. Assistance is required with my precious cargo." He doesn't know which Donovan is the precious cargo, and I hold my breath, waiting for his answer. I'm wanted by the PAX team, but I'm counting on him to never leave a brother behind.

Roger doesn't miss a beat. "We got you. We'll be coming in on bikes. You'll hear us before you see us. Keep heading north and find a place to lose your car. I'll be in touch. Out." His attitude does a one-eighty because he thinks he can be the hero and bring us in.

He hangs up as I grip the steering wheel, praying he gets here before they get to us. The traffic is heavy this time of day, which works in our favor up to a point. I'd rather be in the car than on foot.

I jinx myself as we come to a stop, stuck in gridlock. I throw the car in park as I spot one man jumping out of the passenger seat of the Hummer, heading in our direction.

I grab Quinn's arm. "You need to listen to everything I tell you if you want to make it out of this alive." Her eyes are wide, her breath is shallow, and she nods.

"We'll slip out of our seats and run up the street. We're headed for Union Station. It's our only shot. Stay close."

I tuck my forty-five in my waist and grab the backpack. I leave the key in the ignition, crack the door, and slip out, running around the front to her side of the Jeep. "Stay below the car windows."

I'm betting they won't shoot in a crowd of idling cars with people in them. They don't want to draw attention to themselves. We stay low and travel between the cars and trucks, making our way to the train station.

Once inside Union Station, I'm graced with a crowd of people we can get lost in and look for cameras. People mill about, going in and out of stores and restaurants, unaware of the mayhem that might ensue. We duck behind a pillar.

I hand her stuff from the backpack, including hats, glasses, and wigs. "Put on the hat, tuck your hair, and lose your sweater. Hike up your skirt and tie it up." While she's rearranging her wardrobe, I'm busy putting together my look for the day, including glasses and a hat.

I hold out my hand to her, and she grabs it. "We've been doing a lot of hand-holding lately." She smiles as a drop of sweat runs down her temple.

"There's a lot more to come. Follow me and act casual."

I scan the area and spot two guys dressed in black, looking around as if they've lost someone. They aren't from around here. The tourist crowd dresses in shorts and T-shirts. I steer us toward Gate A and look for the next train out of there. As I look back, one goon points in our direction and motions to his companion.

"Run!" I grab Quinn's hand tighter and make it to the nearest train.

The doors close before they get on, and they pound on the glass window. "Move in the direction the train is moving in."

We push our way through the cluster of people, creating distance between us and them. I point to a seat on the opposite side of the platform. I blow out a breath and look over at her.

"When is this going to end?" Frustration and tiredness cover her eyes.

"We need to unravel what's going on with your mum. I need to make a call."

Roger's irritated voice comes on the line. "Where the fuck are you?"

"We're on a train headed for somewhere. Thanks for your help. Take the Jeep for me. I'll be in touch." I click off before he traces the call or reacts.

"Where are we going?" Her head rests on my shoulder.

"We're going to Arlington, Virginia. We need to find a used car lot and drive back to Pennsylvania. I think we found our mole."

She sits up. "Who?"

"Sam."

She rolls her eyes. "He's not that smart."

"You don't have to be smart to be a criminal. Besides, I don't think he's the lead dog. Someone else is pulling the strings. I need to call Pippa."

Pippa picks up on the first ring. "Hey, are you two all right?"

"We're fine. I need a thorough analysis of a guy named Sam Owens. He's Senator Donovan's assistant. I'll catch up with you when we're back in Pennsylvania."

"Got it. Be safe." She hangs up.

Quinn smiles at me. "You're in charge. It's hot. Have you ever done it on a train?" She wiggles her brows.

"You find the oddest times to get horny, and no, we are not doing it on a train full of people."

"You've never seen *Risky Business*, have you?" Her eyes are bright.

"No, it was before my time," I reply dryly with a smirk.

"Do you know I've watched every movie Tom Cruise has been in?" She curls up in the seat.

"Interesting. The king of action movies, among other things. I've only seen *Top Gun*."

"Watching those movies made me wonder what you were up to somewhere in the world."

I brush the hair away from her eyes. "I was in places Tom Cruise wouldn't even dream about. Dirty for days on end, covered in sweat, and being shot at is not glamorous."

She doesn't ask questions but gives me a synopsis of what happened with her mum.

The automated voice announces the next stop is Arlington. We leave the train and head for the parking lot. I set up an Uber and search for the nearest used car lot.

Once Pippa does her search on Sam, we have to move swiftly and carefully. We're running out of time now that Roger Bane and the PAX team are back in play.

THIRTY-NINE

Campbell

THE UBER DROPS us off at Lou's Used Car Lot as the Virginia humidity hits us like a wet towel. There are a lot of cars to choose from, especially in the old clunker department. I spot an old Honda Civic from across the lot. A salesman lumbers out of a small shack with sweat stains covering his white dress shirt. He wipes his face and bald head.

"Can I help you?" he says with a Southern twang. He coughs into the handkerchief he used to wipe his face.

I point. "How much for the Honda Civic?"

"That one there will run you about two thousand."

He must think because I have a Scottish accent, I don't know anything about cars. "That's a 1998 Honda Civic, with anywhere from one hundred to two hundred thousand miles on it. It's not worth two thousand dollars." I walk across the lot to get a better look at it.

The car has seen better days. Rust has eaten through the front quarter panel, and the gray cloth interior is ripped in spots.

Quinn nudges me from behind. "What about the motorcycle? We need to go back to my mom's townhouse," she mutters.

"We're not going back to the townhouse. It's too danger-ous. I'm sure they are staking it out. We've got to get back to the cabin in Pennsylvania," I say over my shoulder.

As if I haven't said a word, she moves around me and says, "How much for the motorcycle?"

The salesman looks her up and down, trying to decide if he can hit on her, which he cannot. "For a pretty thing like you, five hundred."

"Does it run?"

"All day long."

"Three hundred cash and a full tank of gas," she counters.

He graces us with his yellow-toothed smile as he holds out his hand. "Sold." She looks at his hand without making a move.

"What part of we're not going to the townhouse did you not get?" I say through gritted teeth.

She stands on tiptoe and kisses my chin. "I think you need to pay the man so we can get going."

"Who's running the show here?" This is the second time I've asked that question. I've come too far to give up being the lead on this op.

The salesman leans toward me. "I'd do anything she told me to do if you get my drift." He holds out his palm.

"Trust me, I don't need your advice." I slam the cash in his hand, depleting our reserve of money.

"I'll be back with the key and a gas can. Oh, you're going to need helmets. It's the law. There's a place right next door." He counts the bills as he walks away.

I turn to her with my hands on my hips. "This is a dangerous move."

She leans on the motorcycle and wipes her forehead.

"They won't look for us there. We can call Liam and have him get MAGS to loop the security cameras at my mom's place while we are there."

"His phone is only for emergencies," I huff.

"This is an emergency. I need to get into her place to see if I can figure out what is going on. Also, we need two helmets. I hope you know how to drive this thing."

"You have some form of ADD," I murmur.

The sleazy salesman comes back huffing and puffing with a gas can, keys, and the title. He fills the tank, hands me the title, and winks. "Have a delightful ride." He wiggles his brows and walks away.

Quinn makes a gagging sound, and I laugh. "Let's go get helmets." She nods her head in the store's direction.

"Let me contact Liam so he can get started."

He picks up after several rings, making me nervous. "Cam, is everything good?"

"Yeah, I need you to do something, and we'll fill you in on the rest later." I tell him what we need MAGS to do. "I'll text you when we get there."

"Be careful, Cam."

"Just to be clear, this is not my idea. This is your sister's grand plan."

"Figures," he responds, and I click off.

We get rid of our disguises as we get fitted with helmets and stroll back to the motorcycle. I throw my good leg over it and get it started. The engine comes to life as it coughs and sputters. Quinn straps on the backpack and gives me the address before she puts her helmet on and squeezes in behind me.

The sun beats down on us while we cruise on Route 66 back over the Potomac and head north to the townhouse. As we venture into the affluent area in DC, the breeze refreshes us. The brick facade and ornate fixtures give it a feel of old-world contemporary.

We climb off the motorcycle and head for the front door, where the doorman greets us. An older man stands in a crisp uniform, wearing a hat. His brown leather skin breaks with a smile when he sees Quinn.

"Louie! How are you?" She runs up the stairs and hugs him. While she's doing that, I text Liam about our arrival.

"Girl, I haven't seen you in years. How have you been? I miss you." The gravel in his voice makes him sound like he might be a blues singer, and this is his side gig.

She cups her hand around her mouth. "I've been working on a top-secret project. Highly classified." My heart skips a beat. What's she playing at?

He leans down. "I'm sure your mother would be interested in your project." He laughs at her like she's joking. "She's not home right now." Something changes on his face.

I chuckle at the irony of this day. If he only knew.

"That's fine. I'm going to let myself in. I have some things to get. Let me introduce you to Campbell Creighton."

He takes my hand in both of his. "It's a pleasure to meet you, sir. I hope you take good care of Quinnie. She deserves the best."

"She does, and I'm the man to do it."

Quinn raises her brows and does a quick turn into the lobby. We get in the elevator, and I pull the disguises from the backpack. She has a grin on her face.

"What?"

"You like me. You want to kiss me," she says in a singsong voice.

"I want to do more than kiss you. I want to—" The elevator stops on the top floor. "Keep your head down. I don't know what cameras they have in the hallways."

She lets herself into her mum's townhouse with her key. The door opens to a living room that looks like it hasn't seen visitors in days. We slip in and shut the door behind us.

"We only have a couple of minutes. You look in the bedroom, and I'll scan the rest of her place."

Her townhouse has an odd vibe to it. I can't shake the feeling we are missing something, but my money is on Sam being a huge part of the problem.

The furniture in the living room and dining room appears to be brand new and never used. The kitchen isn't much better, and the refrigerator is filled with half-full takeout containers.

I reach in the backpack for some things I need to leave behind. There's a glass on the counter with a large fingerprint on it that I may need for later.

Quinn meets me in the living room. "He's a psycho."

"We've confirmed that, but did you find anything interesting?"

"He has a tie I bought for him lying on the floor in her bedroom. Who does that?"

"Your psycho ex-husband."

"I told my ex-husband I felt like killing him. He said I needed professional help, so I hired a hitman. You know any?" She smiles.

I don't laugh at her joke. It hits a little too close to home for the situation. "Let's get out of here."

We walk out the door as we hear the elevator ding, and I grab her arm and head for the stairs.

"I get the feeling she hasn't been home in a while. Something is off, but I can't put my finger on it," she comments as we make our way to the lobby.

"He's very controlling. That was obvious."

"But she has always been the one in control. She stepped

up and cared for my dad near the end when he was the sickest and was on top of everything. What changed?"

"I don't know. How do you feel about riding back to the cabin on the motorcycle? We can stop for dinner on the way."

She nods, but her eyes have a faraway look to them. She's in her head, ten steps ahead of everyone else, but I'm not sure where it will lead us. The piece to unlock is Sam's story and how he fits into this picture.

FORTY

Quinn

―――――――

THE WIND WHIPS AROUND US, cutting through the heat as the sun drops behind the horizon. We drive for two hours at a time and take a break at various rest areas.

For most of the ride, I'm concerned about my mom and how things don't add up. She's always been a confident woman who knows herself better than anyone. The woman I saw today was anything but confident, wearing a face for someone else's benefit, but not mine. The two faces of Liz made me take a step back and evaluate the situation. I still can't trust her, but how has she changed so much?

We make it back to the cabin in Pennsylvania after dark. As we step inside the dimly lit cabin, Liam is having a conversation with MAGS like she's an old friend. He needs to get laid.

"Thank God you two made it back okay. I did some reverse engineering and taught MAGS to search for codes on the AI trying to hack her. She did it and identified Ivan's code, shutting him down." His smile spreads from ear to ear.

"I'm sure Pippa will get a nasty email about that." I drop my helmet on the couch. "A nice long bath is calling my name so I can wash the grime away. You two can make some dinner."

"You're awfully bossy," Cam says.

"I'm dirty, tired, and hungry, which makes me bossy." I wave my hand in the air.

Liam gives Cam a sideways glance, and Cam doesn't say another word. Smart man.

I soak in the bath up to my neck, wracking my brain. Based on what happened today, my mom would never give us up. Even though I'm still pissed at her, she will protect us. She would never compromise our project. Then there is the fact she knew the security codes, but Cam thinks it's Sam who's behind the security breach, but how? I take a few deep breaths and relax before my mind explodes.

There's a soft knock on the door. "Can I come in?" Cam says in a muffled voice.

"Yeah."

He closes the door behind him and sits on the edge of the tub. "Are you okay? Today was a lot to take in."

"I'm getting there. There is so much to sift through, and we don't have the pieces in place yet."

He drags his hands through his hair. "Tell me about it." He looks at me with intense eyes. "I placed bugs in your mom's townhouse."

"Good. We need to hear what's going on and sort this out." I push the floating bubbles around on the water.

"You need to get out of there before you turn into a prune. I made some mushroom risotto accompanied by a bottle of red wine." He gives me a tired smile.

"That sounds delicious." I stand up as the bubbles race down my body back to the warm water. My skin is pink, and my nipples pebble as the cool air hits them.

Cam thrusts a towel in my direction. "Here, put this around you before I get any ideas."

I laugh. "Can you hand me my locket by the sink?"

He swipes but misses as it hits the floor, breaks open, and scatters the pictures inside. We both freeze. He kneels to put it together and reaches for the photo of the two of us I keep behind the picture of Liam. He stares at it for a bit.

He looks at me, and I shrug. "A girl can dream, can't she?" I hold the towel tighter.

He drops the photo, moves toward me, and holds my face. "It was always going to be us, no matter what or who got in the way." His lips crash down on mine as he consumes my mouth like it's his last meal. I hold his arms and dive into his mouth with my tongue. He was mine from the moment we met. He didn't know it then. Our tongues swirl and battle. His mouth breaks away, and he holds my wet body close to his in a death grip. My grand plan of keeping him at a distance starts to fall apart. Since we had amazing sex, the pieces clicked together like a code I've been working on for years.

"I didn't know," he whispers.

"Now you do."

"We can't waste any more time. I want to spend the rest of my life with you." Our foreheads touch. "I need to check on the food before I have wild sex with you while your brother is in the next room."

I laugh. "I think we've already done that."

He kisses me again, puts the locket back together, and hangs it around my neck. "I'm glad you keep me close to your heart." He winks.

I pull on a pair of sweats and a top. The cabin is cool, considering how hot it is outside. The aroma of mushroom risotto filters through the air, and I follow it to the kitchen table. They sit at the table and wait for me, both looking worse for wear.

I raise my glass. "Here's to finding out what the hell is going on."

Our glasses clink, and Cam's cell phone goes off. He leaves the table and comes back with his phone.

He puts it on speakerphone. "Go ahead, Red." He laughs.

"I've hit a wall. It doesn't look like Sam Owens exists. The fingerprint you sent me can't identify him."

"Of course, he exists. I have the marriage license to prove it." I can't take another roadblock.

"I've searched for him everywhere. He has a brilliant cover but, as I like to say, it's borrowed," Pippa replies.

There is silence as everyone's wheels turn.

"What about the NSA? Did you check there?" Liam asks.

"No. I can't get in without being detected and arrested. I don't do well in jail. If you know someone on the inside, that would be your best bet. Someone may have many reasons to stay hidden, and most of them are not good. Let me know if there's anything else you need. Be careful. This just took a turn."

"Thanks, Pippa." My hope deflates as I worry about who I was married to years ago.

Cam folds his hands in front of his mouth. "There are several reasons someone can't be found in the system. It usually includes the CIA, or worse, an international mole."

"How do we find out?" Liam frowns.

"I'll call Roger Bane and see if he can connect us with Clay Murphy, the Secretary of Defense. Either way, we're putting ourselves at risk of being captured, but we need to find out about Sam. I think he holds the key to who's behind this."

"Then do it. Call him and see if he is willing to help us. I have a feeling our mom is in danger." I rub the center of my chest and catch my breath.

He nods and presses a button on his phone. "Bane here," Roger's voice comes through the speaker.

"Roger, it's Campbell Creighton. We need your help."

"You called in your only chip. Where the hell are you? My only mission is to bring in the Donovans."

"I can't do that just yet. We ran a search on Sam Owens, the personal assistant to Senator Liz Donovan, and nothing came up."

"What do you mean, nothing came up? He would have needed an extensive background check before he gained access to the Capitol Building."

Cam rubs the back of his neck. "We have one of the best hackers in the world, and she can't find him. No, she did not breach the NSA. That's why I need your help. Can you contact Clay and see if he can get information on Sam Owens through his resources?"

"Why should I do that? How do you know I'm not tracing this call right now?" He's testing the waters.

"Because this call is about to end. I'm the only connection you have to Liam and Quinn. Liam is not your guy. He was taking directions from his mum, or at least we think it was his mum. You don't want to send an innocent man to prison. Sam has answers if I can find out who the hell he is and what he's doing with Liz Donovan."

Roger exhales into the phone. "I'll see what I can do. Call me back in twelve hours." He ends the call.

Questions swirl in the air without answers. Our faith rests in Roger, who we hope will do the right thing. The sound of forks scraping plates fills the space where a conversation should be. No one is hungry as we sit on pins and needles, waiting for answers.

"Boy, do I know how to pick them? I don't even know who the hell I was married to." I throw my fork on the plate and leave to go to the bedroom.

I lie on the bed, staring at the ceiling. Emotions inside me collide with nowhere to go. Who is Sam Owens, and what is he doing with my mom?

FORTY-ONE

Campbell

IF I THOUGHT things were complicated before, they have gone to DEFCON 1. There are many moving parts to this op, and my nerves are getting the better of me. Calling in my team may be my only option to keep Liam and Quinn safe.

I tiptoe into the bedroom, and Quinn is fast asleep. There are no worries about waking her up. I ache from head to toe, and my stump is inflamed. My prosthetic leans against the chair as I stare at the missing piece of me.

This mission has proven I can do a lot, but I can't help but feel I'm not all here. I can't be a hundred percent like I was before my leg got crushed. I wish I could say I'm over lamenting about my leg, but those feelings creep back in to haunt me.

As I slip under the covers, Quinn curls up next to me in the crook of my arm on instinct but never wakes up. I stare at the ceiling, willing myself to sleep, but questions come at me from every direction. One keeps nagging at me. Should we be looking at Liz Donovan as the mole? She's had every opportunity and means to make this happen.

. . .

MY EYES POP open as the sun streams in around the curtains. The bed is missing Quinn's warmth, and the smell of bacon and eggs fills the room. I throw off the covers and examine my stump. It's still inflamed. This requires help from Quinn and Liam. I pick my clothes up off the floor and get dressed. I hate asking for help. "Liam," I yell from the bedroom.

He rushes in as Quinn almost slams into him from behind. "What's wrong?" His eyes are wild.

"Calm down. I need your help to make it into the kitchen. My stump is acting up, and I need to give it a rest." I focus on a piece of thread on the floor, never meeting their eyes.

"Is that all? No problem," Liam says. I stand up, and Liam lifts me under my shoulder with Quinn on the other side.

I sit at the table filled with fruit, eggs, muffins, bacon, and coffee. A buck runs by the window, stops, and stares at me. I would consider the sighting good luck, but this morning, I need to confront what I've been unwilling to say.

"Aren't you hungry?" Quinn says softly with her plate half empty.

"I have a lot on my mind."

Quinn glances over at Liam. "Do you want to share?"

"I need you to keep an open mind on what I'm about to say. Is there a possibility your mum is the mole? Could she be working with Sam?" I wait for hellfire to erupt.

Liam puts his fork down and wipes his mouth. "You and I are on the same wavelength. I suggested that to Quinn this morning. It's not a theory I'm fond of, but it's one we need to consider." He sighs.

The fact Liam can stand back long enough to be objective and let his Ranger training take over is remarkable. What is even more surprising is that this didn't come from Quinn. I look over at her and watch for her reaction.

"How do you feel about that?" I ask Quinn.

She wiggles around in her chair. "She's already proven she can't be trusted," Quinn says between mouthfuls of food. "I won't dismiss Liam's suggestion. Some things don't add up. The phone conversation I had with her didn't make any sense. Her questions and lack of emotion after not hearing from me for so long are not her style. But it was her voice on the line."

"AI has come a long way in many different fields. One of those fields is voice. It is possible someone else was speaking on the phone and disguising their voice to sound like hers," Liam offers.

"Do you have any taped conversations with your mum?" I ask.

"I recorded our conversations when she gave me the security protocols. I needed to refer back to them."

"Was there ever anything unusual when you spoke with her?"

"No, not really. Our conversations have only been about the program. There were times when she probed into areas she knew I couldn't tell her about, but nothing that struck me as odd."

"Since Pippa and Peter already have access to your phone, I'm gonna have them pull those conversations with your mum and analyze them."

There's a false sense of relief as we make a discovery that might lead to a break in this case. I load my plate with food, and we finish eating breakfast.

Liam and Quinn clear the table and clean up while I call Pippa and Peter. I fill them in on the latest development, and they assure me they are on it and will analyze the recordings.

Quinn and Liam carry me to the front porch so we can be outside while we wait for information. We aren't out there long as Liam watches the birds in the distance.

"We've got company. Wildlife always gives humans up. Let's get inside."

He carries me inside and gets my leg as Quinn packs everything up.

"Declan said there's a quad in the shed, and you can ride the motorcycle. We need to keep the engines off as long as possible," I offer.

"They're coming in from the west, so we need to head east through the woods," Liam instructs.

"We need a distraction. Let's close the curtains, lock the doors, and set this place on fire." I'm hoping we can make it out of here in one piece.

We set the fire to start on the inside with gasoline and matches. Liam pushes the motorcycle next to the shed. I get on the quad with Quinn. "Hang on. It's going to be a bumpy ride."

We're ready to take off as the cabin crackles with flames shooting past the roof line. We gun the engines and race through the woods. Quinn hangs on when we hit a bump and catch air.

The rule of any escape is to never look back, but we can hear them. My guess is they traced us through our phone calls and using the computer. They won't stop until they capture us. We're not even sure who we are running from, good or bad.

Up ahead is a river, a perfect cover for our tracks. We race through it to the other side and up an embankment. At the top of the hill is a large cabin with several sheds. The beat-up late 90s S10 pickup parked in front is what we need to get out of here.

I point to the nearest shed. We kill the engines and let them coast to a stop, parking them out of sight. An old man comes out of the cabin with a shotgun in hand. He's dressed in ripped jeans, a flannel shirt, and a baseball hat with a veteran patch.

"What's going on out here?" He points in our direction.

We put our hands up as we walk toward him. I nod to Liam to do the talking. This man might not take kindly to a Scotsman.

Liam whispers, "Q, hold your side like you're in pain." He steps forward. "We're being chased by some assholes. We were hoping we could use your truck to get out of here. My sister needs to go a hospital. She's in a lot of pain."

"What's wrong with her?"

"We don't know. She woke up like this. It could be anything from kidney stones to her appendix." Quinn falls to her knees like she's in pain. Nice touch.

"Keys are in the truck." He nods over to the parked vehicle. "Make sure you return it."

"Any chance you have some extra guns lying around we could borrow, one soldier to another?"

The man stands up straight. "What branch?"

"Army Ranger." Liam smiles.

The tanned lines on the man's face crease as he smiles. He takes off his hat and salutes. "Anything for a fellow soldier."

Liam jumps in the driver's seat and turns the key. Quinn squeezes in between us. The man's face appears in the driver's window. "God's speed. I'll fend them off for you."

Liam covers the man's hand. "Thank you, but you might want to stay inside. You may have just saved the world."

The man frowns and backs up. Liam nails the throttle, and

we're off. I know exactly where we are going, to the hornet's nest.

FORTY-TWO

Campbell
_____

WE DRIVE to the end of the dirt road and hit the interstate into town. Quinn's face is pale, but she's hanging in there.

"Are you okay?"

"I'm fine. It's just a lot of excitement this early in the morning. Who the hell is after us now, and where are we headed?"

"Back to DC, to the apartment. It's the last place they will look for us." Liam doesn't flinch. He knows what I'm thinking, go where they least expect us.

I pry off the back of my cell phone and rip out the SIM card, tossing it out the window along with the phone. "So much for a secure line. We need to stop and get a burner." Liam nods and pulls into a drugstore parking lot.

"We've got to dump this truck and get another set of wheels. They're already looking for this one." Excitement fills Liam's eyes.

"You know what to do." I dig into the backpack and pull out my baseball hat, along with Quinn's disguise. "I'll be back with goodies."

Liam pulls the truck around the back of the store, out of sight and away from cameras. I pick up a few items, a burner and snacks, keeping my head down.

I stroll back to the parking lot and look for them. Liam traded keys with a couple of kids. He and Quinn sit in a vintage '80s Mercury Lynx hatchback that has seen better days. I squeeze myself into the back seat with Quinn. The boys are in the truck peeling out of the parking lot. We're going to owe that old man a truck.

Liam waits and backs up, driving down the highway toward DC. He looks in his rearview mirror for any tails but finds none. Sweat rolls down his temple as my clothes stick to me.

"No AC?" He shakes his head. "Here you go. I thought you might want to be undercover for this trip." I hand him a John Deere hat and blue light glasses. Quinn is already in disguise with her hair tucked under her hat.

I purchased a cigarette lighter adapter to charge the new phone. We drive down the highway at a pretty good clip until dark clouds appear on the horizon. The traffic slows down as sheets of rain cover the road, adding time to our trip.

The raindrops are heavy and loud as they hit the roof of the car, drowning out any conversation. Liam rolls down the window to prevent the windows from fogging up as rain pelts us in the back seat.

Quinn reaches for my hand and looks at me through worried eyes. I pull her toward me and wrap my arm around her shoulder.

"It's going to be okay," I say with a crack in my voice. "Trust me." It's not a question.

She looks up at me. "Yes. We'll get out of this, even if we have to leave the country."

"Someone has thought this through." I laugh, but it comes out as more of a chortle. "The three of us may live in Belize, which wouldn't be so bad, but they would hunt for us for the rest of our lives."

The challenges waiting for us in DC are many and varied. I need to contact Sean to let him know where we are headed. The burner shows a full battery, and I dial his private line.

"Hello?" It's not his usual greeting, but he doesn't recognize the number.

"Sean, it's Campbell."

"What's going on?"

"Someone found us at the cabin, but we made it out of there."

"The US government hacked our computer system and got through our firewall. Pippa and Peter are furious because they thought they built an impenetrable system. They must have tracked you through us. Where are you headed?"

"We ditched everything. We're going to DC."

"Don't go to the apartment. They have eyes everywhere. I don't know how much they got off our server," Sean says with a bite.

"Do you know if Pippa and Peter deciphered the phone conversations Liam had with his mum? We need to know if it's her voice or someone else's."

"I'll have Peter contact you at this number on a secure line."

"That would be great." There is no relief in talking to him. We've gone black.

"Campbell, be careful. They are out for blood and won't stop until they have the Donovans in custody. They've invested a lot in this program. Limit your contact with us to absolute emergencies from here on out."

"Got it. Thanks." I press the end button in under two minutes.

Liam glances at me through the rearview mirror. "We're in the wind, aren't we?"

"Without a parachute. They won't stop searching for us, so the sooner we get answers, the better."

Quinn's body stiffens. "What does that mean?"

"It means we need to figure out what the hell is going on and who's behind this, or our asses are going away, never to be seen again," Liam replies.

A heavy silence fills the air at the gravity of our situation and what being on the run will be like together. We were always the Three Musketeers as kids, but we're playing a grown-up game. The rules have changed.

We cross the Virginia border as the rain lets up. The land is green as far as the eye can see, spotted with wildflowers. The landscape reminds me of Scotland and happier times.

"We need to ditch the car. If they caught up with those kids, which I'm sure they did, they'll be hunting for this piece of shit," Liam comments.

"We can't go to the apartment in DC. The PAX team hacked the firewall. Sean thinks that's how they found us. I'm open to suggestions."

"Let's look for a motel near the center of the city. Here, give me your phone," Quinn says.

"We'll lose the car in Arlington and Uber to the motel. Do we have enough cash to cover us?" Liam asks.

"We've got enough for now, but it won't last forever." My leg bounces up and down.

Liam finds a supermarket and drives around back to park the car. We throw the keys in a dumpster and walk out to the road. Our disguises make us look like tourists as we blend in with the crowd.

We walk a couple of miles until Quinn complains about her hurting feet. She orders an Uber to pick us up at a pharmacy and drive us into DC. The driver drops us off a couple of blocks from the motel. We get one room with two queen beds. It's not the Ritz, but considering we're on the run, there are worse places.

The guy behind the counter eyes us up and down, then smirks. Quinn and Liam are obviously brother and sister.

Quinn leans over the counter and hands him a wad of cash. "Really? You work at a low-rent motel in DC. You've seen weirder shit than this."

The smirk leaves his face as he hands her the keycards. Liam and I roar with laughter. It's a welcome relief, considering the day we've had and the journey that awaits us.

When we make it to the room, Quinn throws her hat on the chair and flops on the bed. Liam heads for the shower, and I turn down the air-conditioning in the room.

"Can we go buy some clothes like T-shirts and shorts maybe? These smell."

The bed dips as I sit next to her and rub her leg. "Sure, but only one of us should go. I'll go. You two stay here. Why don't you take a shower? It will make you feel better."

I lie beside her and run my fingers down her face and neck, peppering her cheeks with kisses. She kisses my lips with softness and reassurance.

Liam comes out of the bathroom wearing nothing but a towel.

"Way to kill the mood," I joke.

"Here's my mood. I'm not getting back into those clothes." He stands with his hands on his hips.

"I'm going, I'm going. Keep your towel on."

Quinn giggles.

"I'll take the phone with me in case Pippa or Peter call."

Quinn and Liam look exhausted. "Two of the smartest and the most wanted people are in this room. We need to keep it together and keep our heads on straight. We also need to prove Liam is innocent."

What Peter tells us about those recordings will determine our next moves. I contemplate contacting Roger to see what he discovered about our friend Sam.

FORTY-THREE

Campbell

I HURRY down the street to a local tourist shop and pick up some T-shirts, shorts, hats, and socks for us. Liam and I are the same size, but I guess on Quinn's size. As always, I keep my head down and have minimal interaction with few words.

The motel buzzes with activity as I scoot to the end unit to our room. I open the door and see Quinn and Liam wrapped in towels, sitting on different beds.

"You two are giving me the creeps. Here are some clothes. Please put them on as quickly as possible." I throw the clothes in their direction as Liam makes a beeline for the bathroom.

"What? You don't like me in only a towel?" Quinn wiggles her brows.

"I do, just not sitting across from your brother."

"Good point," Liam says as he heads for the bathroom. Quinn bolts to get in and change.

Liam gets dressed and sits on the edge of the bed with his elbows on his knees. "Do you think we can beat this? There's a roadblock at every turn." His voice lacks the confidence I'm used to hearing from him.

"Don't give up yet. A few pieces need to fall into place before we can present our case, so to speak." I talk a good game, but I doubt we can pull this off.

Quinn emerges from the bathroom looking like a DC tourist, and it's my turn to clean up before we go out to dinner. Water and soap never felt so good. The salt from my sweat washes down the drain. I stand on one leg as the warm water runs down my stump. The door opens, and Quinn stands on the other side of the curtain.

"Liam begged me not to come in here. He said he felt weird. Here I am." She laughs.

I part the curtain enough to see her. Her smirk says it all. She loves to torture her brother. She leans against the counter with her arms folded across her chest. "I wanted to see how you were doing with your leg."

I close the curtain. "You don't need to do that. I'm fine." I punctuate my words a little more than I want to.

She pulls back the curtain. "I need to do it because I care about you. This is new for me. You need to tell me when you aren't okay or how I can help. I'm not trying to bring attention to your leg. I want to be there for you."

My back is to her, and I hang my head so the water flows down my back. Turning around, I flip my hair out of my eyes. "I'm sorry. I'm not used to someone else worrying about my leg. It's always been me attending to it. I need time to get used to this."

She rests her hand over my heart. "I've always been here." Her hand moves to my head. "Let me be here too. Remember, we're a compound." She'll always think like a scientist.

I bring her hand to my mouth and kiss her palm. "I might need reminders. What did the patient with the broken leg say to their doctor?"

She smiles. "Hey, doc, I have a crutch on you," I answer.

"I'll let you finish up in peace." She kisses me.

My cock is hard as granite, but I have no desire to find relief. I'll save myself for her. I pull on a fresh T-shirt as the phone rings on the dresser. I tap the speakerphone button.

"Hello?"

Peter begins. "Pippa and I dove as deep as we could on the sample you gave us. This voice is AI-generated to match Liz Donovan's voice. The technology is sophisticated. We can't decipher who is actually speaking. Her phone must have been cloned to appear as though it came from her. I'm sorry we couldn't find the voice behind her voice."

"This may be very helpful. Thanks, Peter. I know you two have your hands full right now with the government."

"Those sons of bitches. Payback will come in the form of a destructive virus if they try that again," Peter spits out.

"Don't get too carried away. We may need them. Roger has been cooperative, and I want to keep it that way."

"I'll think about it. Stay safe."

"Thanks."

Liam sits in a chair in the corner with his head in his hands. "I am so stupid for a smart guy. Who the hell have I been talking to, and for how long? Did they give me the security information and I blindly followed along like an asshole?"

"Don't be too hard on yourself. Had I been talking to Mom, this could have happened to me, too. Whoever is behind this knows what they are doing." Quinn tries to comfort Liam.

We remain silent for a couple of beats. "I think we need to let this digest and form a plan. Let's go to dinner and talk it over."

"What the fuck? I've been talking to a stranger. I'm an

idiot," Liam replies as if he hasn't heard me. "How did I not pick up on the fact it wasn't our mom?" His face is red, and tears crest in his eyes. "I've done this to us. We're in this shit pile because of me." He pounds his fist on his chest.

I've never seen Liam distraught about anything. The stress of being under a constant threat and on the run is getting to him. Quinn may not be far behind. The weight of the survival of this program is on our shoulders. If it gets into the wrong hands, it's on us. I'll fight like hell to save MAGS and make sure her creators are safe and sound.

Quinn chimes in, "I think you have to consider your conversations with Mom were all business. I only picked up on the fact that there was something wrong because my conversation with her was personal. Whoever is behind this purposely kept this strictly about the program, knowing you would feed off of that. We've both been a little over-focused on MAGS." She sits on the arm of the chair and rubs his back, but he's lost in his head with a mountain full of guilt. I know the look and feel of a man wracked with guilt.

"Mate, I need your head in the game for this. You can beat yourself up later." My eyes bounce between Quinn and him. "You two are smart enough to get us out of this hole. I know it looks bottomless right now, but I'll keep us on track. I still have a few tricks up my sleeve. One of them is named Roger Bane."

Liam scrubs his face. "You've played that card one too many times. He won't help us. We've got nothing for him to take back to his team."

"He has information on who the hell Sam Owens is, and my negotiating skills are top-notch. I also win at poker a lot. I'll bluff my way into convincing him to help us. There are a couple of ideas I need to toss around. Let's get food. It might help clear our heads." I throw them their disguise before heading out in front of CCTV cameras.

"You play poker?" Quinn asks.

"That's what you came away with, that I play poker?" I adjust her hat and tuck her hair underneath.

She shrugs. "I learn something new and interesting about you every day. When this is over, we should go back to Vegas so I can see you in action, provided we're not in jail or dead. I don't trust that we will get out of this unscathed."

I hold my hand to her. "We're not going to jail, maybe Belize, but not jail." I kiss her forehead and wrap my arm around her. "You will be alive and well." I will lay down my life for her.

Liam follows us out the door. "Too bad MAGS isn't real. I could use some partner support."

Quinn and I turn around. "You really need to get a human girlfriend," we say in unison.

"You owe me a soda of my choice." Quinn laughs.

"If you can get us out of this, I'll owe you a lot more than that."

FORTY-FOUR

Campbell

WE FIND a hole-in-the-wall restaurant in an alley with decent food and walk around while we eat. Staying stationary allows them too much surveillance. This serves to bring normalcy to our lives for a small moment. We come across a store selling wigs.

"These might be useful later on. Pick one out to try on," I say.

We enter the store and leave with three different color wigs in a paper bag. There's not much conversation, and I can see the wheels turning in Liam's and Quinn's heads.

Their goal is to deliver MAGS to safe hands. Even with every technological advancement, humans are always five steps behind. They didn't anticipate having their government turn on them. This mission has taken a toll on everyone, including the MBK team.

We enter the motel lobby, and the same guy stands behind the counter. Quinn waves to him and says, "We can't wait for tonight. It's going to be a blast." Liam and I wave as the guy scrunches up his face.

As soon as we get to the room, Quinn informs us we must

turn around so she can take off her shorts and slide under the covers. We do as she asks as Liam rolls his eyes.

"I don't care if you roll your eyes at me. This whole thing is weird. Good night." She turns her back to us and goes to sleep.

I strip down to my underwear, remove my leg, and slip in next to her as Liam does the same, getting into his bed. "Thank God they had two beds and not one. I couldn't handle it. In some ways, it's strange to see you with Quinn. In other ways, it makes perfect sense. There's no one else I'd rather have our backs than you." His words pierce the darkness.

"I think I've been in love with your sister since I was six years old. When she married Sam, I had to move on, but no woman ever stuck around. As for you, we need to get you hooked up with a real woman without a British accent." I pull the covers up to my chest.

"I'd like to find a human woman, but there aren't many in my field." His voice fades. "What's the plan for tomorrow?"

"I'll call Bane and try to find out more about Sam. I can't shake the feeling he's the one behind this. Let's get some shut-eye. Good night."

A voice in the dark says, "Promise me there won't be any hanky-panky during the night."

I laugh. "I'll try, but I can't speak for your sister."

"Ugh." Minutes later, he's asleep, and I'm left with my thoughts.

Somehow, I find myself in the position of saving my best friend and my new girlfriend. They created a program everyone in the world wants to get their hands on. All eyes are on us, but it feels so small lying in the motel room in the middle of Washington, DC.

There are no explosions, no gunfire, and no smart one-liners like something out of *Die Hard*. Three kids who grew up together are fighting to save the world from an epic disaster if MAGS gets into the wrong hands. I would like to think the US government would do the right thing with the program, but I haven't convinced myself. I'm not sure Liam is sold either.

The morning comes with a kick to my shin from Quinn. She's thrashing around in her sleep. I shake her shoulder to wake her. "You're having a dream and kicking the shit out of the only shin I have left."

Her eyes turn into slits. "Oh, sorry." She rolls over and finds her spot in the crook of my arm, a place reserved only for her.

"Are you all right?" I bury my nose in her hair.

"I guess. It was a bad dream," she mumbles.

"What was it about?"

"MAGS got into the wrong hands, and the world changed as we know it."

Icy dread covers my body, and I pray her dream is not foretelling the future. "We got this." My words lack confidence as her body stiffens.

Liam is sprawled out on his back, snoring, until Quinn throws a pillow at him. He bolts upright. "What?"

"You were snoring," she responds.

"That's what people do when they sleep."

The hard-on I had two seconds ago has deflated with the sound of Liam's voice. "You two can work it out. I have to go across town to make a phone call to Bane and dump my burner." I sit on the side of the bed and put on my leg. The swelling has gone down, which will make walking easier.

Quinn grabs my arm. "Please be careful."

Reaching into the bag, I get a wig and put it on my head. "I've always wanted to be a blonde." I twirl around and put on the baseball hat.

I walk to the lobby and past the counter guy, who doesn't recognize me. An Uber driver takes me across town and drops me off at the Lincoln Memorial. The place is crawling with tourists, which is what I want. Behind the columns sits a marble goliath, the statue of President Lincoln.

His Gettysburg Address speech is relevant today as he references unfinished work and great tasks ahead. The world never learns from history but makes a note with silent disregard.

The Capitol looms in the distance, where battles continue without resolution, as it does with many governments. The war on the horizon is AI-based and has little to do with human-to-human combat but everything to do with humans versus technology. We will destroy ourselves if we don't get in front of it.

My cell phone burns in my hand. Bane may be our only link to what is going on with Sam.

I dial his number. "Bane here."

"It's Campbell. What did you find out about Owens?" I hold the phone close to my mouth, keeping my head down.

"You need to give up and turn in the Donovans. If you're a good boy, they might cut you a deal. Sam Owens is not your guy."

"I'm not turning in the Donovans because they're innocent. Someone is setting them up. The phone conversations Liam had with his mum were AI voice-generated. His calls revolved around security for the labs. They breached the labs without force. Sam is close to Senator Donovan. I need to know who he is."

Roger doesn't respond right away. "I had to call in a favor from a friend at NSA. Clay stonewalled me. Sam is ex-CIA. They pulled him six years ago with a new face and identity. He had a bounty put out on him by the Russians and Chinese.

They did not give me the details. You're barking up the wrong tree. He checks out, which is why he had security clearance for the Capitol."

"Is this the same Sam Owens who worked in Germany with my brother Declan at Bio2Chem?"

"What are you talking about?"

"I'm sending you an old photo." I text him the photo Pippa sent me of the Sam Owens Declan knew in Germany.

"That's him before his surgery, but what's he doing there? This mission isn't in his dossier, at least not the one I was given." There's alarm in his voice.

At the bottom of the stairs, two agents climb out of an unmarked car. "I see you traced the call. Got to go. Thanks for your help." I slide the phone away from my ear and shove it into my pocket.

I walk to the other side of the stairs and head for the reflecting pool, blending into the crowd. When I get halfway to the Washington Monument, I kneel and dump the phone in the pool. Water and technology don't work well together. I continue straight ahead, walking a couple of miles back to the motel.

After the information I gave Bane about Owens, I may have made an ally in the hive. We have to get Liz away from Sam to test my theory about his puppet master skills.

FORTY-FIVE

Campbell

A WELCOME SUMMER breeze accompanies the walk back to the motel northwest of the Capitol. The heat and humidity have taken a break, which my leg appreciates. I've learned temperature has everything to do with how well my leg does during activity. Too much heat, and I know I need to limit the time on my leg. My stump starts to bother me, and I can't wait to get to the room.

My appearance screams unstable and unable, but if this mission has taught me anything, it's that I have a purpose and I'm accepted by those I love. Second-guessing myself has been a monkey on my back for too long. No one has doubted my ability to do this mission and keep them safe. My normal is returning, but I couldn't have done it without Quinn.

I pass by famous buildings, storing messy histories with perfectly manicured landscapes as I check for tails. The National Mall, which stretches from the Washington Monument to the Capitol Building, is immaculate, much like the people in DC. Appearances can be deceiving because this place oozes power plays, dirty little secrets, and high-stake backroom deals. I won't be sorry if this is my only visit to DC. As the Brits say, it's not my cup of tea.

On the way back to the motel, I pick up a new burner to stay in contact with the team. They are going to want to hear this latest information. I open the door. The room is empty of the two people who should be there. My heart bounces up into my throat, and I break out in a sweat.

Quinn and Liam are gone. I look for signs of forced entry. There are none. Liam is an ex-Ranger. He's not dumb enough to open the door for a stranger. Where could they be?

I hurry to the lobby and hear loud music and voices coming from the pool area. Across the water, Quinn lies on a lounger with Liam next to her. At least they are in disguise. I storm toward them. Quinn picks her head up, sensing the impending hurricane headed her way. Her eyes never leave mine as she taps Liam on the shoulder.

"Oh, shit." I read his lips, unable to hear him over the music.

"What the hell are you two doing?" I say over the thump of the bass.

"We were bored," Quinn says as she looks at her fingernails.

"Oh, boo-hoo. I'm so sorry I don't have board games for you. Let's go. Now." My tone sounds like that of a father to two teenagers.

"I'm losing my mind being on the run and cooped up in that room." She grabs her Mountain Dew and shoves the straw in her mouth.

They follow me back to the room and plop themselves on the bed as I pace back and forth.

I stop in the middle of the room with my hands on my hips. "Someone could have seen you, or better yet, a camera could have picked you up."

"We're in disguise. Wearing a wig in the sun is no picnic," Quinn says off-handedly. Liam hasn't said a word.

My eyes bore holes in him to respond. "Well?"

"There was no way I was going to put my sister in danger. We were fine out there in a crowd of people," he responds. "I checked for cameras. Good pick because this shit hole doesn't have any."

I take in a deep breath. Maybe I'm overreacting. "I hope so because things have shifted. The tide may turn in our direction."

I relay the intel I got from Roger. They look at me wide-eyed.

"Sam is ex-CIA?" She curls herself on the bed with her arms crossed over her body.

"So it seems, but it doesn't explain what he was doing in Germany. No one has a record of it."

Quinn turns her head and looks out the window. "I didn't know him at all. I'm such a fool."

"I get the impression he was doing some off-book ops. They're trained to fool everyone around them, so don't feel bad." I sit on the bed next to her and rub her back.

"It would seem being a personal assistant to my mom would be a downgrade for him. Which begs the question, what is he really up to?" Liam offers his insight.

"That's the question. I'll check in with Pippa and Peter and see if they have any new information."

I dial the number I have memorized as Pippa picks up. "Hello?"

"It's me. Any recent news?"

"I need to talk to you privately, no speakerphone," Pippa says.

"Sure." I point to the door and step out into the hall. "What's going on?"

"We've been watching and listening to Liz Donovan's townhouse. She and Sam came home and had an interesting conversation. I'll play it for you."

"You need to find your kids before it's too late," Sam says.

"I know what I need to do and why. You don't need to keep reminding me," Liz replies.

"They are the keys to everything we've worked for. I need to get hold of that program."

"I have no way of contacting them, so we will have to wait it out. I want this as much as you do." Her tone is one of resignation.

The recording stops playing. My heart sinks because my theory is correct. Senator Liz Donovan is playing for the wrong team and wants their program. "It sounds like Liz and Sam want to get their hands on MAGS," I reply.

"I'm not sure."

"What do you mean?"

"Does anything sound not quite right to you? Let me play it again and listen carefully." She plays it again.

I listen to other sounds on the recording. "There are some inconsistencies in the background noise."

"Exactly. The video feed has been sketchy. This is the feed from the bugs you planted, but someone knows they are there and is scrambling them. This is the last recording we got. We analyzed it and discovered someone had spliced it together. The background noise for her voice differs from his. I think someone wants us to think they are in on it together. I bet Sam is setting her up for the fall."

"I need to let Quinn and Liam know, and we need to act fast." I rub the back of my neck.

"I wanted to read you in first, and then you can present it

to them. They didn't need to hear this from me." Pippa may be a hardcore hacker, but she has a heart of gold.

"Can you send this directly to Bane and no one else? Thanks. I'll be in touch."

I walk back into the room, and Quinn unfolds herself and sits up. "What's wrong?"

She reads me too well. I never could get anything by her. "They recorded a conversation between your mum and Sam. Someone wants us to believe your mum is the one trying to get ahold of MAGS. Pippa said they remixed the recording to make it sound like they are in on it together."

"Son of a bitch. He's framing her, but I don't get how he's planning to get MAGS from us." Liam stands up.

"We need to get her away from Sam and talk to her. I'm open to ideas because he's like her fucking shadow. It won't be easy. I don't know how we can contact her without him knowing about it." I have the patience of a saint until I hit a brick wall, then frustration sets in.

The room goes quiet. "I think I might have an idea on how to contact my mom and get her away from Sam," Quinn says.

FORTY-SIX

Quinn

I THOUGHT BEING on the run was complex, and then Cam adds a layer. We have to outwit Sam. Maybe he's smarter than I gave him credit for when we were together. Being ex-CIA doesn't make him a slouch. He must have played dumb for my sake. He doesn't know me well enough to understand that I will stop at nothing to save my family, even if my mom betrays me.

"When I was away at MIT, my mom and I would communicate via a shared email address. We haven't used it in years, but I could send her an email that Sam could never decipher. She is good with codes and keywords. Sometimes simple is better." I sit back with my fingers laced behind my head, ankles crossed.

"That's super, but how do we get her to check her email?" Liam thinks he's smarter than me.

"We're going to have Pippa call her office, posing as a member of the Security Council with an important message for her. She'll use code to tell her to check her email." I blow on my knuckles and rub them on my shirt. "I'm smarter than you, bro."

"Highly unlikely," Liam grumbles.

"I need the laptop and Wi-Fi, which this place doesn't have. In what universe does a motel not have Wi-Fi?"

"A cheap, crummy one," Liam replies.

"There's a coffee shop around the corner, but you'll have to be quick. Write the email here first, then go down there to send it," Cam suggests.

"Great idea." I turn to Liam. "See? He has great ideas."

He throws a pillow at me and smiles. "I'm waiting to reveal my grand finale. Save the best for last."

"Cam, I need a letterhead from the United States Botanical Garden." Cam and Liam stop and stare at me.

"What for?" Cam asks.

"My mom and I used to tour the botanical gardens everywhere we traveled. Her favorite flower is the orchid, and there are twenty-eight thousand varieties. She has a favorite, and it's here in DC. I'll send an email from them inviting her to the botanical garden, and that's where I will meet her."

"Who said you're meeting her? I'm not putting you in harm's way." Cam stands up.

"While she's meeting with Mom, I can call her cell and get hold of Sam to test our theory. This is perfect," Liam adds.

Cam throws up a T for a timeout. "Hold everything. You two are not running the op. I can't put either of you in danger."

"You don't have a choice. You can't do this alone. We know Sam and Mom well enough to know this might work," Liam replies.

Cam sits on the bed, resting his head in his hands, and scrubs his face. "You're right. We need to work as a team. It's as good a plan as any. I'll contact Pippa for the letterhead."

We spent the rest of the afternoon working on my email

with the necessary information to get my mom to meet me at the gardens. I'm sure she's already been there, but this orchid will prompt her to go again. Luck may be on our side for a change.

Cam runs out to get dinner as we wait to hear from Pippa about the letterhead. This is our last hope of finding out more information from my mom and figuring out Sam's role in her life.

Pippa informs us that she has sent the letterhead to my email. I grab the laptop and head out the door in my disguise, with a wig and a baseball hat. Cam and Liam tell me to watch for cameras, and I find a corner spot in the coffee shop with my back to the cameras and windows.

The first thing I do is copy and paste the letter to my mom. I swallow the lump in my throat as wonderful memories of our time together come flooding back. Not all moms are great. Not all moms are bad. Mine falls somewhere in between.

Dear Senator Donovan,

I hope this correspondence finds you well. It's my understanding that you are an avid orchid lover. As you may already know, we have a vast array of orchids. However, we have acquired a rare orchid that may interest you. We like to call her Cinderella.

Our mission at the United States Botanical Garden is to inspire people to appreciate, study, and conserve plants to enrich society locally and globally. Orchids are our ambassadors for exotic plant appreciation. Their unique colors, designs, and growing features draw visitors from around the world to the botanical gardens.

Orchids take a great deal of care, from pruning to just the right amount of water. We must also take special care using a Q-Tip and other delicate brushes.

You are invited for a personal tour tomorrow at lunchtime. Your presence is welcome, and we would like to do a feature article about your interest in orchids. No RSVP is required. Please wear your favorite hat for a photo opportunity.

I'll see you in front of our new golden gem.

Sincerely,

Dennis Davenport

Public Affairs Specialist

I hit the send button and then go off script for the next part of my plan. I wake up MAGS from her deep sleep mode so she can help me. She might be in jeopardy by being active, but this is the best way. I instruct her that we will communicate via text, not speech.

> Me: Hi, MAGS. I miss you. I need your help.

> MAGS: Hello, Dr. Quinn. I am here to help you.

> Me: I found some recordings of the Prime Minister (Chair) of the United Kingdom's Security Council. His name is Sir Colin Barlow. I need you to embed the voice into a file. I'll give you a sentence to say after you put a call through. Do you understand me?

> MAGS: Yes. I'm ready when you are.

I love MAGS. Good God, I sound like Liam.

I give MAGS the phone number to call, connecting her to my mom's office. She needs to make it look like it's coming from the UK, which is child's play. The secretary sends it through to my mom. After my mom picks up, MAGS needs to say, "You have a beaver to check on," using the voice of Sir Colin Barlow, and then hang up.

The MIT mascot is a beaver, and this will trigger her to check the email we used many years ago. When she gets in, the email from the botanical gardens will be waiting for her.

When I was growing up, she would always say my lunchtime wasn't lunchtime since I ate at two o'clock in the afternoon. She is the only one who will get the references in my email.

I shut down MAGS and scurry back to the motel. I walk into the room and have two pissed-off men scowling at me.

"You opened MAGS, didn't you?" Liam is the first to speak.

I nod.

Cam doesn't look any happier. "Peter called. You've triggered something, and we have to get out of here. I hope it was worth it."

"It was. I set up a meeting with my mom for tomorrow. We need somewhere to stay between now and then. Have faith." That is the only thing I have left at this point. I might have to put my trust in a woman who betrayed me but knows me better than anyone else.

FORTY-SEVEN

Quinn

THE BOYS ARE NOT happy with me, but it had to be done. Pippa was not going to get through, and they would have traced the call back to her.

We need to talk to my mom and get information from her. We'll determine whether she's in on it or in danger before making our next moves. As I think like an agent, I can see the flowchart of actions we need to take.

"We need to split up. I've ordered three Ubers to pick us up at various locations." Cam hands us pieces of paper with the address of where the Uber will pick us up and where they will drop us off. "We'll leave the motel in five and seven-minute intervals. We can't get caught together. I'll go first."

We put on our disguises, and Cam leaves to get into his ride. Liam and I stay behind and sit in the lobby. Two black sedans screech to a stop in front of the motel as men in black suits get out and head for the front door.

Liam nods and signals for me to leave through a side entrance to the street. He stands up and heads for the pool area. His gait looks like he doesn't have a care in the world. I wish I felt as confident. I walk out on shaky legs, resisting the urge to run.

My hands are sweaty, and my heart is racing. I hit the door to the street and quicken my pace. The sun beats down on me as dizziness takes over.

I reach in my pocket for the address for my pickup, trying to remember the directions Cam gave me, but my nerves get the better of me. Cam's voice pops into my head, "Don't look behind you. It's a dead giveaway."

Curiosity gets the better of me. I peek over my shoulder as the men get in their cars and drive away. My pace slows as I breathe a sigh of relief. They were too close for comfort. How did they get to the motel so fast? Do they know we're in disguise? Did they get Liam? My mouth goes dry.

The location of my pickup is near a bus stop. I stop to wait, looking at my piece of paper. Out of the corner of my eye, a small car stops before the bus stop as a black sedan pulls up behind it, just missing hitting it. They need to use less obvious cars. Two men in suits get out and talk to the driver. At every turn, they're getting closer.

I take my cue and turn to walk up the street, getting lost in the crowd. Whatever jitters I thought I had before have tripled. I throw the piece of paper in the trash and stay close to the shadows of the buildings, out of sight. I keep my head down like Cam taught me and walk to the motel where he made reservations.

Tears burn in my eyes, and my heart pounds in my ears. What if they caught Cam or Liam? I'll be out here on my own. They might be watching my mom, and she may not make it to our meeting. Questions swirl in my head, taking up space needed for logical thinking.

I find the address of the motel. A brick three-story building greets me with a torn, faded green awning. A bell rings above the door as I open it. The guy at the front desk, if you want to call it that, has greasy hair, a dirty T-shirt, and a brown-stained smile. This place might be worse than the last one. I'm not sure how that's possible in DC, but I'm about to find out.

"Can I help you?" There's a slimy twinkle in his eye. Gross.

"I have a reservation for Maggie Scotland."

"Ah, yes, the men have already made it upstairs." He grabs the key from behind him and then leans over his desk to look at me from head to toe. "After you're done with them, I want a crack at you."

I grab the key from his grimy hands. "Not if my life depended on it. Besides, you can't afford me." I grit my teeth until my jaw pops.

He grunts. "You might want to take the stairs. The elevators are not reliable. I wouldn't want you to be late for your threesome."

"What is with this town and threesomes?" I mumble under my breath.

I lumber up the three flights of stairs. The heat of the stairwell is suffocating as sweat pours down my face. I open the door to the hallway. Stained carpet greets me, the walls are smeared with an array of colors, and it smells like vomit. The room number is three eighteen. The key sticks in the lock and won't open. I hear a commotion on the other side of the door as it flies open, and Cam pulls me into his arms, slamming the door behind me.

"Thank God." He buries his nose in my neck, and his breathing becomes labored.

I wrap my arms around him, unwilling to let go, perhaps forever. "Is Liam here?" I say with a shaky voice.

"I'm here, Q," a weary voice says behind Cam.

I break away from Cam to hug him. "What the hell happened?"

They look at me with a scowl. "MAGS happened. It wasn't hard to put the pieces together. They got the signal from the coffee shop and located the nearest place we would stay." Liam's shoulders slump. "If they searched far enough into the MBK server, the Uber app may have been compromised."

"There's no way Pippa could have contacted Mom's office, and we're on a time crunch." They nod. "I see you picked another five-star hotel for us. This is worse than the last one." I turn to Cam.

"The worse, the better, and less security. They can't check every hotel in DC."

"I had to walk here. They were at my Uber pick-up," I choke out.

Cam looks at Liam. "Same with both of us. Liam had to outrun them through a department store."

Next to Liam on the bed is a fedora-style hat, a Hawaiian shirt, and swim trunks. "Did you do some shopping along the way?"

He holds up the shirt. "It's the first thing I've ever stolen in my life. I'm not proud of it. I grabbed some stuff and changed to get them off my tail. The department store was huge, which was to my advantage." No smile accompanied his adventurous tale.

"Harrison Ford has got nothing on you in that hat." He places it on his head, giving him a dashing look from 1920.

I sink into the bed and lie back. The ceiling is yellow-brown from previous smokers. "You're going to owe me a spa day after this," I say to Cam.

"I'm going to pay for all of us to have a spa day. Right

now, we need food to come to us without using apps or the phone."

I bounce up and head for the bathroom. "I have an idea." Splashing water on my face, I wiggle out of my bra.

Heading for the door, I turn and say, "I need some cash." Cam peels off some bills. "I'll be right back. I hope you like pizza and soda." I leave before they stop me.

The gross guy is still at the front desk as his eyes laser in on my chest. He registers I'm not wearing a bra, and I look sweaty.

"Whew! What a day. Those boys are tiring me out." I lean across the counter and prop my chest up on my arms. "Would you be a sweetheart and get us a large pizza with everything and a two-liter Coke? I would appreciate it."

"What's in it for me?"

I wave a couple of twenties in his face. "You never know. I want to keep it a surprise. But this should do the trick for now, with more to come with the delivery. What do you say?" I smile at him like he's the last man on earth.

He licks his lips. "I don't get off for another half hour."

"Sounds perfect. You know where to find me." I saunter off down the hall to the door for the stairs. His eyes burn my butt and not in a good way. At least I've accomplished something today.

FORTY-EIGHT

Quinn

I ANSWER the door and hand the front desk guy more money. Cam stands behind me like a Brahma bull, but I hold him off. I smile and close the door. "This guy is our lifeline. We need to stay on his good side."

We stuff ourselves with pizza as exhaustion sets in. The room is quiet with speculation about the plausible scenarios for tomorrow's meeting. While I fade to black, the guys get amped up, which is what they are trained to do.

"Let's talk about it tomorrow. We have most of the morning to nail things down. I'm tired and stressed out. Let's get some shut-eye." I yawn.

"You're right. We'll rundown possibilities tomorrow with fresh eyes and ears on the situation. It will take some creative planning to make this work, especially if Sam is watching your mum twenty-four-seven," Cam agrees.

The mattress is lumpy and digs into my hip. I move around, trying to find a comfortable spot. God only knows what's been on this mattress. If I think about it anymore, I won't be able to sleep, which is a stretch for me.

. . .

I'M the first to wake the next morning, anxious about the day ahead. I haven't had time to tell them everything I included in the email. Putting it together brought back a flood of conflicting emotions. My love for her as my mother and her betrayal of an unwritten code among family members collide in unknown territory.

As Cam rolls over and pokes me in the butt with his impressive hard-on, I snap out of my memory. I giggle, looking over my shoulder, and his eye cracks open.

"I feel like it's been forever since we've been together," he whispers as he jabs me again.

I slap his shoulder. "Stop it. It's not like we can do anything now."

A voice comes from across the room. "I can hear you. My ears are bleeding, so please stop talking about doing it," Liam says in a groggy voice.

Liam's voice is a libido killer as Cam turns away from me. We get out of bed and dress for the day, skipping a proper breakfast and munching on snacks until later. We've consumed the All-American favorites of Doritos, cheddar popcorn, and Cheetos for the last couple of days. I top it off with a Dr. Pepper. Why stop the soda trend now?

Cam and Liam question me about what was in the email. We discuss how we will move forward. I recite the email to them verbatim. They remain quiet as they take in everything.

"I see why you used MAGS. It was a calculated risk but worth it," Liam says.

Cam paces the floor, which I have recognized as his way of processing information. "I think we can use the hat thing to our advantage." He taps his chin with his finger. "Do you know what color hat she'll wear?"

"No. She loves to wear beach hats, and she has one in every color." I blow out a breath.

"We'll get some in every color. We can use them as a distraction if she's being watched," Cam offers. "It will eat up more cash, but I don't think we have a choice."

I frown as Liam smiles. "How?"

He sits down next to me and holds my hand. "We're going to buy a bunch of hats to hand out to various tourists at the right time and location. There will be a sea of beach hats. Get it? Sea?"

I elbow him and hit a rib. He rolls away like he's injured.

"Where do these crazy women live? Mad-hatt-an." Cam laughs, and I smirk.

"Is this really the time for one of your jokes?" Liam's face darkens.

"Lee?" I haven't used my nickname for him in years. He looks up at me.

"I'm worried about Mom. I don't know what to think anymore, but I want her to be okay at the end of this. We need to keep her safe." His mouth turns down.

I move to his bed and hold his hand. "That's the idea. No matter what, we'll keep her safe." My words sound convincing, but I have my doubts.

The hours are shrouded in quiet tension as two o'clock comes too soon. Liam will stay here at the sleazy motel and make the call on the burner. Cam and I will walk to the botanical gardens to meet my mom.

The time of day is perfect for the crowd of people streaming into the gardens. Cam buys a bunch of beach hats in different colors and another burner to contact Liam. Our cash flow is dwindling rapidly. We slip behind the building through the service entrance and search for the locker rooms. Cam needs a pair of dress pants and a shirt.

He finds a locker with a pair of pants and a polo with the

botanical garden's logo on it. He'll pose as the Public Affairs Specialist and hand out the beach hats.

Cam stands at the entrance to the orchid exhibit and hands out the beach hats. "We don't want you to roast in the sun once you leave here. It's blazing out there," he says in the worst American accent I've ever heard.

I put a hat on my red wig and mingle with the crowd moving into the tropical exhibit. There is a stream of colorful beach hats bobbing up and down as if they were floating out at sea.

Up ahead is the meeting location, the Yellow Lady's Slipper orchid. A woman stands, observing the magical orchid, wearing a yellow beach hat. I stand beside her and stare at the yellow orchid with Cinderella's slipper in the middle and two cascading brown tendrils.

"I think it looks like every woman's fairy-tale wish," I say without looking at her.

"Wishes don't always come true. There isn't always a fairy-tale ending." She wipes a tear from her cheek and looks at me through pained eyes.

"Cam says we have to keep moving so there's less chance of anyone catching up to us." I loop my arm in hers as we walk together, observing the orchids along the way. "We can get you out of here to safety."

"No. Sam watches me constantly. I can't disappear. It would be catastrophic." Her use of the word catastrophic catches me off guard.

I need to cut to the chase. "When you instructed Liam to change the security system at the labs, did you give anyone else the codes?"

She stops and frowns. "I never talked to Liam about changing the security systems at the labs."

I nod. "We think we can trust a man named Roger Bane.

He works for the government on a special forces team called PAX. If you need help, contact him and only him." I pull her into a corner and hold her hands in mine. "What's going on?"

"I don't have time to tell you everything, but what you think I did and what is actually going on are two different things. I love you and Liam more than my life. Remember that." Her words send chills down my spine.

She holds my face in her hands and kisses my forehead. "This is goodbye for now. You and Liam need to stay safe, no matter what. Use those beautiful minds you both have. Send my love to Liam. I have to go."

She's swept away in the crowd before I can ask her what she means. "I'll be in touch. Check your email." My words are lost in the humid air. I watch as her yellow beach hat bobs down the walkway. Someone grabs my upper arm. I try to jerk my arm out of their grasp.

"We have to go. There are eyes on us. Stay close," Cam says. "We need to get back to the sleaze factory. We'll compare notes there."

"Whatever it is, I get the feeling it's not going to be very good." Despair I've never experienced tugs at my chest, making it difficult to breathe.

I follow Cam out of the tropical exhibit as he shoves me into a car. I grab the center of my chest. We've made it out, but has my mom?

FORTY-NINE

Campbell

My eyes never leave Quinn's location with her mum. I keep track of their colored hats floating down the pathway toward the rest of the orchid exhibit. Their bodies are a symphony of stiffness and relaxation. The conversation is tense and probably not what either of them expected.

A tingling sensation hits me as if I'm being followed. I glance behind me and see a man in black out of his element in the tropical greenhouse. He stands on his toes to look over the crowd, searching for someone. His eyes land on Liz as he speaks to someone on his phone.

Pippa created a new Uber account with an untraceable card. I press the icon to order a car to the pickup location. Anticipating the arrival of others to escort Liz away, I push my way through the throngs of people toward Quinn and her mum. There are two women behind them. I put my arms around their shoulders.

"Ladies, I hope you're enjoying your visit with us today." I position them to block the view of the man in black and steer everyone toward an exit door. I release the ladies to continue their route, and Liz goes with them.

"We've got company, Q." We hit the exit door marked "Employee Personnel Only" and I jam it shut behind us with a chair. I peel off my clothes as we walk, heading to the street.

We cross over the busy street and around the front of the Museum of the American Indian. Our timing is perfect as a tourist bus lets people off for the tour. A compact car pulls up behind the bus as I hustle Quinn into the car. I put in an address a couple of blocks away from the motel.

Between the traffic jam, honking, and swearing going on around us, Quinn hasn't said a word, and I give her space to process. She's never this quiet, which makes me concerned about what was said between her and her mum.

I'm itching to get back and hear what Liam says about his conversation with whoever is portraying his mum. We must be close to cracking open who is behind trying to hijack the MAGS program.

When we enter the room, Liam sits on the bed with his arms crossed over his chest. Quinn and Liam stare at each other with quiet communication. As much as we've always been the Three Musketeers, I'm the outsider here.

"You first," Quinn says in a whisper.

"I can say beyond a shadow of a doubt it is not Mom I've been talking to." He lets out a deep sigh. "I told whoever it is that someone is after the MAGS program. I explained that I'm in the wind by myself, but I can't run forever, and I'm running out of resources. I tried to make the situation sound desperate. She, I mean, they suggested I come in, but they needed to check with someone before they could help me. If this is Sam, he's not the alpha dog in this operation. There's someone he's taking orders from. What did Mom have to say?" Worry covers Liam's face.

"She knew nothing about the change in the security

system at the labs, which is everything we needed to know." Her shoulders round, and her leg bobs up and down in rapid succession.

"We need a clone of a clone." I interrupt the silence. "If Sam has cloned your mum's phone, then we need a clone of his phone."

"Hey, genius, how are we going to do that?" Liam says tersely.

"This is where I throw caution to the wind. Our only hope is Roger Bane. I have a plan that might work. Quinn, can you send another email? We need a new location, but Sam needs to be there. Preferably a noisy, busy tavern. Does your mum have any favorites?"

Quinn nods her head with a curious look on her face. "What's your plan?"

"We're going to have Bane meet up with your mum and act like he's an old friend of Liam's. He'll be able to get close enough to clone Sam's phone or the cloned phone he's using. I think we can get enough information to form our endgame."

Quinn and Liam nod in my direction. "Bee, I need you to write one of those emails to your mum again. This time, we'll call instead of using MAGS."

"You don't need to. I told her to check her email, and she will. I'll use MAGS for less than ten seconds, not enough time for anyone to trace her." She types away on her computer to put together an email her mum has to decipher to get to the location. I lean over her shoulder as she crafts her code.

Dear Senator Donovan,

It was a pleasure seeing you today at the orchid exhibit. We need to follow up with an interview about your experience at the botanical garden. I will keep it off the record until you have reviewed and approved the article. You seem able to roll

*with anything that might come your way, and we appreciate
your flexibility.*

*Feel free to bring any associates for a late dinner and
drinks tomorrow night. I wouldn't want to leave out anyone
who could contribute to the article about your passion for
orchids.*

Looking forward to seeing you.

Sincerely,

Dennis Davenport

Public Affairs Specialist

"How the hell is she going to figure out where to go and
at what time?" I spit out in aggravation.

"Off the Record is an underground bar in the Hay Adams
Hotel where politicians go to be seen. My mom hates it there,
but she'll understand why we need to meet there. I set the
time for 9:00 p.m. She'll know because I always complained
about dinner being too late when she was home. I also told
her to bring fuckface, Sam. Believe me, she can read between
the lines. She's had years of experience," Quinn says roughly.

"Before you press send, let me contact Roger and check
that we're a go."

I take the stairs to the roof for the best reception. "Bane,
it's Cam."

"What's up?" He seems more agreeable each time I call.
That may be a good thing or a bad thing. Either way, I'm
rolling the dice. I'm running out of options.

"I've got a job for you," I say as if I'm in charge. "I need
you to pretend to be an old friend of Liam's from university.
You're meeting with Liz Donovan and Sam Owens at the Off
the Record tomorrow at 9:00 p.m."

"I hate that place," he mumbles.

"You'll approach her like you know her. The goal is to get
close enough to Sam to clone his phone. We need to get

what's on there. I'll be there for backup if anything goes shit up."

"Sounds good, but you're not going as backup. I'll take one of my men from the PAX team without reading them in."

"You're scaring me. You're a little too agreeable and willing to help the traitor."

"Clay has been like a cat on a hot tin roof. I've worked with Clay for many years, and the guy doesn't get antsy. We need to get to the bottom of who is behind this and bring in the Donovans. Let's see if Sam has a role in the manipulation. There are a lot of things not right about this."

"Liam called his mum's line while Quinn was with her mum. Needless to say, Liam did not talk to his mum. We think it's Sam, but he's not in charge. There's someone else pulling the strings. We're hoping to clone the phone to identify the puppet master."

"I'll be there in my best attire, ready to clone."

"Liz is on board, but we're not sure what her role in stealing the program is yet. She didn't know anything about the codes at the labs. Go easy if something goes down. She is their mum." There's a beat of silence. "Why are you doing this?"

"Ever since we spoke last, my Spidey senses have been tingling. I don't think Liam is a traitor, but someone else is, and I have my suspicions. I'll talk to you later."

He clicks off before I can ask him who he suspects is behind this. When I get back to the room, I give Quinn a thumbs-up to send the email. After tomorrow night, I hope we have a better sense of what's going on. I can feel them closing in while we're running out of time and angles.

FIFTY

Campbell

WE ORDER BREAKFAST, lunch, and dinner through the guy at the front desk by bribing him, even as the rain pours in sheets outside. We spend the day watching a channel with reruns of shows from the '80s and '90s like *Seinfeld* and *Friends*.

Quinn is quiet, and her body is stiff. A day of doing nothing is a welcome relief for my leg, but we're sitting on pins and needles waiting for news from Bane. Her reaction seems different.

Liam watches TV from the other bed as he and I comment on what's happening in the show. Our favorite movie, *Top Gun*, comes on as we sing the songs from the soundtrack and quote the lines word-for-word. The words *ride into the danger zone* never had more meaning. Quinn begs us to stop and covers her ears. We tell her it's a guy thing.

She curls up in a ball and turns away from us. I leave Liam to watch the rest of the movie as he nods in my direction. I touch her shoulder. "Hey, are you okay?"

She shakes her head. "I can't go back. No matter how hard I try to imagine life without the lab, I can't picture working there anymore. Being on the run has turned my world upside down." She peers over her shoulder at me. "What if I was wrong about my mom? What if my image of her is the opposite of who she really is?" Tears shine in her eyes.

I push a curl behind her ear. "Time will tell. We don't have the pieces to figure out what's going on and who the players are. You'll be the first to know." I kiss her forehead.

As the clock approaches 9:00 p.m., Quinn turns to me. "She's going to be okay, right?"

"Bane will make sure she's fine. We need to get the information off the phone Bane clones. A big fish is hiding out there who is pulling the strings. I'm convinced of it." I kiss her lips with gentleness. My body has other ideas as I get a hard-on lying beside her. I want to make her forget everything she's been through. I miss being with her in our new world of intimacy, but now is not the time or place. Liam doesn't know he's a great cockblocker, or maybe he does.

The clock ticks past eleven, and my burner rings. "Hello?"

"Got it," Bane says, sounding rather proud of himself.

"I'm putting you on speakerphone. Go ahead."

"Senator Donovan played along beautifully. My acting classes paid off because it was *A Night at The Improv.* We made stuff up as we went, knowing Sam wouldn't have a clue." His voice drops. There's dead air.

"What's wrong?" I ask.

"Senator Donovan wore makeup to cover up bruises on her cheek and around her eye. She did a great job of hiding it, but when the light hit it at certain angles, I could see the dark spots."

Liam projects off the bed and bellows, "I will fucking kill him!" He puts his shoes on as if he's going to leave to beat the hell out of Sam.

I hand the phone to Quinn and grab him, wrestling him to the bed. "You will keep your shit together for the sake of MAGS and your mum. We can't jeopardize the mission." This cools him down for a minute as I speak to the Ranger in him.

"Bane, you're an asshole! Why didn't you get her out of there?" Liam's face contorts with agony.

There's a sigh on the other end. "I tried. I followed her to the bathroom and talked to her. She said he had never hit her before but was pissed when she slipped out to the botanical garden. She was adamant about staying in this to protect her son and daughter. Nothing I said could persuade her to come with me. She's one tough cookie. I'm sorry." Roger's voice softens.

From behind me, there is the sound of sobbing. Quinn's head is in her hands as she weeps. I move toward her and hold her in my arms. "Bane, when you get some information off the phone, let us know so we can make our next move. Thanks for your help. We couldn't have done it without you."

"I'll put a rush on it with a guy I know outside of the agency. It's your only hope of not raising a red flag."

I push the button, ending the call.

"Why?" Quinn asks.

I look at her and rub her back. "Why, what?"

"Why would she stay if he's beating her? This is not my mom. She would never tolerate that from anyone. I still hold some resentment toward her, but I don't want to see her get hurt."

"I will bury his ass as soon as this is over," Liam mutters from the other side of the room.

"Both of you need to calm down. Your mum is smart. She knows the closer she stays to him, the better chance we have of getting the information we need." The negotiator side of me never gets a break, but I'm learning to balance it with the leader in me.

Liam sits on the bed with a scowl, and his ankles and arms are crossed. Quinn's crying has ceased as she wipes her eyes. "I've never cried this much in my life. I don't know how much more I can take."

"That makes three of us. I say we turn in, get some sleep, and wait for Bane's call."

Quinn crawls into bed and faces me. "There's no place for us to go to let off some steam. I'm going a little crazy here, sleeping next to you every night. I could use the relief," she whispers. "Can you hold me until I fall asleep?"

"Believe me, I know. It's giving me blue balls," I reply. I wrap my arms around her. "I will hold you whenever you need me to, always."

"Blue balls are not a thing," she mutters.

"Yes, it is," I say in a loud whisper.

"Can you two shut up and go to sleep? Blue balls are real. Trust me," Liam bites out.

The night is restless as Quinn tosses and turns. Liam snores but wakes up once in a while. I float in and out of sleep, waking up exhausted.

Light filters in through the holes in the brown-stained curtains. Quinn and Liam resemble zombies. Dark circles are evidence of the toll this is taking on them.

While Liam is trained for this, the personal nature of the mission makes it hard to be objective. Quinn is a roller coaster of emotions and wasn't prepared for her world to go sideways.

We go through our routine from yesterday, and tempers are flaring between us. There are arguments over stupid things like what show to watch, which show is better, and who gives a rat's ass because they don't matter.

My burner rings, bringing our attention away from our false security bubble.

"Bane?" This time, I don't put it on speakerphone.

"Yeah, we got some information off his phone. We traced numerous international calls, and there are calls to Senator Donovan's private number."

He pauses. Every time he pauses, I hold my breath, anticipating bad news. "Go on."

"There's another number he calls daily, sometimes several times a day."

"Who is he calling?" This could be the fish we're searching for.

"Your brother Declan."

My heart stops beating, and my mouth goes dry. "Declan? That's not possible."

"It is possible, and you need to call your brother and find out what the hell is going on. Maybe during the years, your brother was gone, he worked for the Russians or Chinese. He knew Sam when he worked in Germany."

"No. He had no memories of anything that happened to him when he worked at the biotech firm."

"That's very convenient, don't you think? Maybe he's a deep mole, they brainwashed him, and he doesn't even know it. I've seen some crazy-ass shit in my time. It's not implausible."

"Let me make some phone calls and get back to you." I click off and stand there, numb. Quinn and Liam are talking to me, but I can't hear their words. Their voices sound like white noise.

I turn and leave the room to go to the roof. The sun beats down on me, but I'm not sweating because of the heat. My heart races at the implications of Declan's involvement.

"Mac, we've got a problem." He listens as I tell him what Roger relayed to me about Declan.

"Not possible. Declan has had a lot of problems, but betrayal was not one of them. Let me do some digging and get back to you. They may have cloned his phone to make it look like it's Declan's number. I'll talk to Sean and put Pippa and Peter on it."

"We need to figure this out because someone knows we're closing in and we're running out of time."

FIFTY-ONE

Campbell

My head is foggy as I trudge back to the room that has held us captive for days. Things blur together, and I need to keep the details straight. Declan and I were never as close as he and Mac. Declan is the oldest of the Creighton clan but acted like the youngest, leaving Mac to clean up his messes and me to run interference. If he's in deep with the enemy, I'll kill him with my bare hands. The pain Liam and Quinn have endured because of a mole is unforgivable.

I enter the room. Quinn and Liam stare at me without a word. I throw the phone on the bed and sit in the tan chair covered with burn holes.

"Declan's phone number comes up on Sam's phone daily. We're not sure what's going on. Declan had a rough go for a couple of years and used to work with Sam while he was in Germany. Mac and Sean are looking into it. It doesn't look good."

There's a long silence. "No. Declan wouldn't do this. He's not part of Sam's plan, but Sam wants it to look that way," Quinn blurts out. "Sam would always say he was playing the long game."

"How can you be so sure?" Liam asks through gritted teeth. He needs someone to blame for his mum's agony.

"If Sam worked with Declan in Germany, he's trying to push it off on Declan and cover it up. This has been in the works for years. We're missing something," Quinn replies with clarity and objectivity.

"Pippa and Peter are working on it. They'll contact us when they find out what's going on." I get the last word out of my mouth when the burner rings.

"Hello?"

"Campbell, it's Pippa. We've traced some of Sam's calls. The number made to look like Declan's number led us somewhere else." She pauses.

"Where?"

"The Pentagon. I can't get much beyond that because of the security. My guess is we're getting closer to finding the puppet master. Declan has a new phone and phone number." She pauses. "He was pissed that you thought for one minute he had anything to do with this."

"I'll deal with him later. Thanks. I'll be in touch." I'm not dealing with Declan's attitude right now.

"What's going on? Is Declan part of this scheme?" Liam asks with worry in his eyes.

"No. I think someone cloned his phone while we were in the Pentagon. It must have happened during our meeting with the PAX team. We were told to turn in our phones before the meeting. The question is, who cloned the phone? There is no one exempt from suspicion." I pace the room as my mind spins. "Quinn, you need to craft another email to your mum. I think she is the key to this, which is why Sam picked her."

Quinn sits against the headboard with her knees tucked under her chin as she grips her legs close to her chest. "Do you think she's involved in this?" she says in a small voice.

"Not directly, but I think she has connections Sam needs." The picture becomes sharper.

"I want you to write an email from the botanical garden guy apologizing for not showing up for drinks. We'll work on it together from there. You have to be very careful with your wording. They have Wi-Fi here, but we can't risk getting caught."

She moves to get her laptop and heads for the door. "We have to go to an open Wi-Fi place again. I think there's another coffee place around the corner."

"Let's keep the ball bouncing," I reply.

"Can I go too? I'm going a little crazy in this room."

I tell Liam to stay put as I follow her out the door, down the stairs, and into the noise of DC. As we walk down the busy street, I fill her in on what needs to be in the email. We keep our heads down and take a corner table in the coffee shop. No one notices us or looks up as they are glued to their phones.

She opens the laptop. "No MAGS this time," I say, and she nods.

I peer over her shoulder as she types.

Dear Senator Donovan,

I apologize for not being able to make our meeting the other night. My son played in a Little League baseball game that went into extra innings. I'm sure you can understand the importance of being there for your family. Inside home plate is always the goal, who gets there and when. The pentagon shape is weird when you consider the shape of the other bases.

The purpose of my correspondence is to set up another meeting with you. I need to discuss and get your feedback on the article I wrote about your involvement with the orchids and the exhibit. I was hoping we could meet at a place where modern sculpture meets the greens. My understanding is your treasured treat is a delicious espresso and gelato.

Let's meet at brunch. I promise to make it this time. I would like some one-on-one time with you so we can dive into this article.

Looking forward to working with you.

Sincerely,

Dennis Davenport

Public Affairs Specialist

"What do you think?" She peers up at me as I screen her from prying eyes.

"Where are we meeting her? I don't get it." She's hit the major points, but I'm lost in the code between her and her mum.

"The Hirshhorn Museum has a wonderful sculpture garden with a cafe where we can drink coffee and eat gelato."

"So basically, we're meeting there because you want gelato." I smile.

"Precisely." She shuts the laptop, and we make our way to the front door.

The streets are busier than before as we weave through the crowd on the sidewalk. I hold her upper arm so we don't become separated. If I lose her, I lose everything.

In a short time, my world has been tilted on its axis as she spins it on her finger. I won't let her get away this time. I know what I have to do.

We get back to the Roach Bait Motel and discard our disguises covered in sweat. We fill in Liam on the message in the email, but he looks depressed, and I know this needs to end soon. Liam needs physical and mental outlets, or he gets gloomy.

"If Sam puts a tail on her again, I'm taking the guy out. Let Sam think he's lost her," I state.

"Maybe we can convince her to come with us." Liam's voice sounds hopeful, but his eyes are dull and less convincing.

"She was set on not coming with us last time. There's something she's not telling us about what's going on. I'm going to press her to tell us what she knows." When Quinn is determined, the people around her need to watch out.

"While you're talking with her, I'm going to check and see if she's being followed. You need to find a secluded spot in the café."

"Are you meeting her at Dolcezzo because you want their gelato?" Liam perks up from the other side of the room.

Quinn laughs and rolls over on the bed, holding her stomach. "Yes," she says in between laughs and out of breath.

"You better bring some back for me," Liam replies through his laughter.

Their laughter gets me laughing. This is the most relief we've had in days. It's much needed, so we don't spiral into the darkness of this op.

Liam and Quinn start a pillow fight, and I join in. We hit each other with pillows, releasing some pent-up energy and frustration. When we stop, Quinn shifts her eyes to us and puts out her fist. We haven't done this since we were kids. Liam adds his fist as I add mine.

I play my part. "The Three Musketeers."

Quinn says, "Un pour tous, tous pour un."

Liam finishes, "All for one, and one for all."

We raise our fists and smile. "Let's hope the fates are on our side tomorrow and we get answers." We sober up quickly from our childhood mantra as reality takes hold.

FIFTY-TWO

Quinn

OUR CONFIDENCE STRENGTHENS as we get closer to finding out what's going on. The pieces haven't come together yet, but I have an idea of where most of it is coming from. My mom has some explaining to do, and I'm not letting her off the hook.

Cam and I walk up Independence Avenue to the Hirshhorn Museum instead of taking the Uber, leaving less of a digital fingerprint. We give ourselves an hour of lead time. I beg Cam to let me tour the garden sculptures. We walk at a fast pace so we can look around before entering the lobby of the museum.

The Hirshhorn Museum is my favorite museum in DC. From its funky giant spotted pumpkin to classic bronze statues and modern free-flow designs, it embodies a garden of art for everyone. I have always loved the idea of time travel. This is the only way to do it for now.

We enter the glass lobby with its huge tree root tables and white curved chairs. The design accentuates the curve of the window, bringing the outdoors inside.

I make a beeline for the line at the café as Cam scans the

area. I grab his stiff hand, trying to calm him down. He stands behind me, wrapping his arms around my waist, and rests his chin on my shoulder.

"Is this what we have to do to snuggle?" he mumbles. "We have to disguise ourselves and create an AI global nuclear program while chasing bad guys."

"That about sums it up," I mutter.

Cam peels off me and stands to my right, continuing to scan the lobby. I order myself a chocolate gelato with an espresso, a perfect combination.

"Mum at your six." I've been around Liam enough to know what he means.

Without acknowledging him, I grab my stuff, turn around, and hand him his order. I see her sitting toward the farther end of the lobby near the escalator. I sip my espresso. "Is she alone?" I say into my cup, but he can hear me.

"Highly unlikely unless she gave someone the slip. Why don't you make your way over there? I have your back." He spins around and drinks his coffee.

"And my front, my side, in-between my legs." I smile. Cam groans in pain.

"Thanks for reminding me of what I'm missing. I've decided you may have a touch of evil, which might work in our favor. See you soon." He turns and walks away, leaving me to face my demons.

I wander over and pretend I'm looking for a spot to sit. My eyes land on my mom several times. Her face is drawn with hollow eyes. Her gaze is frantic, watching through the window outside and at the lobby door for someone who looks like her daughter. She never ceases to amaze me. She's here at 11:00 a.m. and at the correct location. My brother and I got the best parts from our parents, mostly their intelligence.

As I move closer, her hands are clasped in her lap, and her index fingers rub together. "Is this seat taken?"

Her head whips in my direction. Her eyes widen. There's a beat before she recognizes her only daughter. "No, I'm just waiting for someone." Her smile doesn't reach her eyes.

Behind the escalator, a man yells for help. Someone has passed out. Cam's American accent is improving. There's a flurry of activity in his direction, and that's my cue.

"Change of plan. We're going to go to the gardens across the street. I'll leave first." I take a bite of gelato. "Keep your head down."

She stares out the window as if she's still looking for someone but gives me a subtle nod. I stand up, taking my gelato and espresso with me, and move toward the glass doors. Hurrying across the street, I follow the pathway to the area with large old trees toward the center of the garden. I stop in front of *The Walking Man* by Rodin and wait.

"That was quite the distraction," she says from behind me.

I pivot in place and stare at a woman I barely recognize. Her heavy makeup covers her bruises up to a point. She sees the questions and pain on my face. "Don't worry. I'm fine."

"This whole thing is not fine. Why is Sam working for you? We know he's ex-CIA, but he has also cloned your phone and has been talking to Liam as if it's you."

Her eyes widen. "How?"

"AI technology. What's going on?"

"Sam forced himself into my life because he not only wants the MAGS program, but he also wants you and Liam to continue to work on it."

"Why not tell him to go to hell?"

"Early on, he said if I didn't cooperate, he would kill both of you in front of me. He proved to me that he had access to both of you." She blinks back her tears and grabs my shoulders. "He's evil, without a conscious of any kind. I've never encountered anyone like him. He scares me."

"Who is the brains of the operation?"

Her brows furrow. "He is."

"No, he's not. Who do you know that works at the Pentagon?"

She looks away as if she's searching her memory for someone. "The only person I know well is General Clay Murphy. We serve on the Security Council together. Why?"

"I don't have time to explain. You need to leave with us. Sam does not know where we are or how to get to us."

Tears well in her eyes. "I can't," she chokes out. "I wish I could. He's implanted a tracking device in my hip. If it's taken out the wrong way, it will release poison into my body. He controls my every move."

I'm stunned and silent. Cam grabs my arm. "We've got to go. Mrs. Donovan, are you coming with us?"

She shakes her head and covers her mouth with her hand. Tears spill down her cheek. I'm numb as I'm pulled into her arms. I grab her back, willing her to come with me, knowing it's not possible.

"I love you, Q-tip, and Liam too. I'll do anything for you." She kisses my cheek and turns away from us to walk down the path. She stops in front of the next sculpture and wipes her eyes.

Cam leans down and whispers, "We have to go." He takes me by the hand, and I float behind him. The world is a blur of green and brown.

We walk out of the sculpture garden and into the National Mall with its perfect rectangular patterns of grass, loose stone pathways, and trees outlining the edges. Cam guides me across the Mall under the shade of an elm tree, and we sit on a bench.

I hold it together long enough for us to sit down, and I cry into his shoulder. The sobs wrack my body. A wave of emotions takes hold of me, and I'm unable to grab onto any of them. Cam holds me to him, stroking my hair and telling me to let it out.

He whispers, "I've got you, and I'm not letting go until you say so."

His body is big enough to hide me from people passing by. He knows what to do with a bawling woman and doesn't back down from my meltdown. I wouldn't feel comfortable letting go like this if he weren't here. He's my safe zone. He always has been. I know I can trust him with my life.

After what feels like an hour, I calm down long enough to relay to Cam what is going on and why she couldn't come back with us. His reaction is not one of shock, fear, or anger but of resolve and contemplation. He plays his part as the eye of the storm.

"What did you do to the guy who was following her?" I ask.

"Two fingers to the nerve in the throat. Works every time. He dropped like a sack of potatoes." He smiles. "Let's get back to the motel. Liam will not be happy."

"No, he won't be. The bigger question is, where do we go from here?"

"Sam will know we know about him and his under-trained team of bodyguards. I worry about your mum. Beating her up again will not solve his problem."

"Maybe I could trade places with my mom. He'll have at least one of us."

"He needs both of you to complete the AI and the formula

for the micro-nuclear weapons. Besides, I'm not putting you in that position, ever." He hugs me closer.

On any other day, I would argue with him, telling him he doesn't have the right to tell me what to do, but I don't have it in me. My fight drains away, and I find comfort in having someone make the big decisions for me.

FIFTY-THREE

Quinn

THE PAIN in my chest is more than I can bear. My mom might die at the hands of a madman to save her children. I had many doubts growing up about her love and commitment to Liam and me. What I found is a woman who will die for the humans she gave birth to while protecting the world from a potential crisis. I'm not clear about how she ended up with my ex-husband, but maybe he blackmailed her from the beginning.

Cam and I open the door, and Liam leaps off the bed. "Where the hell have you been?" His voice trails off when he sees my face. "What happened? Where's Mom?"

"She's not coming." My lower lip trembles.

Liam's face falls. Cam explains what happened in the garden, and Liam plops onto the bed. "That son of a bitch is using our technology to blackmail our mom. What are our next steps? He's got to know we're on to him."

"I'm going to contact Roger again. He said he's worked with Clay for years. For us to bring this forward to anyone, we need proof. No one will listen to us without proof, not even my team." Cam holds his head in his hands.

"While you're working with Roger, I'm going to bring MAGS online and see if she can gain access to Clay's devices and email for proof of contact with Sam and any other information." Liam's eyes brighten, and his determination is steadfast.

"That could be dangerous and put us in the middle of the hornet's nest. They're waiting for us to use her so they can track us down," I reply.

"Maybe we need to be on the inside. Your mum has sacrificed enough. There's one other thing I thought of that you two are not going to like." Cam scrubs his face with his hands. "We may have to use MAGS as a negotiating tool. You need to decide if you are willing to destroy her or somehow make a copy that is foolproof but doesn't work."

Liam and I stare at each other in a quiet tug-of-war. "Go ahead. Tell him," I prod Liam.

"We developed a program called Ghost 1 for this situation. On the outside, the program has everything similar to MAGS, but it self-destructs within twenty-four hours after being installed. The Trojan is undetectable and buried deep in the coding." Liam wiggles his brows. "Get it."

"This is not the time for jokes." Cam scowls.

"Says the jokester." Liam smiles.

I know we're in uncharted waters when Cam doesn't want to crack a joke. We'll have to hold each other up to get through this, and no one knows what the outcome will be. I'm emotionally exhausted from trying to figure things out with my mom and Cam. I worry about Liam, especially when we talk about destroying MAGS.

"I'm going to take a walk." Cam's face is pale.

"I'll come with you and walk in front of you in case anything happens. I've got to get out of here," Liam demands.

Cam nods, and I watch as they put on their disguises

without thinking. We've gotten used to being on the run, and disguises are a part of our routine.

"I'm staying here. I need some downtime. Have fun, but not too much fun." I yawn.

The quiet of the room surrounds me with an occasional beeping horn from the street below. I stare up at the ceiling and use it as a whiteboard, visualizing the pieces of the puzzle. My mind sees pictures, and I put each image on a card. The cards float around with the other cards with words. This process is similar to the way I code, seeing everything in sequence.

Every card I put in place, there are gaps and missing information. To complicate things, I'm emotionally attached to some of the floating cards, standing in the way of my objectivity. Sleep comes over me, and the floating cards fade away like sand on a beach, and my eyes close.

"What are your intentions, exactly?" Liam's voice sounds far away.

"Is this the time to be asking me this? I don't know, and if I knew, I wouldn't tell you," Cam responds in a loud whisper.

The sound of rustling wakes me up, and I open my eyes. Cam and Liam are in a shoving match, pushing each other on the shoulders. I've got to stop it before it gets too far. I stand between them, sticking my arms out, and push them on the chest.

"You two are half-nuts right now. Keep your alpha shit in check for when we really need it."

They sit down on opposite sides of the room with their arms crossed.

"What did Roger have to say?" I ask to ease the tension and distract them.

"He's going to do some snooping and get someone on the team to follow Clay and Sam. When Clay is out of the

Pentagon, Roger will contact us so we can get MAGS inside his phone and anything stored on his devices. We need to act fast. Otherwise, our cover is blown.

"Timing is everything with this. We have to coordinate with Roger and whoever he gets to follow Clay and Sam. I hope this works." Liam rubs his hands together.

What used to be the three of us living in a tight spiral, turns into an outward spiral sucking in more people and problems. I can't shake the feeling it's going to implode on top of us. We need to make sure we have a way out. My mind goes back to the idea of leaving the country, but it tears my heart away from reconnecting with my mom.

There are so many unexplained things between us, and I want answers and a resolution. In the end, she's my mom. I want to understand and make peace with who she is and why she made certain decisions. I don't have to agree with her actions, but I need to understand the reasons.

We wait in limbo to hear from Roger. Cam and Liam are on edge but keep themselves in check. I whip out a deck of cards, and we play card games using peanuts. So far, Cam has the largest pile of nuts. At least we're laughing, enjoying being together after too much time apart. Something warms deep inside of me when I see my boys back together.

The burner rings as we stop and look at it. "Answer it and put it on speaker," Liam instructs Cam.

"It's not a number I recognize." He hits the speaker button. "Hello?"

"Hey, it's Bane. I had to get a burner. I'm being followed and whoever it is sucks at it. There are two guys I served with and trust with my life, tailing Sam and Clay. When we have an opportunity to track them outside the buildings, I'll let you know when you can do your part. Both my guys report that Sam and Clay are twitchy, which means things aren't going the way they want them to." He pauses. "If you don't hear from me in the next forty-eight hours, head north to the Canadian border. I have a teammate there who can help you. I have read him in, and he can get you over the border. Stay loose." He clicks off, and we're left staring at the small plastic device that serves as our lifeline to the outside.

"They are scrambling and will make mistakes. If Clay is part of this, he's seasoned, but I don't know how big his crew is. We need to stay sharp and think a couple of steps ahead. Once we fire up MAGS, we'll have to leave here. Be ready." Cam stares at us. Liam and I nod our heads without a word. The spiral staircase seems to disappear at a rapid rate.

FIFTY-FOUR

Campbell

ACCORDING TO ROGER, Clay walks every day in the National Mall Park. I figure this is when Roger's team will make their move. If our hunch is correct, he's using this time to make calls he can't dial from inside the Pentagon.

I contact Pippa and Peter to read them in on the plan, so they're on standby. Everything comes to a standstill as we are suspended in time, waiting for the call that could change our lives.

My phone rings. "Yeah."

"I got word that Clay is on the move. That bastard has two phones, and he's on both at the same time. It's go time. I'm heading back inside the Pentagon to see if I can get access to his office. His secretary and I are friendly. I'll be in touch." Roger clicks off, and my fingers can't move fast enough.

The energy in our filthy prison shifts from serene to frantic in a split second. "Liam, get MAGS online," I say as I dial Pippa's number.

She answers. "I take it we're a go." Her fingers tap on the keys. She talks to Peter in tech language I don't understand. I put her on speakerphone so she can coordinate with Liam and get access to MAGS.

Quinn stands behind Liam, giving instructions here and there. While they are trying to download as much information as possible in a limited amount of time, I throw everything we own, which isn't much, in duffel bags. We have three minutes until we leave this hellhole and find another rock to crawl under.

The timer on my watch runs down to five seconds. "We've got to go now." I click off with Pippa and Peter and shut down the phone. I take out the SIM card and crush it under my foot on the bathroom floor.

Liam shuts down MAGS and closes the laptop. "Help me move the bed back."

I move to the other side of the headboard. "We don't have time for this."

Behind the headboard is a piece of cut-out drywall. "What's this?"

"What do you think I've been doing while you two gallivanted around DC? MAGS will be safe here. Trust me. I have a plan."

"You need to get a girlfriend," I mutter.

"So I've heard." His face hardens with worry for whatever is coming next.

We rush for the door. "Let's take the stairs," Quinn suggests.

We pound down the stairs and into the lobby in time to see three black cars come to a screeching halt in front of the motel. Men in black flow from the cars like ants, reaching for their weapons, accompanied by soldiers in tactical gear. Who do they think they're capturing, Jason Bourne?

I put my hands out, preventing Liam and Quinn from moving. A sound of pain comes from Quinn, and a stream of curse words leaves Liam's mouth. We stand there stunned as the glass door opens, and Roger aims his weapon at us.

Quinn turns to me. "You said we could trust him, or did you set us up? We can't trust anyone. This is a town full of liars." Her face reddens, and her eyes glisten with unshed angry tears.

His eyes are steely, and he looks at us as if we're strangers. "Put your hands where we can see them, and don't make any sudden moves." Each word is a cut of betrayal. "Thanks for all your help, Campbell." His smile makes my skin crawl.

Roger stands behind me to lock in the zip ties. Two other men zip-tie Liam and Quinn.

"Say nothing and ask for a lawyer," I say loud enough for both of them to hear me.

"Fuck you, Cam." Liam gives me his parting shot.

My hands strain against the ties to reach out to Quinn. The knife of deception stabs me in the gut as well. This is on me. I took a chance that Roger understood we are not the enemy, but my gamble did not pay off. He outsmarted us. He's proven to be a loyal soldier for the PAX team and the US government. I can't fault him for his commitment.

They lead us away, shoving us into three different cars. The divide-and-conquer method. They don't want us to talk. I stay calm, but I worry about Quinn. They trained Liam and me for interrogation. She is a civilian. The fact that someone has betrayed her again may work to her advantage. If they're not careful, she may bite them.

I expect they will transport us to a black site or take Liam to Leavenworth, but I don't know where they will take Quinn. The need to protect her overwhelms me as my failure sits like a stone on my chest. My insecurities about being the lead on this op come flaming back to life, and my doubts creep in.

We travel in a parade of black cars while historic lime-stone buildings flash by the window on our way out of town. People walking by don't notice because motorcades are a regular occurrence.

We cross the Potomac River with the Pentagon in view, where this nightmare began. The car makes a couple of turns toward the five-sided polygon. We enter the spiraling tunnel as a stream of lights whiz by the window. This is going to end where it started: full circle.

The cars stop in front of a bank of familiar elevators. They haul me out of the town car as they haul out Liam. Quinn gets handled with more care. They push the three of us into an elevator, with Bane and two others behind us.

Quinn glares at me and opens her mouth to say something.

"No talking," Bane barks out. We face forward. If I get out of these ties, I'll rip him to pieces or beat him with my leg, whichever is easier.

They should offer me one phone call, but we're traveling to the bowels of the Pentagon, where people can disappear without a trace. I'm sure they have considered Senator Donovan in their equation. She'll want to know what happened to her children.

As the elevator doors open, they lead each of us by the arm to separate rooms. Bane has a hold of me.

"Don't say a word," I yell out as my voice echoes off the sterile metal walls in the hall.

Bane cuts my ties, pushes open a door, and throws me inside. I falter but regain my balance before falling on my ass.

"Sit." He's down to one-syllable words. Perfect.

I pick myself up and slide into the metal chair as he

attaches my hands to the cuffs on a bar in the middle of the table.

"Is this necessary?"

He turns his chair around with the back of it to the table and straddles it.

"I don't know. Was it necessary to run from the PAX team with two of the world's most prominent scientists?" He cocks his head to the side like a dog trying to understand its owner.

"Liam and Quinn are innocent, and you know that. By the way, you suck ass. I don't know why I thought I could trust you." The negotiator in me has left the room.

His mouth curves up on one side. "Yeah, I'm good like that." He stands up. "We'll see how innocent your friends are. In the meantime, get comfortable. You're going to be here a while."

"I need to make a phone call. My understanding is I get one."

He places his hands on the table and leans down over me. "Maybe and maybe not. Your little team of bandits has no power here."

My automatic response is to wring his neck with my bare hands, but the clank reminds me of the cuffs. "No one better lay a friggin' hand on Quinn."

"Oh, it looks like someone made a love connection. How sweet. Too bad you won't be seeing her again." He smirks. "It doesn't sound like she wants anything to do with you."

He turns and walks out, slamming the door behind him. The Academy Awards called and nominated him for his portrayal of an ally. He's convincing as the double agent.

We've missed our check-in. If I know my team, they are wheels up and already in the air.

FIFTY-FIVE

Quinn

PISSED OFF DOESN'T BEGIN to describe my mood. Roger Bane turned out to be the bane of our existence. I can't even laugh at my joke. I don't know what to think about Cam. Was he duped by Roger, or is he in on it? Roger thanked him for his help. I'm not sure what that means.

My gut tells me Cam is not in on it, but Bane wants us to think Cam is part of the deception. I can't accept that. I've trusted Cam every step of the way.

I should be living in sheer terror. I don't know where we are, and they have separated me from my pillars of strength. Torture better not be on the menu. I'm not good with pain.

My hands are in cuffs attached to a bar in the middle of a metal table. I lay my head on the polished surface, trying to cool myself down. We came this far to be done in by a man I thought we could trust. Betrayal seems to be a continuing theme for me. Desperate times called for desperate measures, but we were too wrapped up in surviving to realize we were being played.

I should be used to this by now and able to see the signs. Cam was in charge of this operation. I want to blame him for this mess we're in and probably won't get out of, but Bane is the real villain.

The door opens. Roger stands there looking at me like I'm an animal at the zoo. His eyes fill with curiosity as he cocks his head to the side and clasps his hands in front of him.

The tactical gear is gone, replaced by a pair of cargo pants and a T-shirt that hugs his torso. If he weren't the enemy, I would have a hard time keeping my hands off him just for a quickie, but it's time to admit my heart belongs to someone else. Bane ended up being the worst kind of human on Earth.

He closes the door, spins the chair around, and straddles it. "Hi."

I roll my eyes. That's his lead? Lame. The camera in the corner turns toward him. I lift my hand enough to flip it off.

He smiles. "I see someone has some fire left."

"Can you take these off me? I seriously doubt I'm a threat to security here."

"Nah, I like to see women in cuffs."

"Of course you do because you're also sexually twisted on top of everything else."

He leans on his forearms as his jet-black hair falls on his forehead. His ocean-blue eyes soften as if he's going to seduce me in the holding room. "Where's the laptop?"

"My God, you have no game." His face sours. "I was expecting champagne, roses, and a five-star meal for our first date. Look, I even got dolled up for you. You need to work on your interrogation skills, traitor."

He doesn't even blink until I say the word traitor, and then his eye twitches. "The only traitors here are you and your brother. That program belongs to the US government, and you're trying to sell it to the highest bidder."

"That program is beyond your comprehension, dumbass. Whoever takes control of it will decide the outcomes of wars around the world. Domination will be like nothing this world has ever seen. We won't need world wars because they will end before they can start. We didn't seek out the highest bidder. They came to our door, which is why we've been on the run. Someone is after this program, even though it's incomplete, and they need us to do it, you moron." I had to get in as many derogatory comments as possible and still sound intelligent.

His lips form a thin line. "You're safe here. We can protect you if your story checks out. The evidence is not in your favor."

"You know our story checks out. Why don't you check out Sam and—" I don't get out the next name because of his coughing fit.

He covers his mouth and waves his hand in front of his face, but I watch his eyes. They are warding me off from continuing my sentence. What's going on? The look is there and gone, making me think I've imagined the entire exchange.

His face turns red, and he stops to breathe. "If we can locate the laptop, you and your brother can continue your work and complete the program. I could always tell him you turned on him and told me where the laptop is."

I grin. "You're an asshole." I lean forward to get into his personal space. "My brother and I are on the same page with everything. He won't believe a word that comes out of your mouth."

"Knowing you could be in prison for the rest of your life, how do you know he won't take the deal? If only one of you goes to prison, the other can visit." He chuckles.

"Cam's radar must have been way off when he thought he could trust you. For your information, I don't know where the laptop is."

He stands up. "Sure you don't. I'm going to talk to your brother. Maybe he will be more willing to cooperate."

"I doubt it."

The door suctions closed behind him, and I'm alone again. Sadness fills my empty soul. I need Cam, but I can't get to him. I don't know where he is or what they are doing to him. My anxiety spikes. I do my breathing exercises to calm down. Sleep is my escape from anything I don't want to deal with as I lay my head on the table.

I don't know how much time has lapsed, but I'm awakened by the door opening. Roger the Dodger and a man I vaguely recognize stand there.

"Uncuff her now," the stranger says as his voice echoes off the walls. His biceps are bigger than my head. Is the entire MBK team made up of huge, gorgeous men?

"You want to keep it down? I just woke up."

"Quinn, I'm Sean Knight. We met briefly at the mine. Campbell works for me at MBK Global Security."

I nod as Roger stands with his hands clasped in front of him, staring straight ahead.

The mine seems like a million years ago, and the moment we should have made a run for it. "Where are Liam and Cam?" My voice is soft.

"They're being taken care of. You need to come with me." He offers me his hand.

"I guess they call you the boss for a reason."

He smiles as we step out into the hallway. He has his hands on his hips. "Bane, I need you to take her somewhere to clean up and get food. Meet us back here in an hour."

Roger nods. "Follow me." He walks in front of me, assuming I'll follow, which I do because I don't know where else to go.

We take the elevator up a couple of levels to a floor with

rows of wooden doors on either side of the hall. He twists the knob, and it opens to a luscious suite filled with everything I could want. He doesn't say a word and shuts the door.

I'm rotating in a circle when the door opens again, and Cam walks in. He rushes toward me. "Bee."

I put my hand out in front of me. "Don't fucking Bee me! He thanked you for the information you fed him. You led him to us. Now what?"

He sits on the couch. "I thought we could trust him. Everything about him, with all my years of training, said we could trust him. I was wrong. I'm sorry."

My lip quivers. "Sorry is not good enough. And now I've lost Liam too. I've lost everyone close to me." The tears fall of their own free will. He hangs his head. "I need you to leave so I can process. I can't deal with you right now. My focus needs to be on how to get out of here and find Liam."

When he lifts his head, he looks like a broken man. He did this to himself and us. "My team is here. We'll work this out." He kneels in front of me and grabs the back of my legs. "You will never lose me. I will always love you, even when you push me away." He doesn't beg but commits himself to me.

"This pain of betrayal is way too familiar to me. I feel like I'm drowning. Please go." I choke on my words, torn between wanting him to stay and craving space to put my thoughts together.

He stands up to leave and looks at me one last time. My stab wounds are too deep and too fresh. I can't endure this with him. Pieces of me break off as I cannot hold them together. The man I thought would be my life walks away.

FIFTY-SIX

Campbell

She sank into my soul with grace and determination. I'm not sure how I can live without her. I breathed her air, drank her water, and craved her skin. Walking away from her was excruciating. All I've ever wanted was to give her everything, and now she wants nothing from me.

Life had become a story of my old habits repeating themselves every day. Old recordings of my lack of self-confidence played repeatedly. I couldn't escape my way of thinking, but she and her brother believed in me. They were the jack under a car changing the bald tires and unable to grip the road.

I'm like an old American muscle car with the body rusted out, the engine won't turn over, and my wheels have come off. I have nothing left to give. They might as well throw me away. I've hurt two people I love like family. As I throw myself another pity party, much like the one I threw after I lost my leg, something stirs deep within me. This time, I need to fix it.

My mind goes back to the last time we made love. With every thrust, she surrounded me, taking me deeper into her body and accepting me without question. Pure love comes once in a lifetime, and I intend to grab the brass ring. I won't let her backpedal out of what we have together. I'm going to fight for us and fight for Liam. Screw Bane.

Trudging back to the suite I came from, I close the door behind me. They must have planted bugs in this place eighteen ways to Sunday. I'm sure whoever is watching us and listening is having a good show, but I don't care.

The automatic light comes on in the bedroom, and I slog my way to the bathroom to wash away my regret. When I come out, there is a pile of clothes sitting on the ottoman. I pick them up and realize something heavy is under them. I take the clothes to the bathroom, hoping there are no cameras in there.

Someone hid a gun at the bottom. I pick it up, feeling the weight of it in my hand. It's light, and upon further inspection, the material is plastic, but you wouldn't know the difference by looking at it. Guns made by a 3-D printer will get past metal detectors, and someone thinks I'm in enough danger to need a gun.

I pull my clothes on and stuff the gun behind my back. My shirt with the sweatshirt is bulky enough to hide it. Who left the gun for me? And who would be brave enough to bring a gun into the Pentagon?

I shuffle back to the living room. There's a knock at the door before it opens. Sean enters. "We're wanted in the conference room. We have some things to share with the PAX team." He smiles with a glint in his eye, but then he notices the look on my face. "Everything okay?"

"Not really. Quinn thinks I betrayed her by giving Roger the information on them and our whereabouts. Nothing could be further from the truth. Roger is playing both sides."

"Technically, he's on our side," Sean says.

"He's the one who hauled us in here when he knows Liam and Quinn are innocent," I say through gritted teeth.

Sean doesn't respond as I follow him down the hall. He opens the double doors to the conference room, where our fates will be determined as we enter the devil's den.

The scene is a flashback to when we met with the PAX team. President Decker sits at the head of the table. Clay Murphy is on one side, and Bea Davidson is on the other side. Next to Bea sits Natalie Palmer, followed by Roger, Dean, Mac, Declan, Quinn, and Liam. Pippa and Peter are on the screen in the background.

I step from behind Sean and lunge for Bane, grabbing him by his shirt. His back hits the wall, and my forearm pushes against his windpipe. "You cost me everything," I say close to his ear so only he can hear me.

"Not everything," he grits out with a curious look in his eyes. His response throws me off.

Two people rip me off him and sit me down in the nearest free seat. Clay smiles as he chews on the end of his cigar. He's the next one I want to punch, but I pull myself together. The President and his staff seem unruffled by the event. No one says a word to let the dust settle. The door opens, and Liz and Sam walk in.

Quinn says the word Mom with a gasp. Liz is pale and thin. The shine has left her eyes. She doesn't make eye contact with anyone. Sam walks in with his shoulders back and head up as he sits next to Liz.

The President is the first to speak. "Senator Donovan, thank you for meeting with us today. Since Drs. Donovan are involved in this, I thought you would want to be a part of the conversation."

"Thank you, Mr. President. I appreciate the consideration." Her mask is in place.

"Let's get started. Bea, would you like to begin with your findings?" The President is cool under pressure.

"We believe Dr. Liam Donovan staged the attacks on the labs to make it look like it was an outside agency. However, we traced calls between his phone and an unidentified burner until he went missing with government property, namely the MAGS program."

Liam goes to stand up, and I catch him by his arm. "That's a lie!"

She looks at him with daggers in her eyes. "Dr. Donovan, the evidence suggests otherwise. Furthermore, we suspect you were trying to sell the program to the highest blind bidder. The chatter on the dark web describes the program without naming it, but the buyers seem to know exactly what is being offered. Currently, there is a bidding war tipping over the billion-dollar mark. Only a group with immense power and assets could afford that bill. We have ears and eyes on our enemies."

She stops to shuffle papers in front of her. "Clay and some of the PAX team members were instrumental in getting this information to us. We are recommending Dr. Liam Donovan be charged with treason. Dr. Quinn Donovan will be charged as an accessory, and Campbell Creighton will be extradited to the UK to face prosecution for international crimes under their laws." She places her hands on the table. Mac and Declan's eyes snap in my direction.

The room goes silent. The only sound is the soft weeping coming from Quinn. I want to go to her and hold her in my arms, making sure she understands everything will turn out in the end, although I'm not sure how. Their case seems airtight unless someone on my team performs a miracle. My eyes bounce from person to person, but no one on my team says a word.

Liz's face is ghostly as two tears streak down her cheeks, one for each child she may never see again.

"But you don't have MAGS," Liam says with an edge in his voice.

"But we do," Clay smirks, reaching down to grab the laptop and placing it on the conference table. "Did you think we wouldn't find it? We tore apart the motel room. Your hiding place wasn't very creative."

"What do you plan to do with it?" Liam's eyes narrow.

"We have scientists who can finish your work and make it operate the way we need it to function."

"No, you don't. They would spend years playing catch-up. That's why you hired my sister and me." Liam smiles.

Clay leans forward. "Maybe we'll have you work on it from a black site. How fitting, considering you came from an underground lab like a mole."

Liam stands up again. "I'm not a mole! I have not betrayed my country."

Clay turns to the President. "Let's get this over with and send in security to take them away. We have spent a lot of taxpayer dollars trying to capture them."

Sean stands up. "With all due respect, Mr. President, we have uncovered information we would like to share with you."

FIFTY-SEVEN

Campbell

SAM AND CLAY are in my line of vision. Neither of them gives anything away, but they shift in their seats. Sean pulls his shoulders back and fires the first shot across the bow. I've never seen fireworks set off underground. This may be a first.

He hands manilla folders marked *confidential* to the President, Bea, and Natalie. "First, I commend Campbell on a job well done. He protected and secured the assets, as directed, by taking matters into his own hands. His decisions were made on the fly to keep everyone safe. His years of training paid off." He turns to Bea.

"We believe the attack on the two labs, the kidnapping of Dr. Quinn Donovan, and the chases have occurred because of a mole on the inside and involvement by Deep 8. We have been tracking Mr. Sam Owens and General Clay Murphy as suspects trying to steal the MAGS program."

Clay smiles. "I can't wait to hear this. Boy, you better have this locked down, or I'll have your ass," he says with a Southern drawl.

Sean doesn't miss a beat. "I'll get to you in a minute. For months, Dr. Liam Donovan thought he was speaking with his mother on her phone. She advised him on the program and suggested he change the security systems at both labs. Dr. Donovan did exactly as she recommended. Why wouldn't he? She sits on the Security Council. However, he wasn't speaking with his mother, Liz Donovan. He was talking with someone who had cloned her phone using AI technology to imitate her voice. It was undetectable as a fake, even to her son." The air stills around us as the HVAC system turns on with a hum.

The President listens intently. "Do you have any proof of this?"

"Yes," Sean explains our setup at the Botanical Garden when Liam called his mum, but her phone never rang, yet he had a conversation with her.

"Did you track the phone?" Natalie Palmer asks.

"It was a burner, which is hard to track, but still uses cell phone towers. We followed the ping from those towers back to the Russel Building, where Senator Donovan's office is located."

"That proves nothing. We have irrefutable proof the doctors are working for the enemy, thanks to Roger Bane," Clay sputters.

Sean stays focused on Natalie. "Someone close enough to Senator Donovan had to clone her phone. That person also had to have intimate knowledge of her life and children to pull off the charade. Sam Owens had the means and opportunity. He was married to Quinn to lay the groundwork for the ultimate goal."

"Of course, you would point the finger at me since I'm closest to her, but you haven't come to the table with any proof," Sam speaks up, unruffled.

"Except we pulled your fingerprints. You're an ex-CIA agent who got burned, had reconstructive surgery, and went off the grid seven years ago. You showed up in Germany five years ago to steal a cancer-causing drug and almost burned Declan Creighton alive because you recognized him as MI-6 when your paths crossed during an op. Is that enough proof for you?"

Chaos erupts when Declan lunges across the conference room table and grabs hold of Sam. They crash to the floor as Declan gets in a few good punches. The rest of the MBK team sits and watches.

"You need to do something about your man," Clay barks.

Mac gets up and grabs Declan off Sam. Sam's lip is bleeding, and he's going to have a black eye. He pulls out some tissue, dabs his lip, and points at Declan. "I saved your ass!"

"After you lit him on fire," Mac replies. "Guilty conscience, or did you need him for something?"

"You took five years of my life from me that I will never get back." He jerks forward as Mac holds him back. "I hope they put you in a black site where you will never see the light of day."

"Let's everyone have a seat." The President hasn't moved a muscle as he glances at Clay. "Mr. Knight, please continue."

Clay pats his forehead with a handkerchief. Sam continues to wipe his lip as he sits to my right.

"The only reason you have Drs. Donovan in custody is because they used MAGS to infiltrate the burner phones and emails of both Sam and Clay. They are very cozy. Roger Bane also got into Clay's office to find more evidence," Sean continues.

He opens the folder and lays out some papers with the Deep 8 insignia. "The infinity symbol with a capital D in the middle is the Deep 8 logo. We know this because we've come across it several times when dealing with this organization. The rest of the evidence can be found in your folders." Beads of sweat run down Clay's face.

Out of the corner of my eye, there's a flash of movement. Sam has Liz in a headlock with a knife to her throat. "I'm getting out of here with the MAGS program, or she dies." Liz's fingers claw at his arm, and her eyes are wide.

I draw the weapon from behind my back and aim it at Clay. "I'll call your threat and raise you one General. You kill her, and I'll kill Clay." Clay's eyes widen.

"You think he's the head of Deep 8?" Sam sneers.

"I think Deep 8 would be very sorry to hear you killed one of their top insiders in the US government. I would imagine he's a highly valued asset to them. You won't make it to sundown. Even if you kill Senator Donovan, you're outnumbered." My eye never leaves the site.

I have Sam's attention. In a split second, a shot is fired. Sam falls to the ground with his plastic hunting knife and a bullet to the brain. Roger is holding a gun similar to mine and lowers his weapon. I nod to him.

Liz falls away from Sam and into a chair as Quinn and Liam rush toward her.

The security outside the door breaches the room with weapons pointed at everyone. "Hands where we can see them," one of them orders.

We have our hands in the air when Sean says to one of the security guards, "Hey, Stan. Clay is your guy. The President has disappeared."

"There's an escape panel behind his chair," Stan grumbles, "just for this type of emergency."

Clay is put in zip ties. His face is red. "You think you've cut the head off the serpent, but you're not even close," he spews.

"Hey, Clay. Why did the spy cross the road? He didn't. He was never really on our side." I can't muster a smile.

Sean stops him. "Who's head of Deep 8?"

"Why don't you ask Roger?" He laughs. "My hours are numbered. This is beyond your pay grade, son."

Our heads turn in Roger's direction. His eyes go wide, and he shrugs.

FIFTY-EIGHT

Quinn

CHAOS ERUPTS. Everyone stands with their hands in the air except for Liam and me. We attend to our mom, who slumps over in a chair, holding her head in her hands. I peer over my shoulder and catch Cam's eye. He nods to me in understanding. If I were him, I wouldn't talk to me ever again.

Paramedics come in to check my mom over and take her away. They'll bring in specialists to figure out how to remove the tracker without poisoning her. Liam raises his chin in Cam's direction. I take the hint and look for Cam, who is standing in the corner talking to Roger.

"Those acting classes pay off every time. I had you fooled. You really thought I turned on you. Not a chance. I've suspected Clay for a while. I just couldn't pin anything on him," Roger says.

"You had us snowed. You were playing a dangerous game with Clay if he found out what you were up to. I'm pretty sure Quinn wants to eat you and spit you out again." Cam stops talking and turns around as he senses me before he sees me. It's always been our way. Science can't explain the energy flowing freely between us that we use as a signal.

I look around him. "Thanks for everything you did, including saving my mom's life. I think Sam would have killed her. There was a lot of hatred running through his blood."

Roger smiles. "You're a tough customer. You wouldn't give me an inch in my interrogation. Maybe you missed your calling and should have become a spy. You've had the training on this mission." He holds my hands in his. "I hope to always be in a position to save the innocent. No thanks needed. You and Liam need to finish what you started."

Cam removes Roger's hands from mine. "Okay, that's enough hand-holding for one day. We'll talk later, Bane. Thanks for the weapon." Roger salutes before he leaves through the door.

My eyes are glued to Cam's chest. I don't want to look at the anger in his eyes. His fingers lift my chin. "I'm not angry. I don't know what I would have done in your position. There was so much to unravel in a short amount of time."

"I trust you. I was just confused by Roger's total change of attitude. In the end, he kept my mom from being killed." My hand clings to his wrist. "I need to go to the hospital to be with her. We have a lot to sort through."

"Yes, you do. Then you and I are going to finalize a couple of things."

I'm unsure what he means, but I can only focus on one thing right now, my mom. He bends down to kiss me sweetly on the lips. The gesture is filled with longing, safety, love, and trust. I leave him with the words I've wanted to say my entire life.

"I love you," I say.

He holds my face. "I know. I've always known, and now you know for sure. I love you too, and I know what I'm going to do about it." His thumb brushes my cheek. "Go be with your mom. I'll get us a hotel room."

"Make that a luxury suite." I laugh.

"You bet."

One of the security personnel takes me to Walter Reed Hospital. Crying babies and people holding bloody appendages greet me. I make a mad dash for the check-in area, and they direct me to the bank of elevators.

Her floor is quiet, with the occasional beeping from a machine. Two guards stand on either side of the door to her room. They ask me for identification, which I don't have.

"Mom, can you tell them who I am?" I yell through the door.

Liam opens the door and smiles, pulling me in and closing the door behind us. My mom's slender frame hides under the blankets. Her eyes are closed with dark circles under them. My heart breaks from her appearance. I don't know everything she's been through, but it took a lot out of her.

I pull over a chair and place her hand in mine. A smile forms on her lips before she opens her eyes. "You came." Her voice is scratchy.

I nod my head as tears spring to my eyes. She pats the other side of the bed for Liam to sit next to her. She tilts the bed up as Liam and I wait for her.

"Now that you are both here, I need you to hear my story." She looks at me with sad eyes. "I would never do anything to hurt my children, ever. Sam came to me before you were divorced and laid on the charm. That's what you saw when you walked in on us. I never let him touch me until I had to."

She puts her head down and bites her lip. "I wasn't buying what he was selling but needed to find out his angle.

He threatened my children's lives when he realized he wasn't getting anywhere with me." I squeeze her hand and wipe my tears. Liam's eyes are watery, but he never looks away.

"He told me if I didn't do exactly what he told me to do, he would end both your lives with long, drawn-out torture he would be sure to share on film. To prove his point, he showed me he had access to both of you at the drop of a hat. I couldn't risk either of you. I had to allow him into my life personally and professionally."

Her words are knives cutting into my soul. I never thought to ask what was going on with her and Sam. I assumed the worst. That's what I will have to live with forever.

Tears stream down her face, and she lays back on the pillow. "After your divorce was final, he became more aggressive with his plan. At first, he was kind, like he really wanted to be with me. For the first time since your father's death, I felt cared for. Things changed when Liam became less cooperative with sharing information about the program. His attention was off me and on trying to get what he wanted. I was not privy to the details of who he was working with, but I knew he wanted the program. He was frustrated that you might be a year out from completing MAGS."

She tightens her grip on my hand and holds my cheek. "I wasn't there for you when you were younger, and I should have been. Foolishly, I strived to make the world a better place. I'm so sorry. I misplaced my dedication."

We lay our heads on her shoulders. "It must be a genetic thing. I think our dedication has been misplaced, too." The three of us lie in quiet contemplation.

"You need to finish the program and decide what you're going to do with it," my mom says with resolve.

We lift our heads, and I look over at Liam. "I'm not sure

that's a good idea. It may be too powerful for what this world is ready for," Liam responds without remorse over losing MAGS.

My mom smiles and brushes the hair from his forehead like she used to do when he was a little boy. "You'll do what's best. I have faith in both of you. Now, get out of here so I can get some rest. I need to get stronger to continue my work and keep trying to make this crazy new reality make sense."

"I'm guessing we will have matching scars to remember this moment." I look over at Liam.

She follows my eyes. "We will always be connected, scars or not."

We kiss her goodbye, making our way to the lobby, where Cam has a car waiting for us. He asked us if we wanted to Uber. I hung up on him. The car pulls up in front of the Jefferson, and the front desk directs us to two different places. Liam and I hug.

"We made it," I muffle into his shoulder.

"Thanks to Cam." He pulls away. "Don't forget that." He kisses the top of my head and turns away.

This place is the exact opposite of the motels we had to stay in while on the lam. Liam makes his way to his suite, while I can't wait to meet up with Cam in the Deluxe Suite. I knock on the door, and what greets me on the other side makes me burst into laughter.

Epilogue

Campbell

MY WHOLE WORLD stands in front of me. Her eyes widen, and she laughs so hard that she holds her sides. I scoop her up, not thinking I might lose my balance and we might fall, but we will always help each other up.

I toss her on the bed as she continues to laugh. "What is so funny?"

"What if I was the maid, and you were standing there buck naked with a wig, sunglasses, and a beach hat? She would have had a heart attack," she says while catching her breath.

"Did you hear about the soldier who snuck behind enemy lines disguised as a Christmas tree? He was a decorated veteran."

Quinn throws her head back as her laughter fills the room. It's the sweetest sound to my ears.

"She would have thought how her man isn't this well-endowed." I wiggle my brows.

Honeybee stops laughing and rips off her clothes as we lie side-by-side. Fingers skate over our skin, leaving goose-bumps in their path and stirring up an inferno that never stops burning.

We feather kisses over each other's bodies, never losing the connection. The rhythm we create is our own and can't be replicated by any AI program.

We spend the rest of the night eating, making love, and sleeping. Few words are spoken, but I throw in a joke here and there. Our bodies speak in quiet desperation, never severing the thread binding our hearts. There is a newness with an old familiarity in the way we explore each other inside and out. I will never get enough of her. I want her surprises for the rest of our lives.

THE MORNING RAYS of sunlight set the room in an amber glow. She's where she needs to be, in the crook of my arm with her leg over mine. A sunbeam highlights the scar on her hip from what seems like a million years ago, but it is a reminder of what she's leaving behind. My finger traces the scar. She opens her eyes, and a smile touches her lips.

"Good morning," she says. I want every one of her mornings.

"Good morning. We're leaving for Scotland soon, so we might need to do some shopping for the trip."

She sits up. "You're up to something."

I shrug. "Maybe. But I guess you'll have to wait to find out."

"As long as I'm with you. You're my forever. We had to

jump through some hoops to get here, but you're worth it. After some of the damage has been repaired with my mom, my heart feels free. I didn't realize Sam's betrayal would color everything I looked at in a red light, warning me to stay away. I'm sorry. I need to make it up to you." The devil is in her eyes.

"I have no doubt you'll think of something." I roll her on her back and begin our dance.

We spend the next couple of days buying clothes and finding creative ways to make love. She catches up with colleagues and tries to patch together the past and the present. I watch her, realizing I've been away from home too long. Home is wherever she is. My leg isn't the missing part. She carried my heart with her, and I am finally complete.

A car waits for us at Edinburgh Airport as we drive through the country to her house. There's nothing like the Scotland countryside filled with emerald fields spotted with lavender thistle. Our timing is perfect. For once, we're exactly where we should be.

There are cars in the driveway, and the lights are on. She sits up. "What's going on?"

"You'll see, Bee."

Her mum waits for her on the front porch with open arms. Quinn rushes out of the car and runs to her mum, who looks more like herself. Gone are the dark circles, but left behind are the emotional scars that may never heal. I recognize those. This is the best ending we could hope for. All children need a mother. Not all are lucky enough to have one.

I enter the house as everyone waits for the big moment. My brothers and father, along with the entire MBK team, fill the house. Everyone looks well-rested and smiles. Declan slips something in my hand, and I know it's go time. I grab Quinn's hand and lead her to her father's office. She has a look of surprise, which is my intent.

We stand by the bay window, looking out over the pasture. It was her father's favorite view. I get down on one knee. Everyone tries to squeeze into the room behind us.

"Cam," she says as her hand covers her mouth.

"Not a word until I'm done." I take both her hands in mine. "You embody everything I want in a woman. I fell in love with you from the minute we met. I didn't know it, but my soul recognized you. This isn't our first go-around, and it won't be our last. There is not another minute I want to spend without you."

I swallow at the words I'm about to say. "Your father told me to let you find your way to me. He understood you. Once you did, I was never to let you go. He always knew we would be together. I honored his request, even though it killed me minute by minute." Tears stream down her face. "Will you give me the honor of being my wife and soul mate for eternity?"

She nods. "Yes, forever." Sniffling plays in the background, but the bubble surrounds us. I take out the engagement ring and slip it on her finger. It's a square-cut emerald surrounded by diamonds.

She looks down at it and then back up at me. "I recognize this ring. It's your mom's."

"She wanted you to have it. In her lucid moments, she told me we were destined to be together. Your dad and my mum knew way more than we did." I kiss her, and everyone applauds. "You better get dressed. We have a wedding to attend."

"Today? Right now?"

"I'm not waiting a minute longer." I point to my sisters-in-law. "They will take care of everything. See you soon."

She hesitates as a book titled *The Chemistry of Love* falls off the shelf. We laugh.

"Okay, Dad. I got the message." She looks up and smiles.

While she prepares, I hang out with my best men, drink a beer, and get into my tux. The crew spent the last couple of days getting the barn together for our celebration. I made sure to have plenty of soda on hand for Bee. An arbor stands at one end. The tables have centerpieces filled with native flowers, including thistle. I notice Neal isn't among the guests.

"Where is Neal? I thought he would be here with Liv's mum." Liv is Declan's wife. They met in Germany and fell in love again.

Sean looks at Mac. "He had some things to take care of. He promised to be here." I don't ask questions. This is my day with my soon-to-be wife.

I pass by Dean and say, "Looks like I beat you to the altar. You're the last man standing." He grumbles a response, but I don't stick around to hear what it is.

My heart beats with excitement at the altar with my brothers by my side. Mac's wife, Marabella, and Liv stand on the other side for Quinn. This is what coming out the other side looks like, and I will savor every moment.

The music plays, and I see a vision of beauty walking toward me. Liz didn't have a wedding dress, so Quinn is dressed in my mum's dress. The off-white dress fits her perfectly while Liam walks her down the aisle. She beams with happiness, and the smile never leaves her face.

With no time to write our vows, we recite the standard verses. Neal walks in as the pastor tells me to kiss the bride. He's looking grim and moves toward Sean.

The reception gets underway as a local band plays our favorite songs. After our first dance, I get a tap on my shoulder. I turn around, and Neal motions to me to go to the house. My teammates are missing from the reception, which is my signal that something is up.

The kitchen is packed with my team and Roger Bane. Dressed in suits, most are smoking a cigar with a drink in front of them. Their faces tell a different story.

"Have a seat, Campbell. We need to have a discussion. First, the President would like to thank you for everything you've done to secure the MAGS program and save the lives of Liz and the Drs. Donovan. The more pressing problem is Deep 8. They are ramping up their game." He turns to Roger. "At first, we thought Clay was trying to pin the operation on Roger's father. His father is the Australian ambassador to the UK, which didn't make any sense. It was a strange connection. We started investigating Roger's father, but as of yesterday, the Ambassador has gone missing." Roger's arms are crossed at his chest, but he doesn't seem worried.

"I'm not sure it's too much to worry about. He'll sometimes lose his detail to go for walks or to his favorite pub. Maybe he wants to spend time with a woman." His face grimaces enough for me to notice.

"Not this time. They ambushed the car, drug him out, strapped him into a harness, and airlifted him by helicopter. He had an engagement at the harbor when it went down. They planned out the kidnapping down to the minute. They got into international airspace and flew below ten thousand feet. Fighter jets were scrambled but couldn't locate the heli."

No one says anything or looks at Roger.

"What's the motive?" Sean asks.

"We aren't sure. Bane, you aren't going to want to hear this. If your father is involved with Deep 8, they may be protecting him, or he's not with them, and they took him for leverage. They have a lot to gain from his expertise. He was a member of Parliament for ten years and served as the Minister of Defense, Foreign Affairs, and Trade. As an ambassador, he served in Iraq, Japan, and Kuwait. He's a valuable asset."

Our eyes turn to Roger for his reaction. "This is not good, but I can't believe he's part of this. He must have something they want, but I have no idea what it is. My father and I aren't on the best of terms."

"Roger, I'm putting you on this case. You'll be taking a train to London first thing in the morning. Here's the dossier with your contact information and background. This will be all hands on deck at a moment's notice. We don't know which way the wind is going to blow. Whoever is the head of Deep 8 is letting their nerves show, and we have to capitalize on it. This last run-in with the MAGS program was a close call. We have to put an end to Deep 8. Do whatever you need to do. World security may rest in our hands."

Way to get the party started, Neal. We finish our drinks and cigars in the kitchen and head back to the reception. Quinn won't be happy about putting off our honeymoon, but duty calls.

Ready for Roger and Harlow's story?

A hidden agenda lurks behind every friendly face, making trust a dangerous gamble.

Grab Torn for the final novel in the Deep 8 series

FREE BOOK

I love staying in touch with my readers.
Sign up for my newsletter and receive **Silent Night** for
FREE at

https://bit.ly/FREEKenzie

Silent Night

She must save her brother. He only sees her betrayal. Will they find love or fall prey in a deadly rescue plan?

New York City. Chloe's dream of becoming a journalist is cut short when she's unable to secure a job. So in order to make ends meet, she takes a job at J. Luc Gallery for the holidays. Her new boss is easy on the eyes and very attentive. But when her brother gets kidnapped, she must do the unthinkable.

Jean Luc has earned his galleries the hard way. As an established gallery owner, he is trusted with a unique exhibition of expensive ornaments. So when he hires Chloe's brother to install the security system, he doesn't expect to be thrown into the dangerous side of the art world.

Chloe makes a difficult choice, forcing her to betray her lover as MBK races to rescue her brother. But the plan may come together too late, leaving Jean Luc in the cold.

Can love rise above betrayal so they can find their happily ever after?

Silent Night is a novella that introduces the entire MBK Global Security team. If you like page-turning action, steamy scenes, and heart-breaking betrayals, then you'll love Kenzie Macallan's holiday story.

https://bit.ly/FREEKenzie

Please consider leaving a review

Reviews are so precious to writers. Writing a review helps other readers find my books and is helpful when deciding what to read next.

If you have a minute, please leave a review. Thank you in advance for taking the time to help others find RISK.

Building a relationship with my readers is so important to me. Join my newsletter for cover reveals, new books, deals, and giveaways

www.kenziemacallan.com

Also by Kenzie Macallan

The MBK Global Security

Truths

Mara is hiding a terrible secret. He's on a dangerous mission. Can Mac protect the love of his life from a ruthless killer?

Secrets- a novella

She wants him to leave. He's investigating his brother. When the Russians close in, will they make it or head for heartbreak?

Edges

Leigha is under threat. Dean is undercover. Will deadly family secrets ruin the romance of a lifetime?

Masks

Raquelle is investigating him. Misha is accused of fraud. Will a sinister conspiracy ruin their shot at unforgettable love?

Deep 8 series

Wild

Jess leaped into a war zone to get the story. Sean will endure hell to bring her home. Sparks fly, but will romance die on the wrong side of a bullet?

King

Pippa is a hacker turned agent. Beck will become king of a diamond empire. Can two unlikely lovers survive a sinister conspiracy?

Burn

Olivia is a scientist fighting to keep her secret hidden. Declan is an ex-soldier with a tragic past and lost memories. Will the chemistry between them ignite lost love?

Torn

(Roger and Harlow's story)

Harlow is undercover to find her father's killer. Roger must find his father before Deep 8 kills him for the software that will change the world.

Acknowledgments

A heartfelt thank you goes out to the readers who took a chance on me and read this book. If you left a review, I'm forever grateful because they are hard to come by. Your support is greatly appreciated and you make every minute worthwhile.

I want to thank my husband who gives me time and support while he rides his motorcycle. It works!

Karen, you are incredible and love your feedback! We will meet someday.

I love this cover and thank you Tiffany Black.

About the Author

Kenzie Macallan is an author who skillfully weaves intricate action-adventure romances as art imitates life. Not really, but her vivid imagination often finds solace within the pages of her books. Having explored the diverse landscapes of Africa, Greece, Switzerland, Holland, France, England, and Scotland, her travels have ignited a relentless wellspring of storytelling.

This fuels her artistic endeavors, from painting captivating portraits to capturing moments through her camera, all while nurturing her green thumb in the garden. While culinary mastery may elude her, she loves to bake, much to the gratitude of her husband.

Kenzie's true passion lies in transporting readers to captivating realms, where flawed yet endearing heroes emerge, intelligent and resilient women take center stage, and unexpected endings leave them in awe. With each new adventure, Kenzie eagerly anticipates the opportunity to further enchant her readers and embark on a shared journey of discovery.

She loves to hear from her fans.
Join her newsletter for cover reveals, new books, deals, and giveaways.
Website: www.kenziemacallan.com

Goodreads: https://www.goodreads.com/author/show/15058012.Kenzie_Macallan

BookBub: https://www.bookbub.com/authors/kenzie-macallan
Amazon: www.amazon.com/author/kenziemacallan
Facebook: www.facebook.com/kenziemacallan
TikTok: www.tiktok.com/kenziemacallan
X: www.twitter.com/kenzie_macallan
Instagram: www.instagram.com/kenziemacallan
Pinterest: www.pinterest.com/kenziemallan
Email: kenziemacallan@gmail.com